I0819067

Praise for *Handle with Care*

"On an ordinary afternoon in a small Southern town, four women's lives collide at the worst possible time. In *Handle with Care*, Whalen delivers an emotionally charged hostage drama where no one's walking out the same. Cleverly written and unexpectedly tender, this one's unforgettable in all the right ways."

—Kimberly Belle, internationally bestselling author of *The Expat Affair*

"This beautiful novel gives readers what we most need these days—a deep breath of humanity and hope. It's a story taut with suspense and uncertainty, but it's also filled with bursts of joy, kindness, and connection. You will love these women. You are these women."

—Gin Phillips, author of *Fierce Kingdom* and *Ruby Falls*

"*Handle with Care* is an edge-of-your-seat thrill ride in the most everyday of settings—a local post office, a place where humanity intersects, where we usually keep our heads down, unaware of each other's private pain. Marybeth Mayhew Whalen crafts a gripping story around this idea, rich with complex characters, a tightly woven plot and natural suspense that will keep readers hooked until the very last page."

—Belle Burden, author of *Strangers: A Memoir of Marriage*

"In *Handle with Care*, Whalen delivers a heart-thumping story with her signature warmth and insight. This moving novel reminds us that every life is a balance of hope and heartbreak, resilience, and regret. With each twist and turn, Whalen reveals that life is fragile, love is fierce, and we are far more alike than we imagine."

—Elizabeth Bass Parman, author of *Bees in June* and *The Empress of Cooke County*

"Marybeth Mayhew Whalen has crafted a gripping novel telling the transformative power to be found in recognizing the humanity of each and every person."

—Katie Young, book influencer @katiereads.sc

"What a precious little gem of a novel. In these heavy times this lovely book is exactly what my heart needed. *Handle with Care* is a love letter to connection, forgiveness, honesty, friendship, grace, and above all hope. And everyone could use some hope in their heart!"

—Stephanie Howell, book influencer @stephaniehowell

"I am a huge fan of Marybeth Mayhew Whalen and will read everything she writes! *Handle with Care* manages to be a pulse pumping thriller but also a women supporting women heartwarming tale. I can't wait to sell this gem at Fabled."

—Elizabeth Barnhill, adult bookbuyer
at Fabled Bookshop and Cafe

Praise for *Every Moment Since*

"*Every Moment Since* will grip you with its compelling, 'just one more page' mystery, then alter your heart with its beautifully drawn cast of characters. Full of real emotional insight and depth, it's a book to finish in the small hours, feeling utterly transformed."

—Hannah Richell, author of *The Search Party*

"*Every Moment Since* is an astonishing work that didn't let me go, even after the last line. This book has it all: rich characters who jump off the page, a present and past that feel so familiar, and a sense of urgency to see how it all unfolds. I miss this book already!"

—Ethan Joella, author of *The Same Bright Stars*

"*Every Moment Since* is unforgettable. Marybeth Whalen takes every family's worst nightmare and uses her amazing talent for exploring the aftermath to bring this story home. How do you go on when there are no answers? What does forgiveness really look like? In telling the story of Davy Malcor's disappearance, she's tapped into a whole new world of emotional family drama. Heartbreaking and suspenseful, this is Whalen's finest work to date."

—J. T. Ellison, *New York Times* bestselling author of *It's One of Us*

"*Every Moment Since* is everything you want in a novel—a gripping story, nostalgia for lost childhood, exorbitant love, a deep sense of place, and page-turning tension. From the opening scene where a child's jacket is found twenty-one years after he's gone missing to the heart-rending conclusion, this story is brought to vivid life with Marybeth Mayhew Whalen's pitch-perfect prose and signature ability to dive into the characters' deepest secrets and desires. As the lives of those left behind draw ever closer, we hold our breath to find out the truth. For those who love the work of Taylor Jenkins Reid and Jessica Knoll, you've just found your next book club read."

—Patti Callahan Henry, *New York Times* bestselling author of *The Secret Book of Flora Lea*

"*Every Moment Since* is a masterpiece, an important study of humanity, grief, and especially hope in the aftermath of unfathomable trauma. In her best work yet, Whalen expertly and delicately paints an unflinchingly real picture of what happens to a family and a town when weathered scars are opened anew. *Every Moment Since* will deeply resonate with all readers. I couldn't put it down!"

—Joy Callaway, international bestselling author of *What the Mountains Remember*

"Marybeth Mayhew Whalen is at her finest in this novel that dissects the harrowing toll on family and community when a child goes missing. This sophisticated and compelling novel establishes Whalen as an unflinching voice in fiction."

—Kimberly Brock, bestselling author of *The Lost Book of Eleanor Dare*

"Full of atmosphere and twists and turns, Marybeth Mayhew Whalen's *Every Moment Since* is a must-read!"

—Catherine McKenzie, *USA TODAY* bestselling author of *I'll Never Tell* and *Have You Seen Her*

"*Every Moment Since* is a heart-pounding mystery that is sure to leave you breathless. Well-crafted with twists and turns around every corner, Marybeth Whalen's latest is a triumph!"

—Liz Fenton and Lisa Steinke, authors of *Forever Hold Your Peace*

"*Every Moment Since* is one of those compelling stories that you keep promising yourself just one more page, then just one more chapter, and before you know it you've plowed through another five chapters and have stayed up well past your bedtime. Fast-paced and cleverly written, Marybeth Whalen tethers you deeply into the dark recesses of this story while unraveling the truth behind what really happened to Davy Malcor."

—T. I. Lowe, #1 international bestselling author of *Under the Magnolias*

Handle with Care

ALSO BY MARYBETH MAYHEW WHALEN

Every Moment Since

This Secret Thing

Only Ever Her

When We Were Worthy

The Things We Wish Were True

The Bridge Tender

The Wishing Tree

The Guest Book

The Mailbox

She Makes It Look Easy

A June Bride

Handle with Care

A Novel

Marybeth Mayhew Whalen

Thomas Nelson
Since 1798

Handle with Care

Published by Thomas Nelson, 501 Nelson Place, Nashville, TN 37214, USA. Thomas Nelson is a registered trademark of HarperCollins Christian Publishing, Inc.

Thomas Nelson titles may be purchased in bulk for educational, business, fundraising, or sales promotional use. For information, please email SpecialMarkets@ThomasNelson.com.

HarperCollins Publishers, Macken House, 39/40 Mayor Street Upper, Dublin 1, D01 C9W8, Ireland (https://www.harpercollins.com)

Library of Congress Cataloging-in-Publication Data

ISBN 978-1-4003-4506-9 (epub)
ISBN 978-1-4003-4505-2 (TP)
ISBN 978-1-4003-4507-6 (audio download)

Printed in the United States of America

26 27 28 29 30 LBC 5 4 3 2 1

This one is for Ingrid Herriott, who lent so much to this story.

And in memory of her mother, Kari Cynar, who made sure we met.

At acceptance, Postal employees will ask, "Does this parcel contain anything liquid, fragile, perishable, or potentially hazardous?"

—United States Postal Service

Hostage or not, sometimes it's just nice to be held.

—Unknown

The Parts of a Friendly Letter

(And the Parts of This Story)

1. heading
2. greeting
3. body
4. closing
5. signature

Heading

This is a story about hope. It is also a story about four women who are taken hostage by a young man with a gun and not much of a plan, but we will get to that later. Before we do, we should spend a moment discussing hope. *Hope* can be a noun or a verb. And while it will likely be used as a verb at some point in the story, for now we are going to focus on *hope* as a noun. A noun, as you might remember from elementary school, can be a person, place, or thing. Our hope is two of those.

While there are places called Hope, hope is not a place in this situation. Instead, our story happens in a little town called Sunset Beach, North Carolina. Depending on which way you are going—north or south—Sunset Beach is either the last beach in North Carolina or the first. It is a lovely little town, a place where nothing much happens, which is what the people who live there love about it. People say Disney is the happiest place on earth, when, actually, Sunset Beach is. But even in the happiest of places, things can go awry.

So if hope is not a place, then you've probably guessed that it is both a person and a thing in our story. And you would be right. Hope is a person, whom you will soon meet. You will also meet Sylvie and Morrow and Blythe and Nadine, and others who will come in and out of this story. (There are a lot of people involved in a hostage situation, as you can imagine.) As our story begins, Hope, the person, doesn't have much hope, the thing, at all. But it's important to remember that no matter what happens from here on out, this is a story about hope. Now, let's get started.

Greeting

Chapter 1

April 16

IT IS SPRING in Sunset Beach, which is second only to fall in Sunset Beach. Summer is a necessary time for the town since most of the people who live here make the bulk of their income from the tourists who arrive in summer, tripling the population for the high season of Memorial Day through Labor Day. But in the spring (and fall) the weather is lovely, the tourists are mostly gone, and the beaches are less crowded. Everything is less crowded. In spring the people who live here year-round are especially grateful they do.

This week is no exception, as the forecast is for temperatures in the seventies and no rain. When Sylvie checks the weather on her phone, she sees only a line of suns. If she had a yard, she'd be outside gardening on a week like this. But Sylvie doesn't have a yard anymore because she has moved to an "active living community." There, retirees like herself and her husband live in a little (less to clean!) one-level (no stairs to climb!) house with a yard the size of a postage stamp (no grass to mow!). Everything about their living situation tends toward less activity, which has begun to suit Sylvie just fine.

Though she doesn't like to admit it, she's not a young woman anymore. In fact, some might call her old. She is confronted with this truth whenever she sees her face. Or whenever she looks at her husband, Robert, who has morphed into an old man, with hair growing out of his ears and eyelids that have pleated, the flesh drooping down over his eyes, reminding her a little of a basset hound they once had. Though she would never say that to him.

How did this happen? She sometimes thinks when she looks at Robert, and always when she looks at herself, *How did we get so old?* Sylvie is thinking about being old a lot more since their son and his family visited for the weekend just a few days ago. The thought of the weekend makes her eyes stray to the large manila envelope she has tucked out of sight in the space between her nightstand and the bed. She'd promised to mail it this week, but the week is almost over. Sylvie turns away from the envelope, leaving it behind by leaving her bedroom.

She goes to the kitchen instead, busying herself with something else besides the envelope and what is inside it. Though she's already made lunch for Robert (she wasn't hungry, but he was), she needs to decide what to fix for dinner. She has been thinking about what to fix for dinner for decades now, yet the question still regularly stumps her. She rummages around in the refrigerator at their prospects, which are not so good. She really needs to make a run to the grocery store, another errand she has been putting off, but not for the same reasons she has put off going to the post office.

Sylvie opens the pantry door as if something magic will appear before her eyes. But, to quote the old nursery rhyme, the cupboard is bare. Sylvie thinks maybe she and Robert will just go out to dinner. They go out to dinner too much now that they are retired. She admits this. But it's so nice to have somewhere to go, to chat with other people, even if those people are only the restaurant owners and servers. It adds some excitement to the day. Retirement is, as her friend Bea says, "six Saturdays and a Sunday." Sylvie used to look forward to weekends. Now her life is one long loop of them. It's not that retirement isn't nice. It's quite relaxing. It's just sort of, if she's being completely honest, boring.

Sylvie shuts the pantry door and goes to stand at the kitchen window, which looks out over their suggestion of a backyard. From the window she spots a large lizard strolling across their back deck. He stops to tip his head toward the sky as a large red plume emerges from his neck. She calls out to Robert, "That big ole lizard is back!" and smiles to herself as she hears a hurried shuffling of feet in response. She doesn't know what it says about their life that a lizard sighting is cause for excitement, but as the young people say, it is what it is.

Sylvie observes the lizard's attempt to attract a mate, both intrigued and horrified by the strange ritual taking place on their porch. Robert comes to stand beside her, and they watch side by side without speaking. Once, a female lizard appeared and the male jumped on her. The two wrestled around in a violent sort of way until Sylvie banged on the glass and they both ran off. Perhaps this will occur again. Sylvie finds herself hoping for it, just for something to happen.

Robert turns to grin at her, and for a fraction of a second she fears that he has forgotten who she is, that he will ask her name and try to introduce himself. It would not be the first time. But no, he is smiling just to smile. Today is one of his good days, and he must know it as much as she does, though they will not put words to it.

She thinks of the envelope again as the lizard gives up his quest for a mate and wanders off. Watching him go, she decides what she's going to do, committing before she can talk herself out of it. She turns away from the window to look at Robert. "I have to run an errand," she says to him. "Just a quick one." She smiles even as a sick dread fills her stomach over the part she is leaving out. A half-truth is not a lie, she reasons.

"We're woefully low on food, so I need to pick up something to make for dinner tonight. What are you in the mood for?"

Instead of answering, Robert takes her in his arms and dances her around the kitchen, humming "I'm in the Mood for Love." Sylvie laughs, and the dread she was feeling dissipates some. Robert takes her on a rotation of their small kitchen before letting her go. He steps back. "I could come with you?" he offers.

"No," she says as her heart picks up speed. If Robert joins her, he will wonder why she's stopping at the post office. He will ask what's in the envelope she is mailing. Sylvie doesn't want Robert to know what's in the envelope. She doesn't want anyone to know what's in there. She wishes she didn't herself.

"I'll be quick," she tells him. "And you hate grocery shopping."

She gives him a reassuring smile, though it's herself she's trying to reassure. She adds, "Just don't come in here and make any food while I'm gone. I'll be back in plenty of time to make us dinner, and I wouldn't want you spoiling it." She gives a little laugh, an effort to make light of what she has just said to her husband, speaking to him as if he were a child, thinking of any other things he could attempt that he shouldn't while she is gone.

"And don't go for a walk by yourself, okay? Wait for me, and we can do something when I get back. I won't be gone long." She says this again, wondering if she should leave him alone at all. But no, she will continue to think positive: He is having a good day. He knows who she is, he's in good spirits, he's recognized the routines of their day, and he's been oriented to his surroundings. (These are all the things Sylvie has learned to watch out for from googling.) A couple of quick errands should be fine. She worries too much.

She huffs out the anxiety that has built up within her as Robert nods his assent to all she has said, not seeming to notice her safeguarding. And if he does, he doesn't mention it. Neither of them ever broaches what is happening to him. Theirs is a tacit pact to ignore it until a time comes when they have to address it. But Sylvie does wish she could talk to him about it. To do so would be to share the burden, just as they always have when hard things have come along. But would that be selfish of her to force the issue if he'd rather not face it? She fears it would, so she keeps quiet. Instead, she asks him for ideas of what they could do when she gets home.

"It's such a pretty day," Robert says. "We could take our chairs out to the beach and sit."

They love to do that. It is one of their favorite things about living in Sunset Beach. They have so much time together now. Time they've waited so long to have. And yet the more time they have, the faster it seems to slip away. *Not yet,* she thinks. *Not yet.*

"Yes," she tells her husband. "That sounds lovely." She is already looking forward to that moment. In just a few hours it will be the two of them with their toes in the sand and the ocean as their vista. They might even take along books to read. Nonfiction for him, fiction for her, just the way it's always been. "Let's do that. Anything you want."

He waggles his eyebrows and she sees the young man he once was. That was a long time ago and no time at all. "Anything?" he asks, and she laughs as he takes her in his arms again, spinning her around the room one more time.

Chapter 2

THIS STORY STARTS with a hot dog. That's boiling it down some (get it—hot dog, boil?), but without that hot dog, it's fair to say that none of the rest of what's to come would've happened. Two postal workers, Martha and Stacy, got a craving for a hot dog, a very specific hot dog from a very specific place called Burg Dog, and decided they just couldn't go on with their workday without one.

They talked about how good those hot dogs were so much that they convinced the new girl at the post office, Nadine, to hold down the fort while they ran over to Shallotte "real quick" to get them all hot dogs for lunch. (Even though we all know no one runs "real quick" over to Shallotte.) Someone had to stay at the post office to take care of the customers, and being the newbie, Nadine was the easy pawn in Stacy and Martha's plan to cut out of there.

It is a Thursday, after all, which in many towns like Sunset Beach is Friday eve. And it is springtime to boot. The flowers are blooming, the sun is shining bold and bright in the sky, and the air feels fresh and hopeful. It is the kind of spring day when you can smell the green in the air. So naturally Stacy and Martha wanted a little field trip away from work. Who could blame them?

Those two were breaking rules and taking risks by leaving in the middle of a shift, but Nadine figured what business was it of hers if they did? It wasn't her neck on the chopping block if they got caught. Nadine's biggest concern was whether she could hold her own with the customers who came in while Stacy and Martha were gone.

"What do I do if they ask to speak to whoever's in charge?" she asked Martha, who actually was in charge, just before they left.

"Tell them *you* are," quipped Martha. Then they all laughed, because that was far from the truth.

Nadine isn't the "person in charge" type. She tends to be more the quiet, unobtrusive, "fade into the background" type. Unless she's singing. When Nadine is singing, she isn't quiet or unobtrusive, and she doesn't fade into the background. She "comes out of her shell," as her mama says. Nadine wants to come out of her shell more often. It's just hard to find the opportunity. People expect her to be a certain way. Case in point, Stacy and Martha expected her to go along with their scheme, and that's exactly what she did.

Through the front windows of the post office, Nadine sees Martha's car pull out of the parking lot and tries to remember if she'd told them to add onions to her hot dog. It doesn't matter anyway. She will get what she gets. She can live without onions. She just hopes they remember that she'd said no mustard. Her mama always taught her never to say "hate" about anything, but Nadine does hate mustard.

Restless, she stands up from the little stool she usually sits on and stretches her back, lifting her arms up into the air as she reaches for the ceiling, then dipping all the way down toward the floor before standing back up again. It feels good to stretch and take some deep breaths. She is tired from staying late at Wednesday night karaoke last night. She knows she should've gone home at a decent hour, but she'd been having such a good time. It was hard to leave knowing she was only going home to her little, empty house. And, she will admit, she likes the compliments she gets from people when she sings, telling her she has a good voice, telling her she should go on *American Idol* or *The Voice* or some such. Like she ever would.

Don't get her wrong. She loves to sing. But she's pretty sure she doesn't have that kind of talent. She's good enough for a church solo, which is how she got started singing back when she was a little bitty thing. But even though she likes singing, she knows she shouldn't have gone out on a weeknight when she should've been getting her rest.

The job at the post office is exhausting. There is so much to learn, so much to remember. It is not easy keeping up with all the rules and regulations attached to mailing a simple package. Nadine doesn't think she'll ever learn it all. Stacy, who's taken her under her wing and been so nice to her ever since she got here, says she'll get the hang of it before she knows it. She hopes so. She needs the job now more than ever, even if it overwhelms her.

At least she has the weekend to look forward to. Tomorrow is Friday! TGIF! Nadine checks the clock to see how much longer till she can go home. She lets out a long sigh. There are still five hours to go. Martha, who hasn't taken Nadine under her wing and isn't really the type to take anyone under her wing, says that if you want to make time slow down, just hang out in the Sunset Beach post office. Martha isn't wrong. Martha rarely is, and she's the first to let you know it.

Wait. She looks back at the clock, registering the time as her heart lifts a little. By now he has the papers. By now he should know. It is a good sign, she decides, that she's gotten no calls or texts. She feels a little glimmer in her heart, the faintest stirring, the stardust but not the whole shooting star. Still, it is enough. It is still hope. *Maybe*, she thinks, *everything will be okay.* Just like her mama said it would. But Mama doesn't know the whole story. There are some things Nadine doesn't want to burden her mama with yet.

Before she can think on it anymore, the entry door opens and a woman comes in carrying a large box, struggling under its weight. The door doesn't swing closed behind her because another woman comes in right on the other woman's heels. Customers. Nadine swallows back her nerves, hoping she can take care of whatever these ladies need without having her coworkers here to back her up. She hopes Stacy and Martha won't dilly-dally, but she isn't counting on it. Now that they have escaped, they aren't likely to rush back. Not on a day like today.

The customer hoists the box up onto the counter between them, blocking Nadine's view of her and cutting off any chance that the woman can see the helpful smile Nadine tries to offer. Later Nadine will recall that moment, how she thought to herself, *It's showtime.*

And what a show it turned out to be.

Chapter 3

Just a little ways down the road from the post office, a woman is running. Not for her life, but for her health. The woman is Hope, the person, who doesn't necessarily like to run but does so because she knows she should since she's not old but she's not getting any younger either. She is also running because she is bored and she knows a run will kill some time before she can shower, then walk the short distance from the place she has been calling home to the place where she works.

She rounds the corner and her heart sinks a little at the sight of the house. She might *call* it home, but it is not her home. Hope has a home, but it is halfway across the country from where she is now. She left that home to come to Sunset Beach, to the trailer everyone in her family refers to as simply "108."

Hope's family has made 108 Live Oak Drive their second home since 1980, not all that long after Sunset Beach was established, which was in 1958. (If you want to fact-check that date, just look at the T-shirts the tourists wear, and you'll see.) But it's a long time nonetheless, especially when you consider that 1980 was almost fifty years ago, which, for many of us, is hard to accept.

Hope's grandmother used to own the trailer, and when she passed it was left to Hope's dad. But he doesn't come here much anymore. So when everything happened and she needed somewhere to land, it made sense for her to land here. She planned to stay a few weeks, but that was eight months ago.

Hope slows her pace as she nears 108, allowing both her and her running partner, a Rottweiler named Rufus, time to catch their collective breath. She can hear Rufus panting as they walk, but she does not make eye contact with him. She knows she probably ran farther than he would've wanted had he possessed the means to say so. Rufus is not old, but he's not getting any younger either. He does not love to run no matter how good it is for him. As they walk the remaining distance to the trailer, Hope reminds Rufus of the benefits of running. She discusses the effects of cardio on heart health and weight loss. She does not say that Rufus could stand to lose a few pounds. She doesn't want to hurt his feelings.

A little truck drives past them, and they pause before crossing to the driveway of 108. "Plus, I have to go to work soon," Hope continues, "and you'll be in your crate the whole time I'm gone." At the word *crate*, Rufus comes to a stop. But Hope tugs gently on his leash to keep him moving. "Now you'll be good and tired and the time will go by faster because you'll be asleep while I'm gone. So really, I did you a favor."

They make their way up the driveway together, Rufus taking his sweet time until they hear the crunching of tires on the gravel and turn in unison to see the same truck that just drove by suddenly there, behind them. She hears the driver put the truck into Park, and her heart rate spikes in tandem. She reminds herself that this is Sunset Beach, not Philadelphia, Pennsylvania. There is no need to be alarmed.

Rufus, however, does not see the distinction and begins barking and lunging at the driver, who is really, she sees as he emerges from the truck, just a boy. A boy who immediately flattens himself against the truck at the sight of the dog, his eyes wide as he says something that sounds like, "Uhhhh?"

Hope struggles to apologize to the kid and wrestle with Rufus at the same time. It takes all of her strength to restrain the beast. Rufus is a sweet dog, but he is trained for Hope's safety and takes that job very seriously.

Once Rufus is still, she scolds him for good measure, using her authoritative voice. She knows that if Rufus could roll his eyes in response, he would. She goes to take a step but discovers that Rufus, in his efforts to get at the truck's driver, has somehow wound the leash around her legs. If she actually needed to run away, she would not be able to. So, in that respect, Rufus has not been thinking of her safety. She alternates between trying to unwind the leash from her calves and maintain control of Rufus. Once freed, she yanks the leash in such a way that Rufus has no choice but to head with her toward the trailer.

She calls out over her shoulder, "Let me just put him up," without even checking to see if the kid is still smashed up against the truck. Inside the house, she unclips the leash, freeing Rufus to go stick his head in his water bowl, which he does, making loud, grateful slurping noises. Hope could use some water too, but first she needs to get rid of the kid in her driveway. If he is even still there. He might've fled after his run-in with Rufus. No one would blame him.

She turns and goes back through the door, running smack into someone as she does. Except she hasn't run into a person. She's run into a massive bouquet of flowers. A floral scent fills the air around her, reminding her of the way the church sanctuary smelled on her wedding day. For a moment she feels dizzy, disoriented.

"I'm sorry, ma'am," says the kid, who is now in her doorway holding the flowers. If Hope had looked closer, she would've noticed the florist's logo on the side of his truck, but she was distracted by her dog. "I just thought I'd bring these on in to you. Are you okay?"

"Sure, sure," she manages to say. "I'm fine." She takes the bouquet from the boy's outstretched hand and gives it a once-over. It seems fine too. No flowers were harmed in this collision.

The kid points at the card that is fastened to the bouquet. "Hope," he says, reading her name aloud.

Hope nods. "That's my name," she says. She does not say *don't wear it out*, but she thinks it.

"Huh," he says. "That's the name of this bouquet too." He points again at her name on the card as if it is proof. "We call it the 'Hope Bouquet.' My mom came up with it." He gestures to the flowers, the wide array of incongruent colors and shapes clustered together. "She puts in all the different flowers that are supposed to symbolize hope, you know?"

She does know. It had been her husband Alex's idea to fill the sanctuary at their wedding with all the flowers that are meant to symbolize hope: lilies and crocuses and cherry blossoms and irises and daffodils. It was a loud, mismatched, beautiful mess. In keeping with the theme, she'd danced with her father to "Wildflowers" by Tom Petty as her mother stood off to the side watching, persistently catching her tears with a tissue to preserve her full face of makeup.

"I guess whoever sent you these saw we had a bouquet with your name on it, so they just had to choose it," the boy says, pulling her out of the memory. "Usually people send it for, like, tragedies and stuff."

Tragedies, Hope thinks. There are several things she could say in response to that, but none of them seem appropriate to tell this boy. So she says, "Yeah, I guess so," then adds, "Well, thanks again," and waves the flowers. "Better go put these in some water."

"No problem," he says. Close up, the kid doesn't even look old enough to be driving. He might not be. He gives her a grin and then hurries away, calling out, "Have a nice day, *Hope*," over his shoulder as he goes.

Hope looks down at her name on the envelope as she carries the flowers inside, knowing without opening the card who they are from. Of course Alex has sent her a bouquet called Hope, observing her birthday even though she'd asked him not to. She knew better than to tell him that she didn't deserve to celebrate her birthday—that would only result in a lecture—so she'd said, "I don't feel like celebrating," which was also true.

She sets the flowers down on the counter and plucks the card from its little stake, tearing at the seal to reveal the tiny greeting that is clearly not in her husband's handwriting because he is far, far away. She looks down at the words he has told the florist to write:

> I always feel like celebrating you. Happy Birthday.
>
> Love,
> Alex

Hope traces her finger across the words and stands in silence for a moment, reminded of the decisions she has to make. But now is not the time. Birthday or no, she has to get to work. She looks at the clock—between the extra-long run and the flower delivery, she's going to be late if she doesn't get a move on. She doesn't have time to trim flower stems and prepare a vase and put the bouquet in water. But if she doesn't, they will wither and possibly die. Hope studies the bouquet for one second longer. She lets herself appreciate the beauty, the aroma, the memories that swirl in the air. Her birthday used to be such a special day, a day that always involved celebrating in some way with her mom. Hope bends over and inhales deeply. Then she stands up, turns away, and leaves the flowers behind.

Body

Chapter 4

And now we return to the post office. Sunset Beach is replete with beautiful, picturesque places to visit. There is the town park that overlooks the Intracoastal Waterway, the old swing bridge that citizens of the town preserved when the new bridge was built, and plenty of lush, green golf courses to beckon enthusiasts of the sport. There is Bird Island, home of the Kindred Spirit Mailbox, which sits in the dunes of the long stretch of undeveloped coastline. In the decades it has stood there, thousands of people have left messages to the Kindred Spirit, containing everything from happiness to heartbreak. And there is the beach itself, recently voted as one of the ten most beautiful in the world by *National Geographic*. You can look it up.

But the town post office would not be considered a beautiful place to include in a visit to Sunset Beach. The low-slung red-brick building is set back off the street, close to the main intersection of town. It is a functional place, which is what post offices are meant to be. Though from the street the building appears to be large, the actual part where transactions occur is quite small. To access that section of the post office, you must walk through a set of double doors in the front, then enter a vestibule area, then make a left and walk through another door. Then you're where you need to be.

Inside you will find exactly what you would expect to find

in any post office: floor space for customers to wait in line and display cases of greeting cards and mailing supplies strategically placed around the room. To the right is the front desk where the postal workers receive customers, and to the left is a bank of windows looking out at the parking lot.

If you were thinking there would be anything cutesy or beachy here, you'd be wrong. It is as utilitarian as any normal, run-of-the-mill government building. It's good that you have at least a nodding familiarity with the post office as, though it might be hard to imagine, we will spend most of the rest of the story here—certainly longer than any of the people in line expect.

Right now the line is not that long. Not as long as it can get during busier times. Sometimes the line is out the door and into the vestibule. But that's usually at Christmas. Not like today. Today there is one man at the front of the line and four women of varying ages and walks of life waiting their turn behind him. Even though Sunset Beach is a small town, these folks are all complete strangers. But they will not stay strangers for long.

The lone man never looks back at who's behind him, as he is intent on speaking to the postal clerk. It seems he is not aware that the four women behind him are even there. One woman stands out because she is talking on her phone. She came in on the phone and has stayed on the phone since she stepped foot in the place. She is one of those people who talks loudly and freely in public places, as if it has never occurred to her that others can hear her conversation or might be bothered by it.

The other three women, who have been subjected to her conversation whether they like it or not, have learned that she has had a session with her personal trainer already this morning and is quite proud of herself for having done so. They also know she is there to ship back some protein powder that is—as she puts it—foul. She would not—under any circumstance—consume it

again, no matter how committed she is to getting a hundred grams of protein a day.

The three women who are not having a private conversation loudly in public glanced at one another as they took their places in the queue, giving a little nod or the kind of closed-lip smile that says, "I acknowledge your presence, but I don't care to engage with you." Which is fair enough. No one has time to engage with everyone they encounter on a given day. Each of the other three women is, after all, in a hurry to run this one errand and move on, like most any person who is running errands would be.

It goes a little deeper than that, however. These three are carrying packages that, once mailed, have the potential to change their lives forever. But they wouldn't want you to know about that. They'd prefer to keep what's in those packages to themselves.

One of the three, Blythe, is also engrossed in her phone, but not to talk. Instead, her thumbs bounce across the buttons in a flurry of motion. It is important to note that, though Blythe is wearing an engagement ring on the hand that clutches her phone, she is texting someone who is not her fiancé. When she is not texting, she is picking the nail polish off her nails. She'd painted them last night for a very special dinner. But that dinner had not gone well, and now the nail polish only serves to remind her.

Another of the three, Morrow, seems rattled, as if something happened to her before she got here. Even if you don't know the first thing about her, it's obvious. This is because something did happen. She has just had a run-in with one of the local cops. He turned on his lights and his siren and pulled her over like a criminal. One of her neighbors drove by and saw the whole thing. At least she thinks it was one of her neighbors. A lot of people in the area drive small white SUVs, so it might not have been. But still. Morrow, a law-abiding citizen with a clean driving record, is mortified. Instead of letting herself think about what the officer said, she grips her long dark ponytail and runs her cupped hand along the length of it, smoothing it, and her nerves, as she does.

Morrow was so sure the cop wasn't after her that at first she didn't respond to the flashing lights and wailing siren when the car came up behind her. She wondered why he wasn't going around her. Then it dawned on her that she was his target. Confused, she checked her speed, but it was not above the limit. (People tend to go slow in Sunset Beach as there is rarely a reason to be in a hurry.) She pulled the car over to the curb and rolled down her window. The warm salty air rushed into the car as she waited to see what the officer wanted with her.

"License and registration," he said, all business. As he bent down to speak with her, his stomach spilled over his belt. Weren't police officers supposed to keep fit? Wasn't there some sort of rule about that?

She tried not to focus on his belly as she handed over her license and registration, then waited in her car while he ambled back to his own. She still didn't know what she had done wrong, and she hadn't been brave enough to ask. Cars passed by, their drivers gawking at her as they did. He sat in the patrol car for what seemed like an excessive amount of time before returning to hand back her license and registration.

"Ma'am," he said, "did you know your car tag is invalid?"

She blinked at him. "Invalid?"

"Expired," he said. He cleared his voice. "The renewal's past due."

"Oh, okay," she said. She almost told him this was her husband Kevin's fault. He always took care of anything to do with their vehicles, so she hadn't the slightest idea of when or if her car tag needed some sort of renewal. She thought that might diminish her in his sight, though. It sort of diminished her in her own.

When the children were little, she had so many other things on her mind, it only stood to reason that Kevin took some things off her plate. He handled things like lawn care and vehicle maintenance while she handled things like well-child appointments and carpooling and getting dinner on the table every night. Now, as she was literally being talked down to by a cop, she wondered if she shouldn't be taking on more, doing more, seeing as how the children are no longer little. She is without excuse. Maya, her baby, is graduating high school in a little more than a month. At the end of the summer her daughter will be off at college and her nest will be empty. Somehow Morrow has worked herself out of a job. Her car tag isn't the only thing that's invalid. Expired. It seems she is as well.

She accepted the officer's paperwork and reprimand with an apology, her cheeks burning hot as more rubberneckers passed them by. After he'd gotten into his car and pulled away to find some other unsuspecting victim, she took a deep breath, put her car back into Drive, and pressed her foot to the gas. Between the scene with Maya this morning and then being publicly humiliated, Morrow has already had quite a day, and it has barely started.

The last of the three women is Sylvie, whom you've already met. She did make it to the post office after all. She is hoping the line moves along quickly because she needs to hurry back to Robert. Sylvie tries not to think about what Robert could be doing in her absence. Instead, she studies the signs about federal regulations for mailing packages as if there will be a test later, clutching the manila envelope in her hand so tightly she realizes she is creasing it. It does not fit in her purse, so she has to carry it, which makes her resent the envelope all the more. She relaxes her hand and, pressing the envelope against her thigh, bends over and tries to smooth it back out. But the paper refuses to cooperate with her efforts. It is permanently wrinkled, like her.

She gives up, her back protesting as she stands up straight again, glancing once more at the lone woman working in the post office today and the rude man who is taking up far too much of her time. Whatever his issue is, Sylvie thinks he needs to step aside and give other people a chance. But that doesn't happen.

The postal worker, Nadine, whom you've also already met, and the man just keep talking and talking, their heads bent close together as they discuss whatever is in his envelope, which he has begun to jab with his index finger. Sylvie, Blythe, and Morrow watch the interaction intently, trying to ascertain what's going on. The woman who is talking on the phone, however, seems not to notice or mind the delay. She has gone on to launch into a list of the merits, and various sources, of protein. Being of a certain age, Morrow knows that protein is important, but in her opinion, this woman has taken it too far. She feels for whoever is on the other end of that call.

Sometimes Sylvie, Blythe, and Morrow give one another sympathetic glances, but they don't speak, only expressing their impatience by alternating their huffing and sighing. Once, Blythe, who is next in line, turns and rolls her eyes at Sylvie, like "Can you believe this?" Sylvie smiles in response, pleased to be in on the joke. Usually young people don't notice her at all.

Sylvie debates leaving. She could go over to the Food Lion and get the things they need for supper tonight, then come back after the rude man is gone. She glances down at the envelope, sees Robert's name there, the familiar address. She flips the envelope over so she doesn't have to look at it. She wants this done and off her mind. Then she can get on with her day. Or she can try to. In truth, she doubts she will think about anything else for the rest of the day except what she is doing here, in this moment.

Still, it has to be done. She agreed. She promised. So she keeps her place, watching the scene at the front of the line a little more intently as she tries to discern what the holdup is. She tries to make out what the man is saying, but her ears aren't what they used to be and the two are less talking and more murmuring. All she hears is his voice, the words like a hiss. It's pretty clear that he is angry. Someone should intervene.

Sylvie looks around the post office, trying to find a supervisor or . . . someone else to help. But there is no one, which is different. Every other time she's been in to mail something there have been at least two people taking care of customers, and usually a third person who serves in some sort of support role. Sylvie wonders if perhaps there *is* someone in the back, if maybe she should try to let another worker—hopefully a superior—know there's a problem up front.

"Do you think maybe we should check back there?" she tries to ask Blythe, but Blythe's nose is back in her phone, her fingers moving again. It amazes Sylvie how fast these young people are with texting. Sylvie can text, and she does. It's the only way she communicates with her granddaughters. But she's nowhere nearly that quick at it. Sylvie still prefers a good old-fashioned phone call. But she realizes she is one of the few who does.

She rises up on her tiptoes, trying to peer at the back of the building, but it is useless. From where they stand, she is not tall enough to see beyond the section where the clerks work. There is a half-wall partition blocking her view, but she can make out some sort of shipping area behind it. Sylvie sinks back on her heels, her arches protesting as she thinks again about walking out, her grip tightening on the envelope anew, as if she can squeeze the life out of it. She's being silly, obviously. There is no life in this envelope. Which is sort of the point.

"Surely he'll move along soon." She says this sort of loudly, boldly, hoping the man will hear her and take the hint. She would like that very much.

The man does not appear to hear, but Blythe does, looking back and nodding before returning to her phone.

"I'm thinking of saying something," Sylvie says to Blythe's back. Then she tries to get the attention of the woman on the phone behind her, but that woman doesn't notice because she is still deep in her very public private conversation.

Morrow, who would like to get this errand over with so she can go home and maybe even have a glass of wine with her lunch—she feels she has earned it—chimes in, "You probably should if it's been a while." Morrow is the last person in line; she has been there for the least amount of time. But she is in favor of moving things along.

"It's been more than a while," Sylvie answers. "I debated leaving, but I don't want to have to come back, you know?"

Morrow nods.

Sylvie looks nervously over at the man and Nadine, still locked in what seems to be a heated conversation. "So you do think I should?"

Morrow and Blythe, who has looked up from her texting again, both nod. They watch as Sylvie leaves her place in line and bustles up to stand right beside the agitated man. It is a little too close if you ask Morrow, but she isn't getting involved. She is a bystander and a bystander only.

"Excuse me," Morrow hears Sylvie say to Nadine, completely ignoring the man standing there. "I was wondering if perhaps you have someone else who might wait on us?" Sylvie gestures to her fellow line mates, though the woman talking on the phone remains oblivious. "We've been waiting quite some time and, well, we all need to be getting on with our day."

"Yes, certainly," Nadine says, looking down at the man's envelope as she speaks. "I'm sorry," Nadine says to Sylvie, then looks back at the man. "I guess you'd better go now."

In response to being dismissed, the man steps back from the counter, indignant. He sways before regaining his footing. His nostrils flare as he breathes in and out, in and out, like a bull who just spotted the matador waving his cape. The noise is loud in a room gone quiet, his face a question mark as his head swings to the left to look at the women in line, then to the right to look at the doorway, then back at Nadine.

"When I call you later, you'd better answer," he growls.

Watching this, Morrow now understands that they were not discussing the mail, that he is not a customer. She sees him snatch up the envelope they appeared to be arguing over and stalk off. But when he does, she keeps her eyes on Nadine, who appears to be about the same age as the man. She's probably not much older than Morrow's own son, a recent college graduate, now off in the world of "adulting," as he calls it. Adulting, he tells her, is not as much fun as he expected it to be. Morrow tried to tell him that all those years when he was so anxious to grow up. Now he has, and now he knows.

Chapter 5

OUTSIDE TOMMY KICKS his way out the set of doors that takes him to the parking lot. He sees his truck, old and rusting, parked as far away from the building as he could manage. He hadn't wanted Nadine to spot him coming. And she hadn't. She'd been so surprised when she looked up and saw him walk in, the envelope containing the papers he'd been served with curled against his chest like he might've held a child. If they'd had the chance to have a child.

But no, Nadine has seen to it that that won't happen now. What happened to vows? To promises? To "for better or for worse"? Sure, he's been pushing the limits of "worse" for a while now—probably longer than he should have. But he'd counted on her love; he'd depended on her grace. He'd always had both. Since they were teenagers, her love and her grace have been as steady as the tides.

He climbs up into his truck, tosses the damn envelope into the passenger seat, and slams the door hard, the whole truck rocking on its axles as he reaches for his seat belt. He pauses, thinks better of it, then lets the belt go, hearing it zip back into its place. He rests his hands on the steering wheel and stares at the post office, thinking of the old man who was in line in front of him when he arrived. Hadn't he waited patiently for his turn? Hadn't he smiled at the old man when he left?

Tommy had listened as Nadine spoke gently to the old man, who was there to return a piece of mail that had been misdelivered to him. She'd explained to him that if that ever happened again, he needed only to place it back in his mailbox, pull the flag, and the postal carrier would bring it back to the post office and see to it that it was delivered correctly. That way he wouldn't have to spend his time driving to the post office, waiting in line, and all that.

The old man had listened to this, nodding along. When Nadine finished, he smiled and said, "I'm eighty-eight years old. I didn't have anything better to do." Then he smiled again and shuffled off to wherever he'd come from.

Instead of turning to greet her husband (he is still her husband, and that's the point), Nadine had watched the old man make his slow way across the floor and exit the building before turning back to look at Tommy. For a few minutes they were in the same room alone. It had been a while since that had been the case, and it took all he had not to reach across the counter and pull her to him or to come around that counter, get on his knees in front of her, and beg her not to do this.

Sure, she'd kicked him out, which he'd accepted as something she needed to do. He even thought the break might be a good thing for both of them. But he'd also thought she'd calm down and let him come home. He thought they'd figure things out like they always had. But then that server had showed up at his work today. His place of employment! In front of God and everybody! Talk about adding insult to injury.

Tommy casts a glance at those papers, thinking that if he had laser eyes like the superheroes he watched as a kid, he'd incinerate them right there in the seat. It'd catch the seat on fire, but he wouldn't care. Those papers would be gone, and there would still be hope for him and Nadine.

But he doesn't have laser eyes, and Nadine is in there with customers, and—she had a point—it isn't right to show up at her work. Not that she didn't send someone to his work today, he thinks. Then he hears his dad in his head saying, "*Two wrongs don't make a right, son.*"

At the thought of his dad, he leans over and hits the button to open the glove compartment. Inside he sees the handle of bourbon he's been swigging from since he left work. The GM—not just his boss, but the damn GM of the whole dealership—had come and found him under a car to tell him, with this pitying look that made Tommy feel worse, not better, that he could go home for the day. Then the pompous ass had flashed a smile—like there was something to smile about—and added, "With pay."

Well, whoop-de-do, Tommy had thought. But he'd left all the same.

Now Tommy takes a long pull from the handle of bourbon, enjoying the burn and the warmth that comes with it. He thinks of the first time he ever tasted bourbon. He'd been hunting with his dad. He'd been a kid—no older than fourteen or fifteen—but it had been cold and his dad had offered him a sip. "It'll cure what ails ya," he'd promised. Tommy wonders if he ever told his dad that he was right. It does cure what ails ya.

His thoughts are coming hard and fast: the old man, the GM, his father, all making him think about the man he's failed to be. He stares at the post office as he takes another sip. He doesn't think anyone has come or gone since he left, so it's still the same ladies in line in there. How many of them were there? Two? Four? He doesn't remember. He was too intent on getting Nadine to tear up those papers. If she will just tear up those papers it will mean . . . what? He doesn't know. He just wanted to do something, to change something. That's what a real man would do.

Tommy caps the bottle and goes to stick it back into the glove compartment but spies his gun sitting in there before he can. He stares at it for a moment before looking back at the post office. He just needs to make her understand. Not that he would ever use the gun, mind you. Just having it on him will up the ante. That's all he intends. A serious device to show how serious he is. He reaches for the gun and angles his body so he can get it into his pocket. Then he picks up the envelope with one hand and rests the bourbon in his lap so he can use his free hand to open the door.

Chapter 6

Morrow can see that Nadine is rattled but pretending not to be as she beckons to Blythe, who moves into the spot formerly occupied by the man who stalked out of the post office. Morrow can't help but notice that Nadine and Blythe are both younger than she is, as more and more people seem to be these days. When she was younger she didn't use to notice people's ages. But that was because she was young. At least, she thinks, she isn't as old as Sylvie, who has returned to her place in line looking pleased with herself. Morrow, like the others, ignores the woman on the phone entirely.

Morrow watches as thirtysomething (she estimates) Blythe walks up to twentysomething (again, another estimation) Nadine and lays a box wrapped in kraft paper on the counter in front of her. Morrow can't be sure, but she thinks she hears the distinct intake of breath that comes from someone stifling a sob. Morrow looks away from whatever is happening. She does not want to witness another person's pain. She has enough of her own, thank you very much.

Morrow smooths her ponytail, gripping the length of it, then looks down into the darkness of her tote bag, which grew too heavy as she waited and is now sitting innocuously at her feet, the small, padded envelope down in there somewhere. Not big enough to be a threat; at least no one would think so if they saw it. Morrow will not cry when she presents it to the clerk. She won't even need to stifle a sob. She will just put down her envelope and smile like she is any other woman running any other errand. *And that will be good*, she thinks. *That will be what's best.*

At the counter, Blythe is indeed stifling a sob. She is doing her very best not to break down and cry as she looks at the box, steeling herself against the threat of tears by thinking of terrible things that happen to other people—identity theft, extortion, abduction, assault. None of these things are happening to her, she tells herself. She is safe. She is fine. And though she might not be certain about what she's about to do, she is making someone else happy, and that's always a good thing. Right?

They all wait politely while Blythe gets herself together. Soon Blythe is able to force a smile for Nadine, who was clearly just threatened by some man. It could be some sort of domestic abuse–type situation, Blythe thinks. That's another thing that is not happening to her right now. This, she tells herself, is nothing at all. It might even be the right thing to do in the end.

She thinks of her mother this morning, sitting at Blythe's kitchen table, coffee cup in hand as she pronounced, as only her mother could, "You'll never know if you don't try. I'd hate to see you realize later in life that you didn't do what you could back when you had the chance." Her mother had sighed, then added, "I should know."

Blythe thinks her mother meant for her to inquire about this added comment. But she had not. She'd left for the post office instead. With any luck, her mother will be on the road back to Raleigh by the time Blythe gets home. Her mother has a big meeting this afternoon, so there's a good chance she will. Her mother always has a big meeting looming.

She pushes the box forward. "I would like to mail this," she manages to say, though the quiver in her voice remains. She brushes her fingertips across the box, a kind of caress.

"Okay," Nadine says, glancing at the address Blythe has carefully written on the box with a Sharpie, the black letters bold and blocky. Blythe looks at the address as well, reading the name written above it with something like surprise. She thinks about the note she tucked inside, thanks to her mother's prodding. Is it too much? Her eyes run along the line of tape she'd sealed the box with. Even if it is too much, it's too late now.

She listens to the clacking of keys as Nadine enters the information. Nadine points at a screen and directs Blythe to approve what she has entered. Even as she presses the button to designate her approval, Blythe considers yanking the box back and running out of here. *If you go through with this*, she thinks, *it could start something. It could end something.* Which does she want? She doesn't know for sure.

"Is there anything in here that is liquid, fragile, perishable, or potentially hazardous?" Nadine asks, her voice taking on that detached tone that says she has done this a hundred times before.

Fragile? Blythe thinks. *Yes. Potentially hazardous? Yes.* What will happen if she answers yes? Will the clerk tell her she can't mail the package after all? That would make things much simpler, the decision made for her.

"No," Blythe says.

"Okay," Nadine says as she types something else into her computer. Blythe reads her name tag. She looks like a Nadine, Blythe decides.

Nadine directs Blythe to punch a button that says that what she is mailing is safe to send through the United States Postal Service. Blythe presses the green button. Green means go. She is going ahead with this, for better or for worse. She twirls her engagement ring around her finger as she watches Nadine sweep the box off the counter and it drops out of sight. Blythe wants to tell her to be careful with it. But she has already said there is nothing fragile inside. She has pressed the green button.

For a crazy moment Blythe thinks about diving across the counter and retrieving the box. But before she can act on her impulse, she hears a rush of air entering the room as the door to the post office opens. Blythe sees Nadine's eyes cloud with concern and turns to see what it is Nadine has seen. At the same time she hears Sylvie behind her take in a breath.

Together Blythe, Nadine, Sylvie, and Morrow watch as Tommy comes back into the post office. This time he is carrying a fifth of bourbon, which he dramatically pauses to swill in the doorway as they all stare, frozen. His Adam's apple bobs as he swallows the liquid he's poured down his throat. The woman on the phone says, "I gotta go," and hangs up.

Blythe and the other women in line glance nervously at one another as Nadine says, "Tommy," in a strangled kind of way. It is the fear, Blythe thinks, that is choking her.

Tommy lowers the bottle of liquor and moves toward them with menace on his face. He is lanky and tall, able to cross the room in just a few strides. "Tommy." Nadine says his name again, and now they all know it, though they don't all know one another's yet. They will in due time, except for the woman who was on the phone.

"You're going to make me lose my job." Nadine smiles like she is making a joke, but Sylvie sees her lips give her away, a quiver that betrays her bravado. Tommy sees it too. He smirks as he lays the same envelope from before back on the counter, then sets the bottle of liquor right beside it, half gone.

Sylvie wonders if he's drunk it all today or only just started drinking. She thinks about how he swayed on his feet when he stepped away from the counter earlier and guesses it's probably, unfortunately, the former. Impaired men are even harder to reason with than sober ones.

He looks to his left at the women in line. "Sorry to interrupt, ladies. This won't take but a minute." He turns to face Nadine, speaking to them as he regards her. "All my wife needs to do is tear up these papers while I watch, and then I'll be on my way." He takes another pull from the bottle, then adds, "Right, Nadine?"

"This isn't the time or the place for this," Nadine says, the words thick in her mouth. "We can talk after I get off work."

Tommy gestures at the four women. "They'll wait." He turns to them again. They all stand, mouths agape, seemingly frozen to the floor with fear or shock or both. "Won't you?" he asks them.

They all nod even as Sylvie eyes the door and considers fleeing. But she is not as fast as she used to be, and running will only escalate what is, for now, a potentially resolvable situation. There is no need for alarm yet. Morrow debates running out too. But she also thinks this will blow over. No sense overreacting. She thinks of Maya, who claims she overreacts all the time. So she stays.

Blythe doesn't think of running because she is debating how she can get her package back. With everyone's eyes on Tommy, maybe they wouldn't notice her reaching over the counter? The woman on the phone isn't on the phone any longer and just stands there looking puzzled.

Tommy faces Nadine. He jabs at the envelope with his index finger as if he is driving a stake through it. "Tear it up," he says through his clenched teeth.

"I can't," Nadine says, lifting her chin in a defiant sort of way. "I worked hard for the money to have those papers drawn up."

"I don't care what you did," he says. "We are husband and wife. And that's the way it's gonna stay."

"You did this to yourself, Tommy," Nadine says, looking her husband square in the eyes. Sylvie knows Nadine is trying to appear big and brave, but she suspects that inside she feels small and scared.

Still, Sylvie sees her words hit Tommy, the barely perceptible flinch in his shoulders and head. "We can talk about that," he says with less swagger. Then adds with a plea in his voice, "We can fix it."

"I don't want to fix it," Nadine says, but her words sound sad as she says them. Nadine turns suddenly to look to the part of the post office that is behind the petition, her face hopeful. Sylvie looks too, as if someone has appeared back there, coming to their rescue. But there is no one.

Sylvie turns back to look at Tommy, and as she does, it takes her a moment to process what changed when her head was turned. It is hard for her to rectify that there is something in Tommy's hand that was not there before. And that something is a gun that is pointed right at Nadine.

Chapter 7

MORROW YELPS, THE noise jarring Sylvie, who still hasn't registered that this is really happening. She is not panicked like perhaps she should be, definitely not to the point of yelping. *No*, Sylvie persists in her thinking, *things like this don't happen in Sunset Beach.*

The yelp gets Tommy's attention as well, and he turns toward the sound, keeping the gun raised, but now he points it at the four women in line. Sylvie reaches back to Morrow and lays her hand on her forearm, hoping to calm her. "I think," Sylvie says to the room, "that we all just need to take a breath here."

She makes eye contact with Nadine, who has gone deathly pale. "Perhaps you two could set up a time to talk . . . later?" She hears the words as they leave her mouth, how inane they are. She fumbles for the right thing to say, scrambling to recall things she's heard before. "It sounds like you've got some things to sort through," she adds.

Tommy grins as he shakes his head. "There ain't nothing to sort through." He faces Nadine and uses the gun this time to jab at the envelope on the counter. "But there is something to tear through." He raises the gun and points it directly at his wife.

"Tear it up," he tells her. "Now."

They all watch as Nadine raises her arms from where they hang at her sides. Her hands hover in the airspace just above the envelope as she seems to consider her options, her gaze flitting from Tommy to the four other women. Aside from their collective unsteady breathing, the room is silent. She lowers her hands toward the envelope as they all inhale in expectation.

With any luck, she will just tear up the papers and, satisfied, Tommy will slink away. After he's gone, Sylvie decides, she will help Nadine gather the bits of paper. She will throw them away for her, get her some water, and assure her that tearing up the papers doesn't mean she's torn up her chance to get away from this crazy man. It is not about the papers but the intent behind them. Even if the step she has taken has failed, it is just a temporary setback.

Nadine picks up the envelope and stares down at it. A feeling of unity hangs in the room as everyone wills her to tear it in two. The ripping sound will be the best thing they've heard all day. "I—" Nadine says.

Just then the door to the post office opens and they all turn to see a woman walking in, her arms full of a large basket wrapped in cellophane and tied with a huge bow. The woman is so focused on managing the basket that she doesn't notice what is going on at the front of the room. She doesn't notice anything until Tommy turns the gun on her. He runs toward her, yelling, "Get the hell out of here!"

Seeing Tommy coming at her, gun drawn, the woman drops the basket and runs out, shrieking. The basket crashes to the floor and the cellophane pops open on impact. The contents spill out over the floor, and Tommy has to do some fancy footwork to miss tripping over the items, which is pretty remarkable considering his level of intoxication. But he continues chasing the woman, who gets away before he can reach the door.

Muttering a string of expletives, Tommy shuts the door that leads out to the vestibule. He pushes a large display of greeting cards in front of the door, then reaches for another display case, this one smaller and full of travel brochures. He attempts to pull a heavier cabinet full of mailing supplies over, but it is too heavy and he only pulls it halfway before giving up. As he does, the women register a shift in the situation: He is barricading them in.

With Tommy's attention focused elsewhere, the woman who'd been on the phone turns and bolts toward the back, darting behind the partition that Sylvie had been trying to see past earlier. The other four women follow her lead. But she has a head start, and she is fast. She wasn't lying about all those workouts. All that protein consumption has clearly served her well.

As she runs, Sylvie hears the blood pound in her ears. She is amazed at the strength of her beating heart, at the ability of her legs to carry her. She would not have thought herself capable of such a feat at her age. But here she is, running alongside women much younger than her. *We can*, she thinks as the doors that lead outside open wide, the daylight streaming through, *do a lot of things we don't think we can do.* She hears Tommy calling for them to stop, but they just keep running through the warehouse area, her eyes intent on the letters *E-X-I-T* over the double doors at the back of the building.

Blythe hears the gunshot at the same moment a bullet whizzes past her head and the doors close behind the woman on the phone, who has gotten away. The bullet hits the exit sign, cracking it as pieces of glass rain to the floor. The four remaining women stop in their tracks, staring at the mosaic of shards on the floor between them and the now-closed doors.

Tommy reaches them and walks across the glass, which crunches under his boots until he comes to a stop in front of them. The exit is behind him, only a few feet away. But they will not be getting out through it now.

"Now, where do you think you're going?" he asks Nadine.

He uses the gun to point at the remaining three. "I'm sorry, ladies, but it doesn't look like any of y'all are going anywhere." He shakes his head. "You should've torn up the papers when you had a chance," he tells Nadine. "Now look what you've done."

"I was going to," Nadine says. "I had it in my hands. You saw me." She gestures at Blythe and Sylvie and Morrow. "They saw me." All three women nod in agreement as Nadine continues. "I just didn't get the chance because of the lady with the basket." Was she really going to tear them up? No one knows. And it doesn't matter now.

Blythe watches with something akin to pity as Nadine softens her voice and says sweetly, "Let's go back up front and I'll tear up the papers and these ladies can all go home and you and I can go somewhere and talk." There is a plea in her voice that borders on begging. None of the other women like hearing it. And yet they understand and even admire her for trying to intervene.

Tommy shakes his head, a grim look on his face. "It's too late," he says. "They're already calling the cops."

He doesn't say who "they" are, but the women know who he means—the woman with the gift basket and the one who just made it out the door to freedom. They also know he's right; the police have probably been notified. And they are relieved at the thought. The cops will come and put an end to this soon. For their part, they just need to cooperate, to do whatever needs doing to get them out of here. Though they never say it aloud, it is understood and agreed upon with the looks they exchange between them.

Tommy backs toward the exit door, the gun aimed at them as he locks it. That done, he spies a chain on the floor, giving a sadistic little laugh as he grabs it and quickly loops it around the door handles, making it even harder for anyone to get in from outside. That done, he turns and waves the gun at them.

"Now, let's all get back to where we were and figure out what to do next." His gaze falls on Sylvie, and he raises his eyebrows as if in question, even though he hasn't asked one. In that moment, with that look, she sees uncertainty, anxiety, the need for reassurance. She sees a little boy playing at a man's game. Now that she has seen it, she can't unsee it. She isn't sure if this glimpse into Tommy's humanity is good or bad. She hopes that soon he will let them go and it won't matter either way.

Chapter 8

The women make their way back to the front of the post office where it all started. They move much slower, their shoulders slumped, defeated as they come to a stop just inside the room, uncertain what to do next. Morrow doesn't suppose she will be mailing her package today after all.

Maya. Her daughter's name comes to mind as she watches Tommy step into the room and pass his outstretched gun in front of each one of them, a warning. It is Maya she thinks of as she watches the barrel of the gun go past her, how like a gun her daughter had been this morning: loaded, aimed in her direction, with the potential to blow things apart. It was that threat and Morrow's need to do something in response that brought her here, to this moment in this room.

They'd been continuing a conversation that bordered on an argument from the night before. Maya wanted a tattoo because, using the timeworn argument, all her friends were getting one. Her latest strategy had been to convince Morrow to get a matching tattoo with her. Though it was an obvious ploy, she had to hand it to the kid. Her tactic was clever, and insightful. Much of Morrow's time was spent trying to do things with her daughter.

"Want to watch TV?" "No."

"Want to go out for dinner?" "No."

"Want to take a walk on the beach?" "No."

"How about we go shopping?" "No."

Nothing worked. There'd once been a time when spending time together had been Maya's favorite thing to do. Morrow remembers longing to go to the grocery store by herself, a rare treat. Maya had been her "mostly companion," a phrase they picked up from reading the Eloise books, a favorite of Maya's. Morrow had thought it would always be that way, a string of days consisting of mother-daughter outings that stretched into the distant future.

But then that changed. One day Maya began pulling away, at first barely perceptibly, then gradually more obviously. Her friends became her "mostly companions," leaving Morrow always on the outside, trying to find a way back in. Oh, she's read the books; she understands the psychology behind it all, how teenagers have to pull away so they can leave the nest, how it is the order of things. But that doesn't make it feel better.

Now she wonders what would've happened if she'd chosen to see Maya's tattoo offer as a sort of olive branch, the beginning of a way back to each other instead of just another one of her schemes. What would it have hurt if she'd just responded, "Yes, I will get a matching tattoo with you. Let's talk about it when you get home this afternoon"?

Instead, she'd said, "You don't put a bumper sticker on a BMW," which is something Morrow wholeheartedly believes but was, in hindsight, the wrong thing to say at that moment. She does not understand the obsession with tattoos that has become all the rage for the younger generation. She can't think of a single thing she'd want inked on her skin forever. She would never do it, and she feels that it's her job to keep her daughter from doing so, even if it's only long enough for her frontal lobe to develop a little more.

But her quip had been enough to incense Maya. If she could

have a sense of humor about it—and maybe she will one day—Maya would laugh at her own senseless dramatics. The crying, the shrieking, the accusations: Morrow didn't love her enough to get a matching tattoo; she was the meanest mother in the world; and then the final one, the one that stung the most. The one Morrow doesn't like thinking about. But since this morning, she has thought of nothing else.

With that Maya had stormed out of the house, gunning the engine of her car as she drove off to one of her last days of high school. Morrow had waited till she was gone, then slowly, resignedly climbed the stairs to her daughter's room. Though the test had since been tossed in the trash, it was there nonetheless.

If not for Maya, if not for the blowup this morning, Morrow would not be here now. But she does not blame Maya. This is Morrow's own fault, her own harebrained idea that got her here. She has brought this on herself with her need to fix things, her compulsion to set things right. "Let it go," her husband, Kevin, is always saying to her. "Just let it go." But Morrow cannot. So here she is.

The women stay clustered together, casting serious glances back and forth, unsure where to stand or what to do. When Tommy goes to the bank of windows that line the front wall to peer out at the parking lot, Morrow steps away from the group and sidles back over to her tote bag, which she'd left behind when they tried to escape.

She picks it up and peeks inside, taking inventory of the contents once more: umbrella (there was rain in the forecast, but so far not a drop has fallen), wallet, phone, makeup, pain reliever, lip balm, the little deck of cards that looks like playing cards but isn't, a notebook and pen, and then the package, right there in the mix of her normal, everyday things. If things had gone as Morrow intended and Nadine had gotten the chance to take it from her, it would be gone already. But it is still nestled right there where she tucked it, looking benign when it is anything but.

Maya, she thinks again. She wonders what her daughter is doing at this very moment, if she senses that her mother is in danger. Is she in danger? Morrow looks over at Tommy, who is pacing in front of the windows, talking to no one in particular.

"I bet they're on their way right now," he is saying to himself over and over. He doesn't say who "they" are, but he doesn't have to. He means the cops, and the women all hope he's right.

With Tommy's attention diverted, Morrow reaches inside her tote and feels for her phone, extracting it in one smooth motion. She could try to call the police, but she probably only has enough time to do one thing before Tommy catches her with it. As Tommy already pointed out, there's a high probability that the woman with the basket called the police as soon as she ran out. Or the one who was on the phone has already used that very same phone to dial 911, probably while she was still running from the building. So Morrow makes her choice.

Holding the phone just inside the bag so Tommy won't see, she glances down long enough to find her daughter's last text. She has, she knows, a mere moment before he turns around again and sees what she's doing. She can't risk him seeing her with it and taking it from her. Her phone is her link to her family, the only link she has now, thanks to him.

If this situation goes badly, if something were to happen to her, she cannot leave things with Maya the way she left them this morning. She can still hear the slamming of the door as Maya left. She can see herself rinsing her coffee mug in the sink, keeping her back turned until Maya was really and fully gone. In the silent house, residual anger still crackled in the air around her head, as charged as electricity.

I did let it go, she tells Kevin in her head. *And look what happened.* She'd let Maya leave without another word, thinking she'd have a chance later to fix things between them. But what if she doesn't get that chance? She cannot leave her daughter thinking that she does not care, that the rift they left between them is not a rift to her core.

Keeping her eyes on Tommy, she holds the phone down and texts eight letters and two spaces without looking at the screen, trusting her fingers to find the right buttons. Then she looks away from him long enough to check her spelling, to make sure her daughter can read the three words she has written:

I love you

There are some things, she thinks, *you can't let go.* Morrow presses Send, then drops the phone back into the tote, leaving it behind as she joins the cluster of her fellow hostages once more.

From a few feet away, Blythe looks at each of the women around her and wonders how long they will all be here. Other than Nadine, she doesn't even know their names. She would feel silly asking. This is not a social gathering. It's a hostage situation. The two words strung together, *hostage* and *situation*, fall on her, heavy and dark. Does this mean she is a hostage? Like in the movies? Blythe can't process that this is really happening. To her.

At the windows, Tommy is clearly drunk, now pacing and muttering, with no plan—at least that Blythe can see—in place. She doubts this outcome was his goal. She doubts he had a goal at all beyond convincing Nadine to tear up those papers. The situation just got out of hand. Blythe can sort of understand this. She understands better than most how things can get out of hand. But that is no reason to pull a gun on people and make things worse.

She decides she should probably do what Morrow just did while Tommy's not watching. She plucks her phone from her back pocket. The first thing she does is hit the single button on the side five times, sending a silent alert to authorities. She doubts the older women know how to do this, so she figures she should. Unless he spots her with her phone, Tommy won't be the wiser, and she can't take the risk that the women who got away didn't call the police.

At least now she has the assurance that comes with doing something, anything to help herself. And isn't that what she was here to do in the first place? To help herself? With that thought she goes to her most recent text. She glances to make sure Tommy is still preoccupied before she reads the words in the little speech bubbles.

First she scans the ones exchanged between her and her mom as she stood in line, waiting her turn. There are her words of doubt, her mother's words of assurance. The last text from her mom says simply:

> What can it hurt?

She checks to make sure Tommy's back is still turned before looking at her last text, sent moments before everything happened.

> HER: I'm at the post office. I'm sending it now.
> HIM: Thank you. That means a lot.

Now she writes, Still in the post office. I mailed it. But now I think I'm in a hostage situation. She wants to add a joke, make light of it. Like, *So if I die it's all your fault.* But she doesn't. Because this isn't something to joke about.

She watches to see if the ellipsis that tells her he is writing back appears on the screen, hoping he'll respond before Tommy spies what she's doing. But no dots appear. She decides it's too risky to keep her phone out any longer, so she sticks it back into her pocket just as Tommy turns back to his captives. His face looks like he is surprised they are all there.

"What?" he asks the room. He huffs and stomps over to the counter where he left the bourbon just before the woman with the basket walked in. He goes to reach for it at the same time that he realizes it's not there. Blythe looks at Nadine, who is looking at Tommy, her eyes wide, her mouth a straight line.

"Gimme my bottle," he says to her.

"I didn't touch your bottle," says Nadine.

"That's a bunch of bullshit," he says. "Where'd you hide it?"

"I didn't, Tommy," she says and sighs heavily. "Doesn't matter to me if you drink the whole bottle. You can drink yourself to death for all I care." She shrugs. If she is frightened, she's doing a good job of hiding it. Nadine points to the shipping area where Tommy fired the gun. "We were back there, and then we came in here. I didn't have time to touch your precious bottle."

Nadine might not be scared. But Blythe is. Tommy is unhinged and armed. Anything could happen.

And to think last night she'd spent the evening believing her engagement dinner was as bad as her life could get. Now she would happily return to Aaron's family home and the cringefest that was supposed to be a special celebration. In her own defense, she wasn't the one who'd invited her mother.

She was going to tell Rosie, her future mother-in-law, that her mother had to work, which wouldn't have been a big leap. Her mother works all the time. This would not have been the first significant event she'd missed. But Rosie had intervened, going so far as to friend her mother on Facebook and inviting her before

Blythe could offer the excuse. To Rosie, known for the from-scratch cakes for every special occasion, slow-cooked pot roasts for Sunday dinner, and family photos placed everywhere because, as she always says, "Memories are what make a family," there was no question her mother would make the nearly three-hour drive to Sunset Beach to celebrate her only child's engagement.

And so, thanks to Rosie's insistence, Blythe's mother had showed up at Aaron's parents' house, registered its quaint modesty, and shifted her countenance to permanent "resting disapproval face" for the night. Blythe had clocked it from the moment she entered the room, her stomach twisting at the sight, taking the joy right out of the joyful celebration.

It is because of her mother that she is here. Her mother, plus unwisely opening a bottle of wine back at her house after the party, topped off with Blythe's relentless inability to stop vying for her mother's approval. She looks at the place on the counter where Tommy's bottle was before it disappeared and thinks about the place behind the counter where Nadine dropped her package. She wonders if Nadine would allow her to take her package back now. Does she want to take it back?

Before she can ponder the answer to that question, her phone vibrates in her back pocket. She wants to see if he has answered the text she just sent, to see *how* he will respond, which will tell her a lot. Maybe all she needs to know. But first she needs to divert Tommy, who is searching for his bottle all around the room. Blythe musters up her courage and tells a lie. It isn't the first she's told today. The other one she feels bad about, but this one she doesn't.

"I think that lady who ran out the back had it with her," she says, ignoring her pounding heart. "Pretty sure I saw a bottle in her hand."

Tommy looks from Nadine to Blythe, then back again. He shakes his head and makes a *pssst* sound, then goes to the windows to resume his pacing and muttering, giving up his search. Nadine mouths, "Thank you," to her, and Blythe nods, then retrieves her phone from her back pocket, sure it is him. Maybe he will say something that will make her feel like she has come here and done the right thing. But it is just a text from the dentist's office, reminding her she has an appointment tomorrow, an appointment she's starting to wonder if she will make.

Chapter 9

Not very far from the post office, Hope is walking to work. She is not hurrying because she has left herself enough time to make it at a regular pace. Tired from her run, she thought about driving to work just this once. But one of the small pleasures of living at 108, of living in this small town, is her ability to walk to work. This was something she could not do back home, and Hope does not take it for granted now.

As she walks, her mind goes back to those flowers. She is feeling a little guilty about not putting them in water before she left. She could've taken the time to take care of the flowers and driven to work, but she didn't. She is pondering why, wondering if she just doesn't care, if she is that heartless, when her phone rings. She does not have to look at it to know who is calling. Hope left a lot behind when she fled Philadelphia, but not her husband, Alex. He hasn't let her. The flowers are just another example of his persistence. When she left, he'd told her to take all the time she needs, but she's pretty sure he never expected it to take this long.

She thinks about ignoring the call—she's almost to work, after all; it isn't a good time—but she knows she's just putting off the inevitable. Better to get to work without the guilt over neglecting the flowers *and* ignoring her husband who sent them hanging over her head her whole shift. He has been understanding. He's kept his word and given her all the time she needs. The least she can do is answer when he calls. It's bad enough she has left his flowers, a romantic gesture many women would swoon over, to potentially die. *But maybe they won't*, a little voice inside her says. *Maybe you'll be surprised.*

"Hello?" she asks, as if she doesn't know it's him.

"Hey," he says. "I dialed before I realized you're probably at work."

"Not there yet," she says. "But close."

"I still can't believe you're working." He gives a little laugh. "You were supposed to be taking it easy." She can hear his smile, can picture his face in her mind as he says, "So like you to get a job even though you don't have to."

"I wanted to do my part. You know, money-wise. It felt weird with you taking care of everything and me not contributing at all. It felt . . . wrong. And besides, it gives me something to do."

"I know—I just didn't think you'd, you know, return. I mean, with everything—" He stops talking, but she hears his unsaid words anyway. With everything that happened, he never thought she'd go back to police work again. He's not the only one.

At the time she'd felt she had no other choice but to leave, at first just the job, but soon it became her home as well as the job. There were too many reminders, too many triggers. It wasn't just PTSD and it wasn't just grief that sent her running. It was some hybrid of the two, a condition that—regardless of the name—had left her rudderless, altered.

The only thing she could think of that might make a difference would be to go somewhere else, someplace not so familiar, to be around people who didn't know her, in a place that didn't hold unpleasant memories. Alex couldn't come—he had a demanding job and was up for a promotion—so he'd let her go alone. She'd left before he could change his mind. Now she understands without him saying it that he regrets that decision.

"Like I said," she finally replies, "it keeps me busy. And it's not like anything ever happens here. It's a very low-risk situation." She gives a little laugh to reassure him. "It's a big night if we get a drunk and disorderly."

She pauses so he can speak, but he doesn't. In her negotiator training they learned to use pauses for effect. If you pause long enough, the other person will feel compelled to speak just to fill the silence. Nature abhors a vacuum and all that. But it is she who fills the silence now.

"Thanks, by the way," she says, changing the subject, "for the flowers."

"You know I couldn't let your birthday go by without doing something," he chides her, but there is a playful tone in his voice. In that moment she misses him, wishes she could click her heels and be back in Pennsylvania.

"Yeah, I guess I should've expected it. I just didn't want to . . ."

"Celebrate," he says, repeating what she'd said a few weeks ago when he suggested he come down and visit for her birthday. He'd made it sound casual, but they both knew it was not.

"Well, I'm just about there," she responds, because she doesn't know what else to say. *Celebrate* is a word that went missing from her vocabulary eight months ago.

"Listen," he says, talking faster now that he knows his time is running out. "I didn't call you about the flowers."

She opens her mouth to ask him if they can talk about this later, but he continues before she can speak. "I called because you got a letter. Or actually, not a letter. More like an invitation. It's an . . . event. They're recognizing you for, you know, what happened. I don't want to say too much—I want you to see it. I think maybe it would help. If you'd like, I could overnight it to you? I could go to the post office right now and—"

Hope can barely hear him over the sound of her heart thudding away inside her chest. She doesn't want to be recognized. She wants to be as anonymous as she is in this town. "Alex," she says, her husband's name like a stranger's as she speaks it. "I'm about to start a shift. I can't really talk about this now."

"Okay," he says. She hears him sigh, the air leaving him like a popped balloon. "We can talk about it later." He must know she will not want to talk about it later, but he has the grace not to say so.

"I really do have to go into work now," she says, which is the truth. She has reached the doors of the combination town hall/police station.

"Yeah, okay," he says. "I'll let you go."

But Hope knows that isn't true, and though it makes no sense, she counts on it.

Chapter 10

BACK AT THE post office, Sylvie does her best to ignore the distinct combination of nausea and wooziness that means she needs to eat, and soon. Standing on the hard surface of the tiled floor, she ponders what will happen if she pushes herself too hard and passes out right there, in the midst of all that is already taking place. She moves over to the counter, balances her weight against it, and silently reprimands herself for not eating before she left the house. She hadn't been hungry when she made lunch for Robert, figuring she'd eat later. Only now it is later and that isn't an option.

She is always pushing herself, denying her age, as if ignoring it will change it. The question comes to mind again: How did she get to be so old? Time went by, that's how. And no matter how much she protests, her age won't change. That is a fact, like gravity. It is, she reminds herself, better than the alternative.

She looks down at her feet, anchored to the floor by an invisible force. But what is keeping her there is not invisible. She glares over at Tommy, though he doesn't see it, what with his pacing and muttering. She wonders what, if anything, she can do to make things better. She wishes for Robert, or at least the Robert of the past, the steady, calm presence of him that once made her feel safe. He took care of her. He always had.

She'd grown complacent over the years, lulled into thinking

that the way it was was the way it always would be. That she would be herself and Robert would be Robert. Until one day he didn't know which house was theirs. Granted, they lived in a planned retirement community where all the homes looked similar, all variations on a theme. It was an easy mistake to make. That's what she'd told herself at first.

Tommy turns from the windows and looks at all of them. He appears as lost as Robert had that day, blinking at the four women in the room as if he does not know who they are or why they are there with him. He's gotten himself into a mess, Sylvie thinks. A mess he doesn't know how to get himself out of. If only he hadn't chased that woman out with a gun. If only he hadn't fired at them when they tried to run away.

He should've let them go and then fled himself. There was a moment when all of this could've been resolved with little fuss. But they have sailed past that moment. As their eyes make contact, she suspects this is all occurring to him now and the reality is amping up his desperation. A desperate man is a dangerous one. Somehow she will need to make him believe there is still hope.

In her mind she sees the verse from Jeremiah they have mounted over their doorway at home. It's been in every home they've ever lived in, hand-painted by a dear aunt and gifted to them on their wedding day. It is a verse people often like to quote, the one about hope and a future. But she will need to give Tommy hope *for* a future. The reality is, if this goes much further or, God forbid, goes badly, his future won't be looking so hopeful. But she can't let him start believing that or it will only make the situation more difficult.

Tommy gestures at Sylvie, at all of them, twirling his finger in a circular motion. "Have a seat," he says, but none of them move. Nadine, Blythe, Morrow, and Sylvie just stand in place, blinking at him like they don't understand the words that have come out of his mouth. Mostly because what he said doesn't make sense. There is nowhere to sit except for on the hard floor that hundreds of dirty shoes have tramped across, tracking who knows what all kinds of germs in their wake. *No, thank you*, Sylvie thinks.

Exasperated at not being obeyed, Tommy uses the gun like a pointer again, jabbing it in each of their directions, then jabbing it at the floor. Sylvie thinks about him jabbing the gun at the papers he wanted Nadine to tear up. Based on what she's seen so far, she can't blame Nadine for filing those papers, for being so hesitant to tear them up even with a gun pointed at her. Sylvie wants to blame Nadine for this mess, but she cannot. In all honesty, she probably would've done the same and stood her ground. Nadine couldn't possibly have known that it would lead to this. Even Sylvie hadn't truly appreciated what was happening until it was too late.

For now it's best to keep him calm. Appease him. And someone has to go first. *Age before beauty*, Sylvie thinks as she steps away from the counter and motions to the others to follow her over to the largest area of floor space in the small room. "Let's all have a seat," she says. The other three pick up their things and slowly move with her.

Morrow, Blythe, and Nadine slide down into sitting positions on the floor seemingly without thinking about it even as it strikes Sylvie that she cannot do the same. She can't remember the last time she's sat down on a floor. There was a time, in her fifties, when she faithfully got herself down on the floor and then got herself back up again every day just because some guest on a TV talk show said that women her age should do so.

Somewhere along the way she'd abandoned the practice, which she both regrets and wonders how much it would've helped as she stares down at the white specks dotting the tile beneath her feet.

She tries to picture lowering herself—thinking of the balance, dexterity, and control such a feat would require. Even if she got herself down there, there is no way she could get herself back up.

She feels as helpless as a child. Worse than a child. A child could throw herself to the floor and pop right back up again. Sylvie cannot. For a moment she is mad at this man who is forcing her to feel this way. But even as angry tears fill her eyes, she reminds herself that anger is not the way out of here. With all the gentleness she can muster, she says to the room, "I'm an old lady." She gives a little laugh as if she has said something funny. "Sitting on the floor is difficult for me." *Impossible*, she thinks.

She stands, immobile, as they all stare at her, uncertain what to do. She is a problem, but she does not mean to be. This is one part of aging she was not prepared for: the humiliation. The degradation. She was never incapable in her younger years. She never allowed it.

"Here, let me help you," says Nadine, hopping up from the floor as if it's nothing. She goes over to the counter and tugs the stool she'd been sitting on as she worked out of its little nook, then drags it across the floor to where the other women are seated. The steel legs of the stool scraping across the tile floor make a grating noise like fingernails on a chalkboard. They all wince at the sound.

Nadine stops when she reaches Sylvie and extends her hand, which Sylvie, with gratitude, takes. With Nadine's assistance, she climbs up onto the stool. Nadine stoops down to tuck Sylvie's purse and the envelope under the stool. When Nadine stands up, Sylvie starts to thank her for the help, but Nadine's attention is diverted to the vestibule area.

Sylvie watches Nadine's mouth make a small, round O of surprise and turns to discover two women standing in the vestibule, eyeing Tommy's hastily constructed barricade with confused expressions. One of them is holding what looks like a hot dog. One of them is getting out her phone. When Tommy walks forward and raises the gun at them through the window, one throws the hot dog to the ground and the other starts talking fast into her phone.

Sylvie feels a mixture of relief and jealousy as the two women turn and run, exhaling for them as the outer front door opens and they both disappear into the bright light, wincing for herself as the door slams shut behind them. She looks over at Nadine, who stands frozen in place, looking like a child who has been abandoned.

Nadine watches Stacy and Martha go but wants to scream at them to come back. Not that she blames them for running away. Not when Tommy just aimed his gun at them. This situation is getting further and further out of hand. Nadine feels helpless to stop it, yet responsible for her part in it. If only she'd torn up those stupid papers when she had the chance. "*This is all your fault, Nadine*," he'd said. Now she says it to herself.

Nadine looks at Sylvie, perched uncomfortably on the stool, looking sad and worried. She thinks of her own grandma, how she'd want to kill anyone who put her in this position. She gives Sylvie a small smile, trying to communicate that things will be okay, even though she doesn't know if they will or not.

She doesn't think Tommy would actually shoot someone—that bullet he fired off in the back went high on purpose. An experienced hunter, Tommy knows how to shoot a gun too well to miss that badly. But she doubts the cops will take any of that into account, especially seeing as how Tommy has now pulled a gun on two of her coworkers. She looks out at the vestibule. The hot dog is lying there, freed from its bun. Sure enough, there's yellow mustard slathered across it. Nadine rolls her eyes and looks away. The sight makes her nauseous.

Tommy strides back to the counter, to the envelope they'd fought over, still where they left it. He stares at it for a long moment as the four women watch him warily, then looks back at Nadine. "Do you want to tear it up, or me?" he asks.

Nadine sighs. Not this again. "It doesn't matter if I tear it up, Tommy. All this"—she waves her hand at the room, at the seated women—"sort of overrules that."

Tommy grimaces, his brows knit together and his eyes squinty. "All this"—now it's his turn to gesture to the room, the seated women—"is because of that. If you'd just torn it up like I asked, given us a chance like I asked . . ."

Nadine cocks her head at him. "Yes," she says, deadpan. "You've made giving you another chance look like *such* a good option." She rolls her eyes as punctuation.

In response Tommy seizes the envelope and, with a dramatic flourish, holds it aloft like Moses with the Ten Commandments. If he wasn't currently clutching a gun in his free hand, they all would probably crack up laughing. Instead, they all watch, frozen, as he puts the gun down where the envelope used to be and uses both hands to tear the envelope into pieces.

Well, they don't *all* watch. Morrow registers both the gun discarded on the counter and Tommy's full hands and carpe diems her way to the barricade, pushing with all her might to remove the smallest obstacle, a display of tourism pamphlets, freebies meant to entice visitors to come to the local attractions. The pamphlets about the local planetarium fall to the ground and fan out as Morrow grunts with the effort even as she thinks of the one time she took Maya to that planetarium. There'd been a laser show featuring Taylor Swift music. She'd thought Maya would love it, but she fell asleep halfway through and didn't want to stop for ice cream afterward.

Tommy sees what's happening, drops the bits of envelope, grabs the gun, and goes after Morrow. Except he isn't prepared for a mother who's already had a very bad day. Morrow turns on him with claws bared. She uses her nails, manicured in a lovely shade of rosy pink, to fend him off, swiping at him in an attempt to keep him at bay as she continues to try to remove the obstacles he put there, straining for her freedom. She uses her hands and feet and elbows. She puts up one hell of a fight.

Though the other three women don't join in, they do live vicariously through Morrow, appreciating every time one of her appendages makes contact with one of his. Later they will wonder why they never moved to help. If they'd all worked together, they will think, they might have gotten free. But they were too afraid to move, too swept up by the danger flowing through the room, cowed by the threat of Tommy's weapon.

Though it seems much longer, the fight is over in minutes. Tommy gains the upper hand and pulls Morrow away from the doorway, pushing her back to her spot among the others. She slumps down, not making eye contact, the picture of defeat. Blythe thinks of saying something to her, something about how brave she'd just been, how she'd done what they'd all wanted to do but had been too afraid. She wants to tell Morrow she is a hero. But Blythe says nothing. She returns to picking the nail polish off her own nails, quietly marveling over how well Morrow's manicure held up in the fight.

Chapter 11

STILL WINDED FROM the altercation, Tommy marches over to the barricade to try to put it back together. As he leans down, his head swims from the alcohol and the exertion of the fight. He's never fought a woman in his life, and he hadn't intended to just now. In hindsight he figures he should've let her run out. Then he should've let them all run out after her. Then this would be over and he could let the chips fall where they may.

But when he saw her trying to escape, something in him had to stop her. He doesn't know what compelled him, but it was something he doesn't like, a deep-down kind of meanness he wishes wasn't there. It is the same impulse that led him to create the barricade, a combination of stupidity and stubbornness that has got him locked into a situation he can't get out of now. He feels a wash of shame flood his cheeks and travel down through his chest and into his belly, coming to rest there like a hot, spreading fire. He has no choice but to see it through.

He turns his focus back to gathering up the tourism pamphlets that fell to the floor as they struggled. It seems odd to him that they have tourism pamphlets in a post office. How many tourists actually come in this post office? Do people on vacation need to mail things? He doesn't know why they would. The whole point, as far as he can figure, is that people go on vacation to take a break from doing things like going to the post office.

But Tommy doesn't know about taking vacations. That wasn't something he grew up doing.

His dad always said, "Son, we live where people come to vacation. Why would we need to go anywhere else?" Tommy figured that was true, but still. He always wanted to go on vacation like he'd seen people do on TV and heard about from kids at school. He and Nadine said they would go on a vacation someday, but money was always tight, and he heard himself saying to her, like his dad, "Why would we need to go on vacation when we can go to the beach here?" He told himself it was enough. He looks over at Nadine. Maybe it wasn't.

He continues with the pamphlets, each one promising a better time than the one next to it. He goes to pick up the ones on the floor, fanned out like a deck of cards. They are for the planetarium, which is right down the street. He went there once on a field trip. He can't remember what grade it was, but he remembers learning about the stars and finding them fascinating. For a while after that field trip he'd asked for a telescope for Christmas. Instead, he'd received his first hunting rifle. Instinctively, his hand moves to pat the gun in his pocket. It was probably a mistake to bring it in here. But right now it feels like security.

As he continues with his task, his eyes fall on a familiar logo. It is a pamphlet advertising the Tiki Bar over on Ocean Isle. "Hey, Nadine," he says, holding it up. "Look!"

From her place on the floor, Nadine scowls at him. "So?" she asks, as if they haven't been there too many nights to count. As if they hadn't stared out at the night sky from the roof deck, trying to name those stars they learned about in school but had long since forgotten, as Jimmy Buffett sang through the speakers. She can try to pretend she's forgotten all she wants.

But he knows she hasn't. Somehow, he thinks, he's just got to make her remember.

Across the room, Morrow smooths her ponytail, wishing for a mirror as she feels around for loose strands of hair and tries to secure them. She probably looks a sight. When Blythe tries to catch her eye, she looks away, embarrassed for reasons she can't name. Because her attempt to escape failed? Because she looks foolish for attempting at all? She tells herself she should be proud she tried. It is more than anyone else in this room has done.

She would do just about anything for a cigarette right now. It is her dirty little secret, a habit she fell into without intending to. She'd smoked in college, like everyone seemed to, but quit almost as soon as she began. She'd never considered smoking again after that. Then one night last fall she'd walked outside to get the dog back inside the house and smelled the distinct scent of nicotine-infused smoke wafting through the air. She'd looked around for the source, fearful she'd find Maya and a friend, but spotted her elderly neighbor, Pat, instead, sitting on her back porch, taking in the view of the Intracoastal Waterway.

Morrow had nudged the dog inside the house, then stayed where she was, keeping her eyes on Pat, who seemed oblivious that she was being watched. Transfixed, Morrow had studied her neighbor's series of actions: lifting the cigarette to her lips, the glow as she inhaled, the smoke floating into the air upon her exhale. Pulled by her senses and, she can admit now, motivated by loneliness, she'd crossed the yard and spoken to her neighbor, someone she'd only had a handful of conversations with since they'd moved in. She'd let their age difference negate the possibility of a friendship, assuming that she, a perimenopausal woman with family obligations, had very little in common with an elderly widow who lived alone. She'd been wrong.

Pat welcomed her that first night, invited her to sit. And though not on that first night, eventually offered her a cigarette. At first Morrow demurred. Then after one particularly bad night, she'd given in, puffing on the proffered cigarette like a rebellious teenager. But instead of hiding it from her parents, she was hiding it from her husband and child.

After that, smoking with Pat on her porch became a regular thing. Their nightly conversations—taking place when Kevin was on yet another business trip and Maya was locked away in her room reigning over the kingdom inside her phone—became a lifeline. Pat went from neighbor to friend, and now the smell of cigarette smoke reminds her of laughter, of long, meandering discussions, of secrets whispered. Which is why she's craving a cigarette. It's not just the nicotine; it's what comes with it. If she had a cigarette right now, she'd be home. Her daughter would be in her room. She'd be telling Pat all about what has happened here today. She would be free.

Morrow rests her hand on her tote bag. *I tried*, she thinks. *I tried to get back.*

Beside her Sylvie whispers, "That was very brave, what you did."

"I just thought we should try to get out of here any way we can," Morrow quips.

Sylvie chuckles at that. "Well, it was certainly a good try. I wish I'd done it myself."

Morrow catches herself thinking Sylvie is too old to attempt what she did. But if there's one thing she's learned from spending time with Pat, it's not to count anyone out just because of their age.

Sylvie extends her hand. "I'm Sylvie. And you are?" Morrow pauses before answering. Somehow, learning the names of her fellow captors makes this seem more real. But, she figures, it can't hurt. They are, like it or not, in this together.

"Morrow," says Morrow.

"Morrow," Sylvie says. "That's a lovely name. Unusual."

"My mother loved the book *Gift from the Sea*, so she named me Anne Morrow. I was called Anne until I reached my teens. Then I started going by Morrow." She laughs at herself. "I thought it sounded more romantic."

"It certainly does." Sylvie nods. "I loved *Gift from the Sea* as well," she says. "I actually made a needlepoint pillow many years ago with a quote from it."

"Oh?" Morrow asks. "Which quote?" Morrow has read the book many times. It was what led to her campaign for her family to move here, her long-romanticized dream of living by the sea, of somehow becoming whatever her mother had intended when she named her. She wishes she could ask her mother just what that was, but she has been dead since Morrow was a teenager, since about the time she changed her name.

"It was about security in a relationship," Sylvie answers. She shrugs. "About living in the present and not in the past or future." A wistful look passes over Sylvie's face. "I haven't seen that pillow in years. I'd forgotten all about it till just now." Sylvie looks at Morrow. "It's funny how you lose track of things."

Morrow nods, agreeing. In their nearly thirty years of marriage, she and Kevin have acquired and discarded several lifetimes' worth of possessions. They keep a storage room they pay for each month, filled with things she couldn't account for if pressed.

She sees Sylvie make eye contact with Blythe. "And you are?" Sylvie asks her.

"Blythe," says Blythe, but softly.

"I'm sorry," says Sylvie. "I couldn't hear you." She points at her ears. "These things ain't what they used to be."

Blythe smiles at that and says her name again, louder this time.

"Blythe," Sylvie repeats. "Also a lovely name."

"It's supposed to mean 'happy' or 'cheerful,'" Blythe says, then shrugs her shoulders. "Which is not so fitting right now," she adds. She tries for a laugh, but it catches in her throat.

"I think it fits," says Sylvie. "You look like a Blythe. No matter what the circumstances are."

Blythe gives her a smile even as she thinks that this is not true. She once heard happiness is dependent on circumstances. Joy, however, is within you, existing beyond the circumstances, in spite of them. But Blythe's name means "happy," not "joyful." Perhaps her name is holding her back.

Her mind returns to the dinner last night, crowded around Aaron's family's table, elbow to elbow with her mother, who sat stiffly, her disapproval wafting off her and onto Blythe, poisoning the air. Just weeks before, at Easter, Blythe had sat at the very same table, elbow to elbow with Aaron, smiling ear to ear as his nieces and nephews chased one another out the door to hunt for eggs. All the while she was thinking, *This is exactly what I want. This is what I've always wanted.* Only one thing had changed, and that was her mother.

Blythe thinks about the package once more, wonders again about getting it back.

"Morrow, Blythe, and Sylvie," Sylvie says, pulling Blythe out of her contemplation.

Sylvie looks at all of them, then over at Nadine. "And we can't forget Nadine," she adds. Blythe sees this is Sylvie's way of drawing Nadine in, of reassuring her that they don't fault her for any of this.

"I'm sorry about this, you guys," Nadine responds.

"It's not your fault," Blythe speaks up.

Morrow looks over at Nadine. "It's not," she agrees with Blythe, "your fault."

"It's certainly not," chimes in Sylvie.

The four of them exchange smiles as Tommy stops messing with the barricade and looks over his shoulder, aware that something has happened. He turns around and takes in the scene. Something has shifted and he knows it. He almost seems afraid.

He should be, Sylvie thinks.

Chapter 12

FROM BEHIND THE counter, a song begins to play, low enough that they all think they are imagining the sound. Everyone except Nadine. She leaps up. "That's mine," she announces, embarrassed by her ringtone. She doesn't so much want to answer the phone as she wants it to stop playing the song they danced to at their wedding. She's been meaning to change it for a long time, but she keeps forgetting. Now her cheeks color as Tommy looks at her while the song plays. Then, blessedly, it stops.

But seconds later, it starts again. "Go see who it is," Tommy says, his gruff tone masking whatever he might be thinking or feeling.

Nadine nods, then goes to retrieve her phone from where she stashed it behind the counter while she was working. The display tells her it's her mother calling.

She looks at Tommy, who is studying her every move. "My mom," she says just as the ringtone goes silent again.

"What's she calling for?" Tommy grouses.

Nadine thinks that perhaps her mom called to see if she'd heard from Tommy since the papers were served. Or perhaps she's already gotten wind of what's going on. Word travels fast in a small town, and her mother has friends everywhere.

But to Tommy she just says, "How should I know?"

"Hand it here," Tommy instructs her. He leaves the tourism pamphlets behind, abandoning his cleanup efforts. Crossing the room to where she stands, he extends his hand at the same time the phone goes off again.

"You'd better answer that or she's just gonna keep calling," Nadine advises him.

He shakes his head. "I don't wanna talk to your mama."

"So you're saying I should answer it?"

"I don't know," says Tommy, sounding irritated and put-upon when he's the one who created this whole situation.

Nadine answers without waiting for further permission, ignoring Tommy as she says, "Hey, Mama."

"Put it on speaker," Tommy orders. "I wanna hear this." Nadine rolls her eyes but does as he says.

"Nadine, honey." Nadine's mama's voice comes through loud and clear. "You there?"

"Yeah, Mama, I'm here."

"I had to call and make sure you're okay. I got a call from Alice up at the police station, and she said there's something going on at the post office. She said they're having to send cops over there. I was worried to death." She exhales loudly into the phone, the sound like a rushing wind. "I'm just so relieved you're not involved. Phew!"

Nadine raises one eyebrow as she looks at Tommy. "You wanna tell her or should I?"

"I ain't telling her nothing," Tommy says. Though his voice is truculent, his face is downright scared.

"Tommy?" Nadine's mama, whose name is Earlene, says. "Why is Tommy there? What's going on? Am I on speaker?" Nadine knows her mama hates to be on speaker.

"He's got a gun, Mama," says Nadine. "He's taken us hostage and barricaded us in the post office."

"My Lord in heaven," says Earlene. "Can he hear me right now?"

"The whole room can hear you," says Nadine. She almost adds, *That's how the speaker function works.* But now is not the time to be sassy.

"Tommy!" Earlene says. "You'd better not harm a hair on my girl's head. You hear me? Not a hair."

Tommy, who has always been more than a little afraid of Earlene, doesn't know how to answer that.

"He held a gun to my head, Mama," says Nadine.

"Nadine," Tommy hisses, "you didn't have to tell her that."

"I can tell her whatever I want to, Tommy."

"Tommy," says Earlene, "now you'd better just stop this nonsense right now. You hear me? I mean it. This is gonna lead nowhere good for anyone." She pauses. "This is not like you at all. Not at all."

"I didn't mean to," says Tommy. "I was only trying to fight for my marriage, Earlene. And then it just . . . got out of hand."

"So take it *in* hand," says Earlene matter-of-factly. "I don't want to hear your excuses."

"But I just . . . I don't . . . I can't," says Tommy. His face has shifted from scared to bewildered.

"Don't hand me that *can't* stuff. Can't never could do anything. Nadine?" Earlene says. "You still there?"

"I'm here, Mama."

"If he won't take the situation in hand, then you should."

"And how am I supposed to do that, Mama? He's the one with the gun. I'm not in charge."

Earlene's voice softens. "You're a smart girl, honey. You'll figure it out." She pauses again, then continues. "And, Tommy? I mean it. You harm that girl, or anyone else, and the cops will be your least worry. Ain't no wrath like a mama's wrath. You got it?"

Tommy is silent. The whole room is silent. So silent that they can hear the sound of tires on asphalt. All heads turn to the windows. "Hey, Mama, pretty sure the police just got here," Nadine says.

"Tommy!" Earlene hollers. "You keep in mind what I said. You hear me?"

"I hear you," says Tommy, but his voice is already moving away from the phone toward the window, where he can get a better view of the onslaught of authorities as they make their entrance.

"I'd better go," says Nadine.

"I'll be praying," says Earlene.

"I know you will, Mama," Nadine says. Then she ends the call.

One by one, Nadine, Blythe, and Morrow join Tommy to watch the law enforcement presence grow. But Sylvie stays seated, leaving Morrow to wonder why. She is concerned about the older woman, about the strain of the situation on her. But help is here. With each vehicle that arrives, she feels a mounting sense of both the hope of help and the heft of the situation.

Morrow stands shoulder to shoulder with her fellow captives in front of the windows as more and more emergency personnel collect in the parking lot of the post office. The fire department arrives and more cop cars, some marked, some unmarked. A collection of uniformed authorities of various associations stands at the outer edge of the asphalt, as far away from the building as they can get yet still keep an eye on it, alternating between glancing at the building and talking to one another.

Morrow watches it all unfold, counting the number of helpers who are there. She thinks of that quote by Mr. Rogers. At least she thinks it was Mr. Rogers. "*Look for the helpers. You will always find people who are helping.*" Morrow sees the helpers, a whole collection of them, right there on the other side of the glass. But she cannot get to them. She thinks of trying again to escape. Maybe this time Tommy wouldn't fight her. Maybe he'd just let her go.

She glances over at Tommy, who is cursing a blue streak as he, too, watches the helpers assemble. Though he overcame her with force, would he actually have harmed her? He doesn't seem like a killer, but do killers always seem like killers before they kill? She could risk another attempt to escape but decides it's not worth it. Better to go along to get along and hope for a peaceful resolution.

Beside Morrow, Blythe's phone vibrates in her back pocket, the sensation sending a little jolt of fear through her. Tommy has moved to the far window, trying to talk to Nadine in a low, pleading voice. Though from the looks of it, he's not getting anywhere. All that matters is that he is not paying attention to Blythe. So she takes her phone out to see that Bryan has responded to her text about being a hostage.

You're joking, right?

She frowns and shoves her phone back into her pocket, recalling as she does her conversation with her mother after the party, how she got from there to here with a bottle of wine and just one question: "Do you ever talk to Bryan?"

Lulled by the wine and her mother's attention, she had answered honestly. "Funny you should ask that. We've actually exchanged a few messages on Instagram."

Her mother had leaned forward, her eyes sparkling with interest. "I never understood what happened between you two. Now *he* was a catch." Despite the amount of wine she'd had, Blythe had caught the inference: Bryan was a catch. Aaron was not.

Just like that, panic had filled her. Was she making a mistake?

As they talked into the night, her mother's opinion became clear: She was. But it wasn't too late to change course, her mother insisted. So Blythe had revealed her crazy idea. And her mother told her it wasn't crazy at all.

"Go for it," her mother had said, engaged and invested in a way she rarely was where Blythe was concerned. And so, because she wanted to please her mother, to do the right thing in her mother's eyes, she had. And now she is here.

Blythe looks over her shoulder to the desk, to where her package was dropped moments before everything went crazy. Could she get it back? She eyes Tommy again. He is intent on Nadine. She could slide over there and slip behind the counter. Pluck the package out quickly and get back to her place as if nothing ever happened. Would the others realize she is holding the package she already mailed? And if they did, what could they do about it?

She is concerned that retrieving the package would be breaking some sort of law. The mail is part of the government. They are in a federal building. She pressed the green button, after all, and that information went somewhere; the transaction was processed. But, she reasons, there should be an exception if one is taken hostage. One should be allowed to un-mail what one has mailed. She is, she thinks, already a different person than the one who walked into the post office holding the innocuous-looking package. She should be allowed to reverse course.

Blythe takes a sideways step, keeping her eyes on Tommy and Nadine. They are still talking, their voices low and rushed. She does not wonder what they are saying. She does not really care. She has relationship problems of her own. She takes another step. Then another. She is halfway there.

She looks down at her engagement ring, uses her thumb to make it rotate around her finger just once. Is an engagement a promise or merely a promise to make a promise? She'd told herself she had not made the important promise yet. And yet she wanted to. She'd fully intended to until last night. Until her mother showed up and told her that to marry Aaron was to sell herself short. Until her mother pushed her to come here.

She takes several more steps before she hears Tommy call out, "What are you doing?"

She tries to swallow, but her mouth has gone bone-dry. "Nothing," she says. "I was just stretching my legs." Blythe likes to think she despises lying, but today the lies are coming easier and easier.

Tommy looks past her, takes in the other women. They all stare back at him. He opens his mouth, and for a moment Blythe thinks he is going to tell them to go, to set them free. But if he were to let them go, her package would stay behind. She is caught between wanting to be free and wanting to get to that package before the USPS carries it away. She was sent here on a fool's errand. She let herself be cajoled into pleasing her mother instead of doing what her heart had told her to do. Now she must rectify it.

Tommy, however, does not say that he is letting them go. He just tells them to sit down, to be quiet, to let him think. He just, he says, needs time to think.

Chapter 13

Hank, the chief of police, is waiting in the lobby, standing right beside the receptionist's desk, when Hope walks into the station. She does not realize that he is there waiting for her until he beckons for her to follow him to his office. He doesn't even give her a chance to put down her things. Something is happening. Something that must involve her. She feels her heart pick up speed a little at the thought of a chance. But a chance to do what, she doesn't know.

She pushes the thought out of her head as she follows Hank into his office, then pauses by the seat Hank indicates for her to take. The chair he has pointed at is full of odds and ends in a sloppy pile: file folders, books, a box marked "Evidence" with who knows what inside. In her short time as part of the Sunset Beach Police Department, she has learned that Hank is a fastidious cop but a messy human. It is a dichotomy she didn't know could exist together. But Hank makes it work.

"Oh, just push it to the floor," he tells her. So she does, hoping the evidence—whatever it is—isn't compromised by its encounter with the cold, hard floor. That done, she doesn't so much sit as perch on the chair.

Hank dispenses with preamble, which she appreciates. "We're getting calls from over at the post office. Looks like there's a situation there. A barricade."

"Hostages?" she asks. Without warning the little zing of a challenge being presented whizzes through her body, her muscle memory activated. For a moment she forgets that challenges can bring heartbreak and devastation. She forgets why she is here, in this police station, and not the one in Philadelphia she came from. It all comes rushing back, but she doesn't let herself dwell on whether that is good or bad.

"Might be too early to say for sure," Hank answers, measuring his words. "But they've taken several calls from witnesses and . . ." Hank pauses for a bit before finishing with, "It's looking that way."

Hope's body inclines toward Hank, whether a reflex or an impulse, she can't discern. Something is happening, and ready or not, she is going to be part of it. She thinks of what she said to Alex as she walked to work: *"Nothing ever happens here."*

"What do you need from me?" she asks.

Hank pauses, a frown turning down the edges of his mouth as he studies her. "We haven't talked about this because there wasn't a reason to, but I know you've got experience with this type of thing." He takes a deep breath. "And I know that experience is part of why you're here. I, um, talked to your supervisor up there when I hired you."

Hope nods. She appreciates that he is choosing his words carefully and that he refrains from mentioning her sudden departure back in PA. Though she had the blessing of her superiors and team, she doesn't like to spend too much time reflecting on her decision.

Hank presses his palms down on his desk and continues. "Protocol says I need to call in the county. And since it's a federal building, possibly the FBI." He shrugs. "I'm gonna let the two figure that out between themselves. Either way it'll take some time to mobilize everyone, and I fear it's not time we have since this is already in progress. So"—he moves his hands to press his fingertips together—"because you've got more experience than anyone here with this type of thing, I'd like you to head things up over there."

He leans back, crosses his arms across his ample midsection, and continues before she can answer. "I mean, I can do it, but I'm gonna be tangled up in bureaucratic red tape for a while, I'm afraid. It'd be nice if I could be working over here until I've figured it all out. My best bet is getting the county team here. But they've gotta get the team pulled together from out in the field, the equipment, SWAT, you know the drill." He looks at her and she thinks she sees compassion in his eyes. He knows that this will not be easy for her, that this is the last thing she expected. "Think you can do it?" he asks.

She looks down at the floor, at the evidence box turned on its side. The box's lid has stayed on. She blinks at it a few times. She does not know if she can do what Hank is asking her to do. But there are hostages in a post office not far from where she now sits who need her to try. She looks up, meets his eyes, and nods.

He claps his hands together and grins for the first time since she walked into the building. "That's what I wanted to hear! I've already sent everyone who's available; plus the emergency personnel are there too. They're all in the parking lot, getting sorted out. You'll see when you get there. I'll let them know you're coming."

She nods again, stands.

From his seat Hank looks up at her. "This sounds like a domestic situation that has escalated. I'm sure you've seen it all before."

"Yes," Hope says. In her mind's eye she sees another man in another place. She sees the gun, hears his voice, his wife's, and smaller voices besides. She pushes away the threat of her memories. That man is not the man in the post office right now. This is not that.

"We don't have too many facts except what's come from some witnesses who didn't stick around long enough to ask questions."

Hope takes this in. "And it's just a gun?" she asks.

Hank purses his lips. "We don't know. So far reports are just a gun."

"But no explosives?" Even the threat of a bomb can change everything.

Hank holds up his hands. "Not that we've heard so far." Hope knows that in a situation like this, anything could come up. Expect the unexpected.

"So I don't guess anyone has made contact with the suspect?"

"Not yet. They're getting our guys ready to approach, just to get a visual, confirm what the witnesses are saying if we can, but we can't do much past that without backup." He grimaces. "We're, uh, a little out of our depth with this one." He looks away from her, out the window beside his desk, as if he can see the post office from there, which he can't. "That's why it'll be good to have you over there."

"Thank you," she tells him, "for trusting me." He shrugs as if it is nothing, and perhaps it is for him. But it is a lot for Hope. Her mind goes back to the flowers left behind on her kitchen counter. Happy birthday to her. If she'd come into work in Philadelphia today, she would've found all kinds of nonsense waiting for her, meant to tease and taunt her, all part of tradition, all in good fun. There would be jokes and gag gifts and, eventually, cake. For a moment she feels homesick.

"I know you walked to work, so I've arranged for an officer to give you a ride over there." Hank rises from his desk and Hope heads toward the door.

Hank pauses before he opens the door, looking awkward as he says, "Good luck out there." He waves his hand in the air. "Or whatever you're supposed to say at times like these. Like I said, we don't have them very often."

Hope manages another thank you before he opens the door to reveal an officer waiting in the hall, a woman with her hair slicked back in a no-nonsense blonde ponytail, whose name tag reads "Brower." The two nod in greeting before Brower waves at Hope to follow her, so she does. They walk out to a marked SUV and wordlessly drive over to the post office. At less than a mile away, it is a quick trip.

Brower puts the car in Park and looks out at the scene, then over at Hope, speaking for the first time. "Weird, huh?" she says. Hope nods in agreement. It is, indeed, weird.

Brower cuts the engine and opens the driver's side door. "I'm supposed to take you over to talk to the witnesses."

"Okay," says Hope, feeling her nerves sparking just below the surface of her skin. She hopes all of this will be like riding a bike. And that could be the case. Just as long as she doesn't let herself think about the last time she did this, all should be well. "I'll follow you," she tells Brower.

Brower's blonde ponytail bounces girlishly as they cut through the clusters of cops milling around. Brower explains as they walk that they have two witnesses on the premises, women who work at the post office who had, according to their story, gone out to get lunch when everything occurred. "They moved them over here," Brower says, gesturing toward where they're headed, another office building several hundred yards away with a separate parking lot.

They cross blacktop and ragged strips of grass before stopping at the civilian car with the front and back doors open and two figures visible inside it. A uniformed officer hovers nearby, his car parked behind theirs, blocking them in. Whether that's on purpose or just happenstance is unclear.

"This is going to be the staging area," Brower adds, pointing at the building and the empty parking lot. "The chief says it's a good place for the NOC and equipment and such."

Hope nods and does not say she'd already assumed that. "I guess we should see what they have to say," she says instead and walks over to the two women who are smoking cigarettes and watching the goings-on in the post office parking lot like some might watch a sporting event. The deputy who seems to be guarding the women nods at Hope and Brower as they approach, allowing them to pass. Hope raises her hand to the two women, hoping to appear friendly. She sees them sit up a little straighter.

One, as if caught doing something wrong, drops her cigarette to the ground and grinds it under her shoe, then looks up at Hope and sheepishly picks the butt up again, pinching it between her thumb and forefinger uncertainly. Beside her, Brower sticks out her hand and the girl drops it into her palm, looking relieved.

"Don't want to be a litterbug," the sheepish one says. Brower walks away, probably to dispose of the butt, as Hope asks for their names. The girl who dropped her cigarette says, "Stacy." The one who holds on to hers says, "Martha," exhaling a plume of smoke as she does.

"I'm Officer Sherwood," Hope says. She almost says *Detective*, out of habit, but catches herself. She had gained the rank of detective in Philadelphia. But here, by choice, she is just a part-time patrol officer.

Brower appears again at her side, so Hope yanks a thumb in her direction. "And this is Officer Brower.

"Can you tell me about what happened today?" Hope asks. They both start answering at the same time. Stacy, the younger one, talks faster and has a higher pitch to her voice, while Martha is lower and slower with her words. Hope holds up a hand and points to Martha. "Why don't you go first?"

Stacy looks dejected but keeps quiet as Martha continues, detailing how they'd hatched a plan to go get hot dogs over at Burg-Dog in Shallotte for lunch. Martha admits it was totally against the rules, and they'd talked the young postal clerk, who is now trapped inside, into staying behind so they could go. Hope can feel the guilt emanating from her as she speaks.

Stacy interrupts Martha. "But have you ever had a Burg Dog?"

Hope has not and says so.

"Best hot dog you'll ever eat." Stacy nods to herself like this is justification of their unauthorized errand, but something about her face tells Hope she doesn't really believe that.

Hope turns to Martha. "Let's get to the part where you returned from lunch," she prompts, an attempt to move the story along.

"Right," says Martha. "We went around to the back like we'd usually do, but the door was bolted. We thought maybe Nadine got scared, you know, being there all alone, and locked herself in." She pauses to light a new cigarette and inhales as she says, more to herself than to Hope, "She hasn't been there all that long. We shouldn't have left her." She exhales and continues. "Then we figured we'd just go around to the front."

Martha looks over at Stacy, then down at the ground. "Stacy had Nadine's hot dog in her hand and was doing this silly little dance until . . . until we went in, and, well, we saw all the shi—I mean, the stuff he'd pulled in front of the doors. We looked through the glass and we could see all of them in there. And they just looked so . . . terrified."

"How many hostages did you see?" Hope asks.

Martha shakes her head. "Two, maybe three customers? It all went down so fast. And of course Nadine—" Martha's voice breaks, and she stops speaking long enough to swallow back tears before taking another drag from the cigarette to steady herself. "Next thing we knew, he had a gun pointed at us. And I ran for my life even though I wanted to stay. I wanted to push through that barricade and wring his ever-loving neck."

"Who is *he*?" Hope asks Martha. She's been told this is likely a domestic situation, but she wants to hear it from an eyewitness.

"Nadine's ex. Tommy Harrell."

"And are you familiar with Tommy Harrell, with their situation?" Hope presses.

"I mean, she's worked here less than a year, so I don't know a ton," Martha says. "But yeah. I mean, until they separated recently, he'd come by to see her sometimes." Martha looks over at the post office as she says it, a memory likely playing in her mind. "He used to bring her lunch," she adds with a wistful tone to her voice. "I thought it was sweet."

"You said they separated recently. How recent?" Hope asks. This is the information she needs. This is the background that will aid her in reaching the suspect. The coworker is giving her enough to at least get started. She will learn more about the situation as she goes, as she talks to Tommy Harrell. She feels her heart hitch upward a notch, but whether that is due to excitement or fear, she can't tell.

"A month? Maybe six weeks at most?" Martha shakes her head. "Long enough that she finally decided to file papers and make it official." Martha and Stacy both make stricken faces as something dawns on them. "I think maybe that was today." She looks at Stacy to clarify. "That he was going to get served the papers."

Stacy claps her palm to her forehead. "We're so stupid! Why didn't she remind us? She should've told us not to go. Today of all days!"

Martha shakes her head grimly as she says, "This is all our fault."

"The truth is," Stacy adds, her face beseeching, her need to confess obvious, "we ran by the Walmart too. It's just across the street, so it was right there, but we . . . started looking at the clothes and all. Walmart has some real cute things now." She pulls a frown. "We shouldn't have done that. We weren't thinking." Stacy's big blue eyes leave Hope's face and stray over to the post office, which looks placid at the moment except for all the emergency personnel clustered around it. "If we hadn't gone, maybe this wouldn't have happened."

Hope pats Stacy on the shoulder. "Or maybe you'd be trapped inside there right now too," she says, an attempt to assuage some of her guilt, though it likely won't work. In situations like this, it's hard to know what would or would not have changed the outcome. People can make themselves crazy trying to figure out if they could or should have done something different.

A horn blares, and Hope turns to see what's happening. Out on the street that runs by the post office, cars are slowing as curious drivers try to see what's going on. They will need to get a patrol officer out there soon to keep traffic moving, maybe even reroute traffic entirely to keep the main road clear in case of emergency. Hope hopes it does not come to that.

Chapter 14

INSIDE THE POST office, Sylvie remains on her stool, knowing she should conserve her energy, fearing that if she does get up she will pass out straightaway. Her hypoglycemia is in full effect, and all the stress has weakened her further. So she stays put on the stool, and away from the action, for as long as she can.

But when Nadine starts hollering that the cops are approaching the building, her body comes off the stool and goes toward the windows without her mind giving consent. *Curiosity killed the cat*, Sylvie thinks as she finds a spot at the window, *and old ladies who have FOMO.* (She learned from her granddaughter that FOMO means "fear of missing out.")

She makes it to the window and leans against it as she watches a group of three uniformed officers move toward the building, one of them holding a shield up to protect them, which—depending on what kind of arsenal Tommy could have inside the post office—could be about as worthwhile as holding an umbrella in a hurricane. They can't know for certain that Tommy only has the one gun. They for sure don't know that though he waves it around liberally and has fired it, he is, Sylvie is willing to bet, unsure about actually using it on a person. Not that anyone in the room is anxious to test that theory.

They need a negotiator, Sylvie thinks. *A good one.* She scans the collection of vehicles assembled. SWAT isn't here yet. There's no mobile command center either. So the negotiator is still to come. Sylvie scans the landscape, spotting a building farther away with its own parking lot. She squints and sees people out there and a lone cop car. She bets they'll create the staging area right there, far enough to factor in concern for safety but close enough to monitor what's going on.

She looks back to see that the uniforms have come to a stop and wonders what will happen next just as one of them speaks into a walkie-talkie, then nods at another one. That one raises a bullhorn and yells into it, "Thomas Clayton Harrell, come out with your hands up!" All eyes turn to Tommy, who screeches in response.

He points at the men outside, armed with their shield and their bullhorn. "They know my name!" he says. "How do they know my name?"

Beside him, Nadine rolls her eyes and answers, "Stacy and Martha told them, stupid."

Sylvie thinks it is not a good time to be calling Tommy "stupid," but she doesn't say so. He seems to take the insult in stride, too preoccupied with the policemen calling his name while ignoring entirely their command for him to surrender. His eyes are wild, rolling from the cops to the women around him to the barricade he constructed, keeping all the cops out but also keeping all of them in. Sylvie imagines he regrets that barricade now. She imagines he regrets ever coming back in here in the first place. It is funny, she thinks, the way your life can get away from you.

When they get no response, the three officers advance again, this time toward the main door. Sylvie thinks, *Who's in charge here? Who is authorizing this?* even as the officers enter the building. The hostages and their captor watch the duckwalk advancement the policemen make, then their pause when they see the barricade. Sylvie sees one officer peering over the shield, attempting to count heads inside the post office.

She is watching him assess the situation, trying to determine what his next move will be, so her attention is elsewhere when Tommy grabs Nadine and puts a gun to her head. Nadine starts to cry as Sylvie's heart rate hikes up to an unnatural high. It is not good for an old woman to be in a crisis like this. Not good at all. She wonders how many years of her life this situation could potentially be subtracting. For the first time she wonders if she will make it out of this. She came here to mail an envelope, not to die.

She lets herself have this one, scary thought and then decides, *No. This is ridiculous.* She hasn't met her match in Tommy Harrell. She did not come to this post office to die, and neither did these other women. They need a negotiator outside—she prays one is coming—but she can do her part from inside. She can use what she knows.

On the other side of the glass, the cops acquiesce to Tommy's unspoken demand and resume their duckwalk, but backward this time, their hands, or whatever free hands they can manage, raised as they retreat.

"They're gone, Tommy," Sylvie says to him, working to keep her voice low and measured. She needs to sit down again, needs to get back to the stool, but first she needs to make sure Tommy is going to lower the gun and let Nadine go. "It's okay now," she says, hearing the ridiculousness of her words as they leave her mouth. Because clearly it is not okay.

Tommy looks over at her, his eyes wide with fear. She nods slowly and sees his head begin to nod along with hers. They all exhale as he lets go of Nadine and tucks the gun back into his waistband. "They were coming in here!" he says, as if that is a good explanation for threatening Nadine's life. He sounds like a petulant child, pointing the finger of blame at anyone but himself. But now is not the time to tell him this.

Instead, she says, "I understand," and makes a little shooing motion to the group to indicate that they should go back to whatever they were doing, which is nothing at all except waiting for this siege to end.

Chapter 15

After the cops exit the building, Tommy's paranoia intensifies. "Bastards!" he screams at the window that looks into the now empty vestibule. It is so loud that the hostages all jump. But Tommy doesn't notice. He just continues his tirade, moving away from the bank of windows at the front of the room toward the back of the room near the counter, gesturing at the windows like they did something wrong.

"I can't look out those windows now 'cause some trigger-happy cop might decide to shoot me dead," he says. He peers at the scene outside with a scowl. "They're too close to the building. They're going to keep trying to get in here. I need them to move away."

He isn't, Nadine knows, so much angry as he is scared. She's seen that look before. Tommy greets nearly every situation in life with anger. Sad? Get angry. Feeling vulnerable? Get angry. Bad weather? Get angry. Car won't start? Get angry. His anger—and his drinking, which lately seems to come with the anger—is basically why they are all trapped in this room.

Plain and simple, Nadine reached a point where she couldn't take it anymore. It wasn't that he was violent or threatening toward her. For a time she consoled herself with that—it could be worse, she reminded herself often. And yet his anger felt insidious, a poisonous gas filling their home a little more each day with a dark heaviness. Despite her love for him, Nadine didn't want to spend the rest of her life living with the anger. It dwelled in their house like a terrible roommate they couldn't evict.

For so long she was resigned that Tommy's anger was part of their life, something unavoidable, like balancing the budget or cleaning the toilet. Then one day things changed. She saw things differently, felt hope—the barest suggestion of it, but there—within her, waiting to unfurl. Quietly, intentionally, she started feeding the hope, and as with anything you feed, it slowly grew. Until one day it was large enough to sustain her, large enough to move her past being stuck in a situation she couldn't get out of. It took some doing, but she convinced Tommy to leave, that they'd be better off apart than together. She thought he thought so too. She looks over at Tommy. But now here she is, stuck again.

As if he's read Nadine's mind and wants to give her more proof that she was right to end things, Tommy snaps his fingers at all of them, getting their attention. "I can't get near those windows," he says to the four women. "But you can." He smiles at whatever he's thinking. "You bitches can stand up there and remind them that I got hostages and they'd better back up. Otherwise I might just do something crazy." His smile goes wider.

Might do something crazy? Nadine thinks that at this point he is only piling crazy on top of crazy. With a shudder she wonders when—and how—this is going to end. She hears her mother's voice in her head, telling her to take charge of this situation. She just has to figure out how. Nadine is not the take-charge type, but it seems she might have to be today.

"Get on up there!" he hollers, and Nadine sees Blythe's back go ramrod straight, her eyes go wide. Slowly, they all obey him, moving grudgingly, cautiously, toward the bank of windows. Sylvie has a hard time sliding from the stool, and Morrow gives her a hand. Nadine sees that Tommy see this and hopes he is thinking of his own grandmother, whom she knows he spent Easter with if this year was like all the others. Nadine always enjoyed going to his family's house for holidays. To part with him was to part with them too. It was a trade she accepted, but not without the pang of loss. People always ask why women don't leave terrible situations. Nadine can tell them. It's because you never just leave a man. You leave a whole life.

Tommy goes to where shipping envelopes in various sizes are displayed for purchase, yanking down four of the largest size. *He is stealing those envelopes*, Nadine thinks. When this is over, she will tell the postmaster about this, offer to have him take the cost out of her salary. This is her fault, after all. Tommy wouldn't be here doing this if she didn't work here.

She watches as he goes to the counter where she was sitting when all of this began, worrying he's going to see the bottle of liquor where she stashed it, way back, tucked behind some rolls of packing tape. But he's too focused on whatever it is he's going to do with those envelopes.

He gropes around until he finds a large black Sharpie marker and writes something on the back of each envelope, in the white space where nothing is printed. He is turning the envelopes into placards. On one he writes, "Back away!" On another he writes, "I have hostages!" On another he writes, "Am armed!" Then on a fourth and final one, he writes, "No cops!" He examines his efforts like a child admiring his artwork before handing an envelope to each woman.

"Hold them up against the windows!" he demands. When they don't do what he's instructed, he repeats himself, but louder. This time they comply, obediently pressing his makeshift signs to the glass with shaking hands. Behind them, Tommy marches like a drill sergeant, back and forth, supervising their performance while they serve as his human barrier. He nods to himself, pleased as he peers over their shoulders. The cops are using binoculars to see what the envelopes say. They begin nudging one another, stepping farther back from the building.

"That's right, you sons of bitches!" Tommy hollers, drunk on this bit of power he's achieved. "You damn well better get back!"

Sylvie keeps her eyes straight ahead, focusing on the retreat of the people who are supposed to be helping them. As time passes, her arms and shoulders begin to ache from holding the envelope. She can feel a fight-or-flight sensation filling her with a hot, pressing urgency. She steals a longing glance at the barricaded door. She wants to go home. She wants to see Robert, to know he's okay. It is wrong to leave him unattended with no word as to where she is. She longs to find a way to get in touch with him, to hear his voice.

She hopes he hasn't wandered out of the house or tried to take a shower and slipped or turned on the stove and left it on. She hopes he's watching golf, unaware of how long it's been since she left the house. But she knows that is likely not the case. On his worst days he is still aware of her, only instead of a husband being aware of his wife, it is more like a child being aware of his mother, needy and anxious instead of forthright and take-charge like he once was. It breaks her heart a little more each time it happens, seeing this man she loves going backward, retreating into a time before she knew him. Having someone leaving you even as they're standing right in front of you is an odd experience.

She feels tears, hot and stinging, fill her eyes, turning the post office parking lot into a watercolor landscape. A tear runs down her cheek, and she lowers the envelope so she can wipe it away. Beside her she hears sniffling and turns to see that the others are also trying, and failing, not to cry.

"Old lady!" Tommy says, oblivious to the emotional state of his captives. "Hold that sign up higher!"

When he speaks his voice sounds far away. A whistling noise fills her head. She knows she must move fast to keep from falling. Tommy has gone too far, pushed her past what she can bear. She lets go of the envelope, and it drops to the floor. The high-pitched whine in her head drowns out all other sound. She sees Tommy coming toward her but focuses instead on the stool she was sitting on. She needs to get to it. If she can just sit down, then maybe she will be okay.

This is what she is thinking as the floor, once inert, rises toward her.

Chapter 16

Outside, hope has walked back to the staging area. She eyes the post office in the distance, picturing the four women who were lined up inside, forced to stand on display in the windows like puppies at a pet store, holding signs with brief, bold threats etched across them, the words penned by a panicking, cornered man trying to buy more time. Hope does not think the suspect realized all of the women were crying as they faced the windows. But Hope saw. And now she can't unsee. She walked away from them, but only to make a call to Hank, to tell him about the escalation she just witnessed, to find out when help will arrive.

She dials the number and holds her phone to her ear.

Hank answers. "I was just about to call you."

"I know you've got people on the way, but I don't think we should wait to make contact much longer," Hope says, keeping her eyes on the windows for any sign of the women returning.

Hank exhales. "I know. I heard. And I agree, we can't keep waiting around. The county is en route, but there's been a massive car wreck on Highway 17. Several cars are involved and some serious injuries. Maybe even a fatality. The traffic's backed up in both directions and nothing's moving. It's bad enough that if it weren't for the situation at the post office, I'd have sent some of my people up there to help them. 'Course I can't do that with what we've got going on down here. It's all hands on deck everywhere. When it rains it pours and all that."

Hank sighs into the phone. "Since the county team is stuck in that traffic, some of 'em have exited their vehicles to help. I'm afraid it's gonna be a while longer. The FBI still might join, but that's a cluster of its own. I thought about scrambling a team farther up in Wilmington, but they'd still have to come through all that 17 mess, and if they take the back roads to avoid the traffic, that'll end up taking even longer. I could try to access the folks down in Myrtle, but that's crossing state lines, and you know what a predicament that can be."

"Are you telling me to hold off till they get here?" Hope asks, trying to keep the frustration out of her voice.

"No, I'm telling you that you're going to have to fly solo. Except"—he pauses—"and I'm not sure how much help this is going to be, but there's a guy who got in touch with me a bit ago. I know him from golfing. He was FBI, retired now. He and I have shared some war stories. Enough for me to think he could be of assistance. I know you're not exactly, uh, comfortable with being put in this role. And certainly not without a team around you. If—"

"It's okay," Hope rushes to say. She doesn't want to talk about whether she's comfortable or whether she's capable. She's just here, in this place, doing this job. There is, it would appear, no one else to do it.

"Anyway, he said he wouldn't mind coming over there. His name's Bo. Like I said, I don't know how much help he'll be, but if anything he can serve as moral support."

"Sure, yeah," says Hope. She doesn't really want some retiree hanging around looking over her shoulder, but it doesn't seem like she gets a choice. She was relieved when Brower, who'd been her shadow ever since they arrived, got called on to go direct traffic out front. From the sound of it, she's going to get a new shadow.

She hears the clatter of Hank's fingers on a keyboard, then he speaks. "We've shut down the phone line going in or out of the post office so the only calls going to or from will be between us and the people in there. I'm sending you an access line and a code that will enable you to dial in from your cell." He sighs, then adds, "The county's got the technology we need, but for now this is the best we can do."

"I understand," says Hope.

"I'm also sending you what intel we've gathered. It should show up on your phone any second. It's a list of who we think the hostages are and the little bit of information about them I've gleaned from the license plates of the cars in the parking lot. There's also some background on the suspect—name, age, criminal record—which I will say there isn't much of."

He pauses before continuing. Hope can tell he's choosing his words. "The suspect is a local boy. Lived here most of his life. I know some of his people, in fact. He's got no serious record prior to this—a ticket for public drunkenness, a ticket for speeding. Nothing out of the norm for a guy his age. Nothing that would indicate his doing something like this. So just keep that in mind. This isn't some career criminal who's known to be dangerous."

"You didn't see what he just did to those women," she says. "They're traumatized."

"I'm not saying he's not capable of violence—I haven't met a human being who's not if pushed to their limits. I'm just saying I don't think this is something he set out to do." Hank sneezes into the phone. Spring in Sunset means everything is blooming, which also means a lot of people are coughing, sniffling, and sneezing. You have to take the good with the bad, even in the happiest place in the world.

“Excuse me,” he apologizes, then continues. “What I was saying is, I bet he could benefit from talking to someone.” Hank pauses, the silence stretching out longer than Hope expects. “I’ll be honest with you. One of my guys had a clear shot at him earlier when he was standing in front of those windows, but I didn’t authorize it. I think this could be rectified peaceably. And I’d like it to be—” He sneezes a second time, excuses himself a second time, then adds, “With you.”

“Okay,” Hope says. She appreciates the vote of confidence. And yet she is rusty. Out of practice. She won’t say that aloud, though. She will fake it till she makes it. Or something like that.

“Okay, then,” he says. “I’ll be here, staying up on the latest with this county delay. But if you need me, just say the word and I can come over there.”

“I will,” she promises, even as she hopes she won’t need him. “I just have to get the conversation started.” She gives a little laugh, intended to put him at ease. “Maybe it’ll be resolved before the folks from county can even get here.”

Hank’s laugh sounds as forced as hers. “That would be nice.”

They say their goodbyes, and Hope ends the call wondering if he could hear the wobble in her voice. She wants Hank to think she’s got this whole situation in hand, but she suspects he knows that she’s uncertain and unprepared. Whatever happens today, she decides, it’s less about how she feels and more about what she does.

As soon as the information Hank sent pops up on her phone, she downloads it, scans it, then decides to try the access line he sent to see if it works. This is far from the technology she’s used to having at her disposal, but she has no other choice.

She listens to the unusual ring on the other end, but no one answers. Someone picking up on her first attempt would’ve made things easier. She doesn't expect easy, but it would be nice. In her fantasy, she makes contact with the suspect, he surrenders, and the situation is in hand in record time. She knows this is not realistic. But very few fantasies are.

She hangs up and busies herself with reading the full report Hank has sent. It includes information about each hostage, including a best guess as to a contact number for each one. She feels certain that if the suspect hasn't taken their phones yet, he will soon. She wonders if she should attempt to make contact with the hostages individually. If he won't answer the post office line, perhaps one of them will respond to her calling them directly. It's risky—it could set him off, take away his illusion of control if she goes around him to get to them. She thinks again of them holding those signs, trying to be brave. She wants to let them know she is here, working to free them.

Hope is sitting in Brower's car with the air conditioner running, pondering her next move, when a car pulls in and parks beside her. It is an older Toyota Camry, dark green, and the driver sits hunched over the steering wheel like a teenager who has crammed himself into a toy car he has long ago outgrown. She watches as the man doesn't so much exit the car as unfold himself out of it, his knees and elbows sharp angles he navigates around. He stands up, a tower of a man, and surveys the parking lot, his hawkish eyes hooded by bushy gray eyebrows that could use a trim.

Without introduction, she knows this is the man Hank mentioned, the retired FBI agent who has offered to assist. But what does assist mean to him? If he's like a lot of men, it means to take over. And though Hope wouldn't have chosen to be here, now that she is, she's not excited about having someone else try to hijack her role.

She debates staying put in the car and not engaging with this person. She can't help but feel that he is here to babysit her. That it was Hank who reached out to *him*, asking him for his help, instead of the other way around as it was presented. With the team from county being delayed, Hank is likely relying on the only backup he can find. She wants him to think her capable of handling it on her own, but he must not. She both resents and accepts this fact.

The man takes a moment to survey the scene, turning in the direction of the post office. He stares at the building's facade, the suspect's battered truck, and the three cars still parked in front of it, the customers' cars they thought they'd come right back to. Hope wonders what he's thinking as he takes it all in.

When he looks over his shoulder, she waves to get his attention. "Are you . . . Bo?" she calls out.

He peers at her, his bushy eyebrows meeting in the middle, then starts walking in her direction. When he gets to her, he smiles, looking down at her with an expression that is a mixture of curiosity and magnanimity. "Yes," he says. He reaches into his pocket and pulls out his wallet. "Would you like to see some identification?"

He goes to open the wallet, but Hope holds up her hands. "That won't be necessary," she says. "Hank vouched for you."

He smiles down at her. "Okay, then," he says and puts the wallet away.

She squints up at him, feeling like a child under his gaze. Perhaps it is because of his size, or perhaps it is because of his presence, at once authoritative and gentle. She feels herself relenting in spite of her misgivings about him being there. She is still worried he will be bossy or in the way. But he is here. She cannot change it, and there's no use worrying about it. Not when there is work to be done.

He looks again at the post office. "What do we know about

this situation?" he asks, gesturing at the building. "Who've we got in there?"

She tells him what they've gathered about the hostages so far, reading aloud the information from her phone's screen. "We've got a married, fifty-four-year-old mother of two named Morrow King. She lives on Shoreline Drive and has one child still living at home. Isn't employed as far as we can tell.

"Next is a thirty-one-year-old woman named Blythe Howard. She waits tables at the Grapevine Restaurant in Calabash, lives in a home she inherited from her grandmother, and is recently engaged.

"Then we've got a seventy-four-year-old woman named Sylvie Lawson, who retired to the area several years ago with her husband, Robert. She lives in Ocean's Path, that new retirement community."

"They call them 'active living' communities now." He gives her a little smirk. "It's supposed to make us feel better."

Hope smiles and continues. "Finally, there's Nadine Harrell, wife of the suspect, who served him papers this morning for divorce, which I'm sure put all this in motion. There's no concrete information about why they split up. Apparently she was pretty private with her coworkers about the whys and wherefores. And she hasn't been working for the USPS for very long."

"And what about the suspect?" he asks.

"His name is Thomas Harrell, goes by Tommy. Hank says he's a local boy with nothing alarming on his record. Not known for violence or criminal behavior."

"Till today," says Bo.

"Till today," Hope agrees.

"You've initiated contact?" he asks.

"I tried," she says. She fills him in on the police's attempt to enter the building, on her ignored call. "I was just thinking about what to do next when you arrived."

"And what did you decide?" he asks. She is surprised, and grateful, that he doesn't assert his opinion.

She does not tell him she was torn about what to do. She just says what comes to her mind in the moment. "I thought I'd try again," she says. "Try to get him to respond, or maybe try the hostages directly if he won't."

Bo nods once, his large head dipping down and back up again. When he looks her in the eyes, Hope feels like the pupil who got the right answer in front of the whole class. "Then let's get to work," he says. He points at the post office, and they both take it in for a moment.

Those poor women, she thinks. *Trapped like that.*

"We need to get them out of there," he says, an authentic tone of concern in his voice.

"Yes," she agrees. "We do."

Chapter 17

When Sylvie falls, it is Morrow who moves toward her instead of freezing like the others in the room do. *This is motherhood*, she thinks, *this instinct.* She did not use to have it. It showed up with her children. With the arrival of her son, then several years later, her daughter, she came to understand why mothers fought wild animals, faced off villains, lifted whole cars to save their children. It starts with your child, then extends to the world. This kindness, this love, this grace that comes with opening your heart as wide as motherhood does. No one child—or children—can hold it all. So you give it away any chance you get, knowing it is a renewable resource. At least it has been that way for Morrow.

Her fall happens so fast, so unexpectedly. One minute Sylvie is leaving the window in spite of Tommy's protests. The next she is pitching forward, her arms scrambling for something to hold on to as she goes down. Morrow rushes to her side. "Are you okay?" she asks as she kneels beside her. Sylvie nods, momentarily confused as she focuses on Morrow's face. Morrow sees that she hit her forearm on the edge of the stool as she grasped for it. She will have a bruise.

The phone rings, a shrill burst of sound that startles them all. But everyone is focused on Sylvie, so no one moves to get it, and then the ringing stops. Gingerly, Morrow helps her to her feet and rights the stool so she can sit. "I—I—" Sylvie tries to speak.

"Yes?" Morrow prompts her. She sees that Sylvie is gesturing at the fruit basket the woman dropped when she ran out of the post office. Apples and oranges lie scattered about on the tile. There is a package of cheese crackers and a package of peanuts and other things besides that still inside the basket.

"Are you hungry?" she asks Sylvie.

"Hypoglycemia," Sylvie manages to say, looking ashamed, her voice barely above a whisper.

"What'd she say?" Tommy asks, the concern plain on his face. *He should be concerned*, Morrow thinks. He has further victimized an elderly woman.

"She said she has hypoglycemia," Morrow tells him, her voice clipped.

Tommy looks confused by this. He turns to Nadine. "Is that like that dog your sister got?"

Nadine's laugh in response to his question is more like a jeer. "That's hypoallergenic, Tommy," she says. She rolls her eyes and shakes her head.

Morrow sees Tommy bristle at her reaction and hurries to cover over Nadine's derision. "Hypoglycemia is a condition where your blood sugar drops, and it can make you quite weak," she tells the room, as if Tommy isn't the only one who might not know what hypoglycemia is.

She pats Sylvie's shoulder. "My daughter had it when she was little." She gestures at the contents of the spilled basket. "You just need some food, and you should be right as rain," she tells her.

Blythe makes herself useful, hurrying over to the food items, grabbing an apple, an orange, and the package of peanuts, then running back over to Morrow and Sylvie. She thrusts it all in Sylvie's direction, as if to ask, *Will this work?* and Morrow smiles at her effort, then takes the package of peanuts and tears it open before handing it over. When Sylvie accepts it, her hand is shaking.

Nadine goes over to the basket as well, crouching to paw through it as Tommy intently keeps his eyes on her. Not for the first time, Morrow wishes he would let the customers go, since it is clearly Nadine he is here for. He couldn't care less about the rest of them. So why keep them here? Morrow does not understand.

Nadine shrugs and stands up. "I was hoping there was a bottle of water in there. Might be good for her to have something to drink too."

Morrow remembers the bottle of water in her tote. "I've actually got one," she says and stands to go and retrieve it. She reaches inside and paws around, pretending to look for her water as she sneaks a peek at her phone. Nothing from Maya.

She pulls out the water bottle and takes it over to Sylvie, who is already looking a little less peaked. Sylvie takes it, looking grateful but still ashamed. Ashamed, Morrow knows, of falling, of being weak, of needing. Morrow would feel the same if it were her. *In a few years*, Morrow thinks, *I will be you.* She can't believe how quickly she has already become a woman in her fifties. Time just keeps moving, faster and faster.

Sylvie finishes the small pack of peanuts, then tries to get off the stool to throw away the wrapper, but Morrow stops her. "I'll do it," she says.

"Thank you," Sylvie says, her voice a bit stronger now.

"Happy to help," Morrow replies. And it is true. She's been thinking lately about what she can do next year when Maya is off at college and her nest is empty. She will need something to fill her days. Perhaps she could do something with the elderly.

Nadine, also wanting to do what she can, goes behind the partition and gets three more stools, ignoring Tommy's hollering that she can't go back there as she drags them across the floor one by one, creating a little circle for them all to be able to sit.

"Where's mine?" Tommy asks when she is done.

Nadine gives him a look. "This is all we've got," she says. She bites back a smile at the look on Tommy's face when he doesn't get a seat. But he doesn't protest as the three women tuck their belongings under their stools like Sylvie's and settle into their places.

They sit silently as Sylvie sips Morrow's water and the clock on the wall *tick, tick, tick*s away the time. It is the only noise in the room until the post office phone rings again, startling them a second time. It is not a normal ring, so loud and shrill it makes a person want to answer it just to make it stop.

"That'll be the police," Sylvie says to Tommy. Her voice is stronger, and the color has come back to her face, thanks to the food. Blythe thinks of the woman who carried that fruit basket into the post office and the fear on her face as she dropped it and ran from Tommy and his gun. And yet it was good for Sylvie that she had left that fruit basket behind. Her gran used to say that everything works out for a reason, and in this case, it is true.

Tommy doesn't answer the phone, which doesn't surprise Blythe at all. Instead, he looks at the four of them, as if the obnoxious ringing noise is their fault. The phone rings again, then again, the shrill burst of sound sandpapering Blythe's frayed nerves.

Mercifully, the phone stops ringing and Blythe sees her fellow captives' shoulders relax in tandem with her own, hears the rush as they exhale breath they were all holding. No one says anything as they sit in the silence. Blythe thinks about her dog, Murphy, a Lab mix who passed away just six weeks ago. Blythe misses him all the time, is still surprised when he's not there to greet her at the door when she comes home. He was a wonderful dog, the best. Except for when the phone rang. He would bark and bark and run around in circles till she answered it. Murphy would really lose it if he heard *that* ring. She smiles despite the lump in her throat.

Just then, Blythe's phone goes off. She pulls it out of her pocket and places it in on her lap, but she doesn't dare answer. She doesn't move. She just waits for the ringing to end. They all look to Tommy as Sylvie's phone goes off next, then Morrow's after that, then Nadine's, a sequence of buzzes and beeps and song. Tommy raises the gun again. Blythe wonders if the more he does that, the less it will impact her. For now, the action still resounds, her heart picking up speed at the sight of the barrel's hole pointed in her direction.

"Not a one of you'd better answer," Tommy says to them through clenched teeth.

Blythe holds up her hands, an expression of surrender. Tommy passes the gun by them all, going counterclockwise around their little circle. "No one's talking to the cops," he says. He seems to ponder this, then adds, "If anyone's going to talk to them, it'll be me."

He lifts his gaze toward the ceiling, then looks back at them and holds out his free hand. "In fact, give me your phones." When they don't move at his command, he makes a grabbing motion. "Hand 'em over," he tells them, impatient. They look at one another, conferring with their eyes as they grip their phones.

Should we give him our phones? their eyes say.

What will he do if we refuse—shoot us all?

That's a bit extreme.

Blythe can read the whole conversation just from their expressions. She looks to Sylvie to see what she will do. Sylvie simply stares Tommy down, stone-faced, not surrendering her phone. Blythe's gaze travels from Tommy to Sylvie and back again. She can see Tommy begin to waffle on his demand, realizing that, beyond shooting them, he has no recourse if they refuse to give him their phones. *This is good*, Blythe thinks. They are standing their ground together.

But the spell is broken as, one by one, Tommy simply goes around the ring of stools and takes the phones from their hands. They do not fight him, releasing the phones along with whatever power they may have momentarily reached for. Blythe feels a sense of defeat that goes beyond the loss of her means of communication as Tommy walks away with her phone. They should've stood up to him. They should've fought back like Morrow did. But Blythe will not fight back alone, and everyone else has given in. So she does as well.

Blythe watches Tommy try to balance all of the phones, plus his gun, as he goes behind the counter and deposits the phones into the same box where Nadine dropped her package hours ago. Again she thinks of asking to retrieve it. Again she keeps silent.

She looks away from Tommy and wonders if she will get out of here. And if she does, if she will be able to take that package with her. She made a mistake in mailing it, repeating an old pattern of appeasing her mother. The one good thing in all of this, she thinks, is that perhaps her mistake can be rectified. There is still time, she hopes, to undo what's been done, still time for everything to work out for a reason.

Chapter 18

THE TIME PASSES. No one speaks.

The post office line rings again, the same obnoxious ring as before. This time Sylvie speaks up when the ringing starts. "They're going to keep calling until you answer that," she tells Tommy, who, since he's decided to stay away from the windows, has taken to lapping their circle of stools like a deranged game of "Ring Around the Rosie."

He doesn't respond to the ringing, but he does stop circling to try to peer out the windows, pacing back and forth from window to window, surely not really seeing anything from the distance. He only stops moving when the phone stops ringing.

"If they can't make contact with you, they'll resort to other kinds of attempts," Sylvie tells him.

He stops, glares at her. "Oh yeah? How do you know that?"

She considers her response. "I'm a retiree. I've got a lot of time to watch cop shows."

He chuckles at that, shakes his head. "That sure don't make you an expert."

She shrugs. She doesn't care about his opinion. "Time will tell," she retorts.

She turns to see the other women looking at her expectantly. But she's got no real answers for them. Urging Tommy to communicate with whoever is on the other side of that barricade is their best hope. And until he does, they are stuck. She will do her best to keep up morale, but the boredom and stress are taking their toll.

When the phone starts up again, Tommy claps his hands to his ears, exaggerating like a child would. "Make them stop that," he says, looking at her like she can.

Sylvie crosses her arms, eyes him. "You're the only one who can make it stop," she tells him. Then she thinks about him forcing them to stand in the windows with signs. She does not want a repeat of that. "Would you like me to answer it and tell them to stop calling?" she asks.

He thinks about this, blinking slowly as he does. He is no longer as drunk as he was, but he is not what someone would call sober. He nods, looking down. She gets up and goes to the phone, ending the shrill ringing by raising the receiver to her ear.

"Hello?" she asks, just like she would answer any other call.

"Who am I speaking with?" a female voice—female!—says on the other end. What a surprise!

"This is Sylvie," says Sylvie. She does not give her last name. She'd prefer that Tommy not know it.

"Okay, Sylvie," says the voice. "I'm Hope."

Hope, Sylvie thinks. *That's just what we need.*

She listens for a moment to Hope's instructions before hanging up and looking at Tommy, who is still trying to see out the windows yet keep his distance, a hangdog expression on his face. "What'd he say?" he asks her, his voice sullen.

"*She* said that they'd like to know what you want."

"What I want?" Tommy asks. "What does that mean?"

"It means that when someone takes hostages, they usually have demands to go with it. Things they want in exchange for the hostages' release," Sylvie explains.

"You learn that from your cop shows?" Tommy sneers at her.

Blythe watches Sylvie's shoulders tense, then release. "The nice lady on the other end just told me so," she replies. Blythe sees her manage a smile for Tommy. "She's going to call back in a little bit. So you should probably be thinking about what you're going to ask for."

Tommy makes a show of shrugging his shoulders. "How do I know?" he says, his voice like a wail. He points at the windows. "I *want* to be out there," he says. "Free." He cocks his head at Sylvie. "Think you can negotiate that deal?"

"I'm not a negotiator," Sylvie says. There is something, Blythe notes, in the way she says it.

"Then what are you?" Tommy asks.

Sylvie straightens up to her full five-two height before replying, "I'm your hostage, trying to help you get us all out of here safely."

Tommy looks away, stares at the ground for a moment, chastened. No one says anything as he studies the floor for a long time. Finally, he lifts his head. "I don't know what I want." And for the first time since this all began, Blythe feels a flicker of sympathy for Tommy. She hates him for keeping them all here, but she also understands what he means. It is harder than it looks to decide what you want. Harder still to ask for it.

And so, they wait. They wait for Tommy to think about what he wants and for the phone to ring again. From her vantage point in the circle of stools, Morrow can see out one of the windows that looks out onto the parking lot. It is not a full vantage point but enough to see movement, to see the life happening outside of this room. People come and go, vehicles drive past. Her car, and the others' cars, are all still parked in the spots where they left them. She supposes they are evidence now. But of what? How good they had it this morning, walking around of their own free will? Able to come and go as they pleased?

She'd been so burdened by that little package as she got out of the car, her tote had actually felt heavier on her shoulder. Now she would happily send that package off if she could, happily hug her daughter and tell her what she did this morning, then watch as her daughter gave her that smile that told her she'd done the right thing, that their relationship has been salvaged once again.

Morrow notices the press has started to gather. People with microphones and cameras draw as close to the building as the police will allow. Morrow looks away. She cannot watch the goings-on outside the window for too long; the longing it stirs up inside her is too painful to bear.

Once she was on a plane, sitting in the first row behind first class on a cross-country flight. When they dropped the sheer curtain that separated first class from the plebeians behind them, she could still see everything that was happening. She recalls watching as the first-class patrons were served a real lunch with napkins and hot cloths to clean their hands while she made do with cookies as dry as sawdust and water to wash them down. *This*, she thinks now, *is like that. I can see it. But I cannot have it.*

Maya, she thinks. She looks at the watch she wears, her mother's. Morrow inherited it years ago and wears it still, even as so many people strap technological miracles to their wrists to count steps and heart rates and calories, keeping track of every aspect of themselves. But Morrow continues to wear this most basic timepiece, consistently good at doing what she needs it to do: tell time.

Her watch tells her it is 3:10. By now Maya is out of school. She wonders if the police have figured out it's her car parked there. She wonders if her family has been notified that she is in this post office, trapped. She thinks of Maya learning this and wonders if she will worry or if she will toss her hair and decide that in this situation, as in everything else, Morrow will find a way to work things out.

When Morrow was a few years younger than Maya, she learned that her mother had been diagnosed with cancer. She can't remember if she was seized with worry immediately or if it took a while for her to realize how serious the diagnosis was. She wonders if Maya will appreciate the seriousness of what is happening today. She wonders if Maya will replay their fight this morning on a loop like Morrow herself has done. Though it is probably wrong to think this way, Morrow hopes so.

When Nadine speaks up, they swivel their heads in her direction. She has said little beyond her barbs at Tommy, quiet with the shame of what her actions have brought on others. Even if they insist that's not the case, she can't help but feel it is. But now she lifts her head in a defiant sort of way. She thinks of her mother's words to her as she speaks. *"You're a smart girl, honey. You'll figure it out."*

"If you don't know what you want, Tommy," Nadine says, "then I know something I want." She points toward the vestibule. "There's a bathroom out there. I think we should all be allowed a bathroom break."

Tommy points at his barricade in front of the doors, blocking them in. "How do you think we can go out to the bathroom when all that stuff is in the way?" He says this to Nadine like she is the dumb one now.

"You'll take it down," Nadine says.

"I ain't taking all of that down and then putting it all back up again."

"You won't have to," Nadine says. She smiles at Tommy. It is her "I am so much smarter than you" smile.

"I'll give you the keys to the doors," she says to him. "Then you can lock us in once we get back from the bathroom. You'll have the keys, so you won't need the barricade anymore."

He looks at her skeptically. "Without that barricade they might just bust in here."

Nadine gives the barricade the side-eye. "It's not like that barricade was ever going to stop them from entering. It's a few pieces of furniture. Not that hard to get past."

Tommy thinks about this. "Yeah, I guess," he says. He gestures at his gun. "This is what's keeping them out more than anything."

"Right," says Nadine. She goes over to the counter and picks up the keys they keep on a little hook underneath. She returns and drops them into his palm. Quickly, as if she will have second thoughts and take them back, he shoves them into his pocket.

Tommy looks at her like he thinks she is helping him, like she is coming around to his side. Nadine lets him think whatever he wants. She keeps her seat as he tells Morrow and Blythe to come and help him remove the barricade. They slide off their stools and help him push the cabinet and the display rack back to where they were before. The tourist pamphlets are still askew, and the other things have been jostled in all the shifting around. She makes a mental note to fix them later. Her mama always taught her to leave a place better than you found it.

Chapter 19

Hope hangs up with Sylvie for the second time, calls the commander nearest to the building to warn them about the hostages' movement, and turns to Bo, who's been quietly listening in. This whole situation is so rudimentary, so far from what she's used to. There is no Negotiation Operations Center, which they refer to as the NOC. There is no technology to assist them in getting eyes on the suspect or hostages. No negotiation team to serve in different capacities, to add ideas, to confer with. Bo can't even properly listen in on what's being said. It's probably what he's used to. Like they did in the old days.

"He's taking them to the bathroom," she reports. "It's out in the vestibule area, so he's removing the barricade and walking them out to it. The guys close to the building will be monitoring it."

Bo's eyes widen at the mention of Tommy removing the barricade. "Getting rid of that barricade," he says. "That's progress."

She thinks this over. "Not really," she admits. "He's just going to use Nadine's keys to lock them back in once they get back to the room. That was the agreement."

"But with the barricade out of the way, we can use drones and have better visibility through the glass if we need to go in."

"Not yet," Hope says, her voice clipped, anxious at the suggestion of going in this soon. They've barely gotten started. She knows that words are every bit as powerful as tactical force. But that power takes time to build. "I don't want anyone going in yet."

"To be sure," Bo says. When he smiles at her, his bushy eyebrows nearly graze his cheeks. "We're nowhere near the trigger point."

Relief floods Hope's body. When Hank told her Bo was former FBI, she hadn't bothered to ask what he had done for them. She didn't know if he'd been on the tactical side or the talking side of a negotiation. Though they are there for the same outcome—resolution—the two sides often approach things differently.

Bo lifts the binoculars to his eyes as if from this distance he'll be able to see what's happening inside the vestibule. He watches the building for a while, then speaks to her. "I see movement. Can't count heads from here, but it looks like they're all walking as a group." He heaves a sigh, and she can't tell if it's from weariness or sincere worry. "So far, so good," he adds.

"Yes," she agrees. "So far, so good." *Now,* she thinks, *just to keep it that way.*

Chapter 20

As tommy directs them out the door and into the vestibule, Morrow falls into step beside Nadine, thanking her as they head for the bathroom. "I'm so glad you asked for this. I've had to go for the past hour, but I was afraid to say anything," she says. "Funny how something as simple as going to the bathroom can feel like a luxury."

Nadine thinks about what Morrow has said, how when something you once took for granted is taken away, you're that much more grateful for it when it is restored to you. She looks over at Tommy and thinks of all the things they took for granted, things that will never be restored to them, especially now. She thinks of what they would be doing if things were different. Probably planning one of their "Sunday Fundays" for the coming weekend, heading to the beach with sub sandwiches from Publix and a cooler of cold drinks to spend the afternoon listening to Jimmy Buffett or Morgan Wallen while lying in the sun. Though nothing particularly special, those were her favorite days. They were happy once; she remembers this fact whether she wants to or not. They did love each other. Which makes what's become of them even harder to accept.

Ahead of Nadine and Morrow, Sylvie walks beside Tommy, who isn't keen on the idea of taking them to the bathroom. He hasn't said so, but Sylvie is betting he's probably worried about losing control once they are out from behind the barricade. Still, they could all use a bathroom break. They've been inside that room for hours.

And so, like a kindergarten class with the meanest teacher in the world, they shuffle their way out into the vestibule. They pass the dropped hot dog, and Sylvie wonders if she should get some paper towels in the bathroom to clean it up but then rethinks it. Tommy did pull a gun on the two women who came in. Sylvie recalls the women's terrified faces, the way they ran for their lives. Oh, how she wishes she could've joined them.

Tommy gives orders as they near the door to the ladies' restroom, embracing his authority. "You go in there, you do your business, and you don't dawdle," he says. "I'll be waiting out here, and if you don't come out in a reasonable amount of time, I won't hesitate to come in there."

"Tommy," says Nadine, with that past-tense way of saying his name that says she's done with him, only he doesn't seem to notice. "There's no exit out of this bathroom," Nadine continues. "Just a little window not a one of us could fit through. We have no choice but to come out."

Tommy attempts a look that Sylvie supposes means he is not to be trifled with. "All right, then," he says. "Go on." He makes a little shooing motion with his hand.

Released, they hurry behind the bathroom door, each of them stopping as the door closes between them and their captor. No one goes into the stalls. Instead, they just look at one another, knowing this is their chance to communicate apart from Tommy. But to say what? No one seems to know the right words for a moment like this one.

Then Sylvie reaches out her hands, grasping Nadine's on her left and Blythe's on her right. Nadine looks over at Sylvie, then reaches out her free hand to grasp Morrow's. Blythe does the same. They cluster in a tight circle and hang on to one another.

"We will get through this," says Sylvie. She makes eye contact with the other three women as, one by one, they each nod. Sylvie adds, "Amen." Then they let go and take turns in the stalls before convening again at the sinks to wash their hands.

When Morrow goes to open the door, Nadine stops her. "One more thing," she says, keeping her voice low. She reaches into her pocket and reveals a set of keys.

"But you just—you gave those to him?" Blythe says, her mind struggling to catch up with what she sees.

"There're two sets," Nadine says. "But he doesn't know that." A little smile crosses her face. "One thing about Tommy. If he gets bored and sits still long enough, especially after he's been drinking, he'll pass out. And when he does, he sleeps hard. If that happens, I can quietly go to the door, turn the lock, and we can *run*." She raises her eyebrows for confirmation. They all nod just as Tommy hollers in to ask what's taking so long.

Nadine calls out that they're just finishing up, promising they'll be right out. "When I make a move, you guys be ready." They all nod again, absorbing this bit of hope. It might be a flimsy plan, but it's more than they've had before.

When they exit the bathroom, Tommy is zipping up his fly and tucking in his shirt. "I had to go too," he tells them and grins as he juts his chin in the direction of a potted ficus near the entryway.

"That poor tree," Morrow mumbles as they make their way back into the post office.

When they get inside, Tommy makes a big show of locking the door. With his back turned, they exchange cautious, brief smiles. Tommy moves to the center of their circle and jingles the keys at them like some sort of threat. He is their captor, their jailer, he thinks. But not for long.

The besieged women return to the stools and resume their seats as Tommy checks on the scene outside the windows, still keeping his distance. Blythe sees him casting about for something to do, nervous energy wafting off him. He is jittery, vibrating. He wanders over to the counter and paces the length of it, then goes behind it and walks the length of the other side. Then he just stands there, pawing around with his hands along the counter, agitated and purposeless.

Tommy's restlessness reminds her of Bryan, the guy she was texting this morning, who is the reason she is here. He'd been restless too, never able to relax. If he sat down, he'd only last a few minutes before popping back up and roaming around, looking for what that next thing might be. One day he'd up and decided the next thing would be law school. And then he'd gone without her.

He'd broken her heart, leaving her to wonder what she'd done wrong. They'd talked of marriage. They'd even gotten Murphy together, a rescue they'd both adored. That he'd left Murphy behind as well was a small consolation. After he was gone, she'd cried many tears into Murphy's fur, stroking the velvety softness of his ear as she posed questions aloud for which there were no answers.

She doesn't know how she would've gotten through that time without Murphy. And without her gran, who'd invited her here to Sunset Beach to live. "Change your view, change your life," her gran had said. Blythe had done both, and her gran had been right. She thinks again of the question her mother posed last night: "*Do you ever hear from Bryan?*" She should've said no, not let on to her about the messages between them on Instagram that had quickly led to texting. But the wine had done its work, loosening her lips and making her hope that her mother could be the mother she needed rather than the mother she has always been.

It was no secret that Bryan had been her mother's pick for her daughter. When marriage was mentioned, she'd taken them both out to dinner and promised them the wedding of their dreams. "No holds barred," she'd said. "Anything you guys want." In hindsight, it was probably that dinner that sent Bryan running off to law school, but she would never say that to her mother. Though Blythe had eventually moved on—hence the engagement dinner at Aaron's house the night before—her mother never got over the breakup with Bryan. Last night was proof she still held out hope that they would get back together, that Blythe would marry someone more "suitable."

Blythe sees Tommy suddenly squat behind the counter, his face disappearing into the area where her package dropped. She hears a sharp inhalation of breath and looks over to see concern on Nadine's face. She has hidden his liquor in that spot, Blythe realizes, and he is dangerously close to discovering it. Someone needs to throw him off.

Should she ask him to get her package for her? Tell him she's decided not to send it after all? That would deter him. But then he'd probably want to know why. She looks around at the women she is trapped with. She'd have to explain it to them all, and that's not something she wants to explain to anyone. She's still trying to figure it out for herself. Blythe glances down at her engagement ring, the one her mother frowned at, just as Nadine speaks up.

"Tommy," Nadine hollers. "Get out of there. That's federal mail. You shouldn't be poking around in there. That's people's private business."

Tommy stands to his feet, puts his hands on his hips. "I don't care," he says.

"Well, you should," Nadine retorts. "Would you want someone reading something you wrote? Something personal that's not for anyone else to see?"

Now everyone is looking at Nadine. But she had to do something to get Tommy away from that spot. She thinks of the envelope they fought over, of his gun jabbing at it as he demanded she tear it up. There was part of her that wanted to tear it to bits, and that is the truth. She never wanted any of this. She wanted more beach days together.

Defiant, Tommy stoops down again, reaching into the cart where the packages are deposited. He keeps his eyes focused on Nadine as he gropes around without looking, then he randomly extricates one, grinning like a man who's pulled a winning ticket from a hat. He looks at what he's grabbed, squints as he pulls it closer, shakes his head, and tosses the envelope on the counter.

He drops his head, his eyes still on the envelope. The room is silent as they all watch Tommy, who can feel their eyes upon him.

"What is it?" Nadine asks him.

Tommy shakes his head as he continues to look at the envelope. It is nothing really, just a magazine renewal. But Tommy can't help but stare at the familiar logo of the hunting magazine his father subscribed to for as long as he can remember. When Tommy was little and bored, he'd page through whatever recent issue was around. He'd look at the full-color photographs and make up stories about the people in the pictures, the fathers and sons and dogs featured prominently. They all looked happy in the pictures; even the dogs seemed to smile. In his stories the little boys lived with their daddies all the time instead of only seeing them every other weekend, and they had lots of fun adventures together. Remembering all that, Tommy hits upon something he can do, if only to buy himself more time.

"It's nothing," he says, wondering as he says it why of all the mail he had to pull from in that box, this was the one he chose. He has to think it means something. He picks up the envelope and pointedly drops it back into the mix where it came from, then looks to Sylvie. "I want to talk to that woman," he says.

Sylvie's eyes get larger behind her glasses. "Okay, we can do that. But . . . why?"

"I figured out what I want," he says. "I know what I'm going to ask for." He glances down into the cart where the envelope disappeared. "I want to talk to my dad."

"Tommy, you can't do that," Nadine pipes up. "You—"

Sylvie cuts her off. "Sure you can," Sylvie says. "This is what they want. For you to tell them what *you* want. If you don't, there can't be a negotiation. The sooner they can get you what you want, the sooner they can get this all resolved." She gives Nadine a look. It is a look that says, "For now it's best just to keep quiet."

"Well," Tommy says, "then that's what I want." He nods, agreeing with himself. "I want to talk to my dad."

"Okay, I'll get Hope on the phone." Sylvie starts to rise but pauses, raising her eyebrows at him. She is bone-weary, yet she feels a rush of adrenaline. "But they're going to need to hear from you this time. They're not going to want to hear what *you* want from me."

Tommy nods, and there is a broken look about him. Sylvie wonders what envelope he extracted from the cart full of mail that made him decide so quickly that he wanted to talk to his dad, but she doesn't dare ask. Instead, she stands, goes to the phone, and picks it up. She knows that out there in the land of the living the authorities have done something to make it so no other phone calls are coming in or going out of this line. It is a direct line, Sylvie hopes, to freedom. It is a direct line to Hope.

Chapter 21

Outside the post office, Hope sits in Brower's car with Bo beside her as she holds her cell and waits for the suspect to be put on the phone. She hears a bit of muffled discussion, an insistent female voice, before a male voice gets on the line. The voice is younger than she expected. They've been referring to him as a man, but he doesn't sound like much more than a teenager. This softens her a bit. Hope holds on to this scrap of sympathy mustered for this man she hated earlier when he had the women line up at the windows, crying and holding signs. Better to dwell in the sympathy than reach for the anger. Whatever she holds on to will come through in their conversation. You catch more flies with honey than with vinegar, as they say.

"Who am I speaking to?" she asks.

"Tommy," says Tommy.

"It's nice to talk to you, Tommy. I'm Hope," she tells him.

"I know," says Tommy. "She told me who you were."

"And who is she?" Hope asks, thinking it would be good for him to have to say the name of one of his hostages. She needs to make them as human as possible.

"The old lady," Tommy replies.

So, not the personal aspect she was hoping for. She tries again. "What is the old lady's name?" she asks. Beside her, Bo raises his eyebrows. She rolls her eyes.

"I forget," Tommy says. Hope is betting he hasn't forgotten. She is betting, as much as he doesn't want to, he knows every one of those women's names. But now is not the time to push him. She lets it go, takes a different tack.

"So, Sylvie"—she uses the name he refused to say—"tells me that you've got a demand for us." She cringes a little at her own choice of wording. *Demand* is a strong word, too forceful. She is rusty, but her training will come back to her the more she talks. It has to.

"I mean, it's not a demand," he says. "Just, um, something I'd like to—"

He is cut off by a voice in the background, another woman, who yells loudly enough that Hope can hear her perfectly. "Tommy!" she says. "This is not right! You shouldn't be asking for this!"

That is probably the soon-to-be ex-wife, Hope surmises.

"I can ask for whatever I want," Tommy retorts. His voice goes from shaky to surly, a switch flipped. "And this is what I want."

"Tommy, Tommy," says Hope, making her voice sound gentle as she redirects him. "Let's just you and me talk right now."

Tommy makes a scoffing noise. "Fine by me. I don't care if I talk to that bitch ever again." Hope knows that is not true or none of them would be here right now.

"So why don't you tell me what you want?"

"Okay," he says. There is a long pause. Hope waits. Most of negotiation is waiting. She looks around, notices that Bo has his own cell phone out, texting someone. He does not see her notice. She wonders if he is sending reports to Hank. Probably, she decides.

"I'd like to talk to my dad," Tommy says finally. She can hear the weight of his words. There is a history there. This is not nothing to him.

"Okay," says Hope. "We can work on making that happen. I'll just need your dad's name and address. And a phone number if you've got it. Then I can reach out to him and see if we can get him here. To talk to you."

"Okay," Tommy says. "I could send you a contact number from my phone, I guess. Then you could call that number?"

"Whatever works best for you," Hope says. She has a creeping suspicion that Tommy's father is likely in prison and that Nadine knows that. If so, he's asking for something they cannot make happen in a reasonable amount of time. Nadine doesn't want this to drag on any longer than it has to, and Hope doesn't blame her. Still, Hope tells him her phone number so he can send the contact. Her phone buzzes as his text lands. It is a start.

"I got your text, and we will get right on this," she says. "But before I do, I need you to make me a promise."

On the other end, Tommy exhales in frustration, but Hope presses. "You're asking me to do something for you—and I'm making you a promise that I'm going to do what you're asking, right?"

"Yeah," Tommy says.

"So isn't it fair that I ask you to make me a promise in return?" *Quid pro quo*, Hope thinks, but she hears it in the voice of her old boss and mentor, Rich. He taught her this. He taught her many things. But sometimes all the lessons in the world don't prepare you for what life dishes out. Everyone in that post office is aware of that fact right now.

"I guess," Tommy says, annoyed.

"Okay," says Hope. "It's a pretty simple promise." She smiles as she says it. You can hear a smile through the phone even if you can't see it. She wants him to know this is a good promise, one that will benefit everyone.

"I'd like you to promise me that no one will be harmed today."

She waits a beat, lets that sink in. "Not any of those women you've got in there. Not Sylvie or Nadine or Morrow or Blythe. Not any of the law enforcement folks or any of the emergency personnel who are here for everyone's safety. Not me or my partner here, Bo," she continues.

At the sound of his name, Bo looks over, surprised to be included.

She waits a beat, trying not to let the last time she did this encroach on this time. "And not you either," she finishes. She allows a pregnant pause before asking, "Can you make me that promise, Tommy?"

"Aw, man," Tommy argues. "I don't wanna hurt no one. That's not—"

"I don't think you want to hurt anyone, Tommy. I don't think that for a minute." Hope knows she sounds honest because she is being honest. "Most people don't set out to hurt other people," she says. "But sometimes, when a gun is involved, it happens anyway. It might happen on accident, but it happens nonetheless. And I don't want any accidents today. Do you?"

"No," he says quietly.

"Hey, I've got an idea." She pretends this has just occurred to her. "You know what you could do?" She waits for him to respond; this is a partnership they are forming, and his reciprocation only strengthens the partnership.

"No, what?"

"You could open that door and push your gun out into the vestibule. I could send someone in to take it away, and then there'd be no chance of an accident."

"This gun is the only thing between me and prison right now," he says.

"I see why you would think that, but that's not entirely true. We have a lot of options we could talk about."

"I tell you what," he says, and just like that she can feel Tommy shift out of the lull she'd created and go right back into control mode. This is always a one step forward, two steps back process. "You see about my dad, and I'll think about your promise," he says. She can hear the smirk in his voice just as clearly as he heard her smile.

"So you're giving me your word that you'll really think it over? Maybe even surrender your gun?"

"I ain't surrendering my gun, lady," he says. "But I'll think about the promise."

"Okay," she says. She will not push any further. "I'll let you think about it. And I'll be in touch as soon as I have something for you. About your dad."

"Okay," he says. And then he is gone. Round one is over.

Chapter 22

Tommy hangs up with Hope like nothing has happened, his face blank as he turns around to find all four women out of their seats and standing behind him. Four pairs of eyes bore into him. "What?" he asks, indignant. He makes a shooing motion with his hands in the direction of the stools they were sitting on. "Y'all go sit down." He narrows his eyes. "Or would you rather go back to the window and hold up signs?" He rests his hand on the gun he has tucked into his waistband as he says it. Morrow wishes it would accidentally go off, that he'd blow his balls off. That would bring his siege to an abrupt end.

It is a crude and sadistic thought, but Morrow lets herself have it. It isn't nice to think such things, and it certainly isn't what a respectable, refined woman of a certain age would go around thinking. But the longer she is held hostage, the less respectable and refined she feels. As she follows the others back to their stools, something occurs to her. Somewhere along the way, she lost her edge. She went from a defiant young woman making her own rules to a doting midlife caregiver who makes up rules for the people she loves, rules intended to keep them safe. All of her giving and sacrificing have softened her in a good way, yes. But in this world sometimes you need an edge.

She thinks of sneaking cigarettes with Pat, of wishing Tommy would blow his balls off, and deep inside, she feels a little proud, maybe not of herself as she is right then and there, but proud of her potential to change, to become a new person at a time in life when she thought all the versions of herself had already existed. That person doesn't need her daughter to validate her; she isn't defined solely by the roles she has played. *Maybe*, Morrow thinks, *there is another chapter after this. Maybe it could be a good one.*

Tommy goes over and hops up on the counter. His long legs dangle over the edge of it, and he kicks his feet against it like a little kid. For a while they all sit in silence, the rhythmic thudding of his heels reverberating against the steel cabinet drowning out the sound of the second hand on the clock. Morrow wants to tell him to quit that, but she doesn't want to engage him. Better to leave him to it and hope that negotiator calls back with some miracle solution that involves his father. She wonders what kind of father he must be if his kid is doing this.

She is instantly ashamed at the thought. She would not want to be held accountable for her children's failures. With kids, she has learned, you can do your very best and it still isn't enough. You can do your very best and still be guaranteed to make mistakes. She thinks again of Maya this morning, of the tires squealing out of the driveway, and she hopes once again that she will get a chance to apologize to her daughter. This time, though, she won't say, "I'll try to be a better mother." This time she will say, "I'll try to be a stronger me."

Tommy raises his finger and points across the post office. They all turn to look at what he is pointing at. At first they all think he means something outside the window, but when they follow the direction of his finger, they see he is indicating a poster of the symbol of the United States Postal Service.

"What do y'all reckon that is?" he asks.

"Looks like a bird," Morrow answers, playing along, partly because she is bored and partly because she feels a tiny bit guilty for wishing Tommy would accidentally blow his male parts off. She looks closely at the poster. She must have walked past it every time she's been in here, but she's never actually seen it before.

"It's a bald eagle," Nadine says with a hint of disappointment in her voice that she's the only one who knows the answer. All four of the other heads in the room turn to look at her. "It's called the Sonic Eagle?" She poses it as a question, but they all shake their heads. None of them can pass this quiz.

With everyone's full attention, Nadine continues, stating the explanation in the same automated tone she'd used when she posed the question to Blythe about things being fragile or perishable. "It was introduced in 1993 as the official logo of the United States Post Office. It's on basically everything: mailboxes, our uniforms, every envelope we sell, every box we use." Again they shake their heads. None of them have paid attention. Nadine rolls her eyes. "See how it's facing forward? It's poised for flight. It's supposed to symbolize how the postal service has to change with the times. It's ready for whatever comes along."

"How'd you know that?" Tommy asks, incredulous.

Nadine pats the symbol affixed to her uniform. "It's my job," she says.

Morrow studies the Sonic Eagle. *Poised for flight*, Morrow thinks. *Facing forward.* She is about to ask Nadine to repeat the other stuff she said. But then the phone rings.

Tommy's eyes widen. He jabs his finger at Sylvie. "Answer it," he orders.

Sylvie gets that determined set in her jaw that, as Morrow and probably everyone in the room is starting to recognize, means she's ready for a fight. Sylvie doesn't often pick her battles, but when she picks them, they are learning today, she digs in good. She starts to say something, but Tommy, who is learning this as well, says, "Fine, I'll get it myself."

He hops down and walks over to the phone, picking it up before another jarring ring can split the silence. "Did you find my dad?" he asks without bothering with a hello.

Hope counters with, "Did you think about your promise?" Tommy has been yanking her around, and she doesn't appreciate it.

"I haven't had a moment's peace to think," Tommy complains. "These women have been in here gabbing my ear off the whole time."

Hope wonders if this is true. She'd like to have eyes on the situation beyond spying on them through the windows with binoculars. She hopes the team from county will arrive soon so she can have access to the resources they will bring with them. She wonders if, by the time they arrive, she will be ready to hand off the negotiation to someone new, someone who can establish a better rapport with this suspect. At the moment the thought is appealing. Tommy has just strung her along, and she is angry with him and angry with herself for falling for it.

"Tommy," Hope says. "I think you know what I'm going to say. I think the request you made was just a way to buy time."

Tommy argues, "No, it wasn't. It was the truth. I do want to talk to my dad."

She pauses, chooses her next words carefully. "But you know you can't do that."

When he responds his voice is thick, and Hope thinks he is trying not to cry. "Doesn't mean I don't want to. You asked me what I wanted, and I told you."

Hope, seeing the futility of continuing to argue, says, "I'm sorry for your loss." She pauses to let Tommy speak, but he doesn't. So she asks a question. "When did he die?"

There is a pause before Tommy says, "Last year."

"Your mom said it was a hunting accident," Hope says.

"She's my stepmom. Not my mom," Tommy corrects her.

"I apologize, your stepmom," Hope says. "She said she'd be willing to come here. Or maybe she could record a message for you that you could listen to. Would you like that?"

Tommy snorts. "I don't need to hear from her."

"She said she could bring Covey. Said she'd let us bring him right up to the windows so you could see him if you'd like."

"Covey?" he asks, and there is something like awe in his voice. "She'd bring him here? Now?"

"That's what she said." Hope already knows the answer to this, but she wants to hear it from Tommy, in his own words. "Who is Covey?"

There is a long pause. Hope wonders if he is going to answer, but she sits with his silence. She waits. "He's my dad's hunting dog," he finally says. "He was with him when he died." He goes quiet again, but Hope hears what he isn't saying: The dog was with him, but Tommy wasn't. Hope understands this. She understands more than he knows. But Tommy doesn't care about Hope's feelings. He has no reason to.

"Would you like to see Covey?" she asks.

This time his answer is quick, immediate. "Yes."

"You never made me a promise, though. I'll need that from you if I'm going to be able to bring Covey here."

"Fine," Tommy says. "I promise."

"Okay," Hope says and turns to look at Bo, who is folded in the front seat of Brower's car where they are both sitting, the car serving as a de facto NOC for the time being. He nods his assent to the decision to bring the dog to the scene. It's unconventional, but it makes a certain sort of sense. A big drawback is that the stepmother lives two and a half hours away in New Bern, North Carolina. They just extended the length of time for this to be resolved. But, Hope thinks, if she can convince Tommy to come outside, bait him with the opportunity to put his arms around this animal that clearly means a lot to him, then maybe she can also convince him that, once he's outside, he can surrender. A seamless, peaceful solution. It won't be that easy. It never is. Still, it's good to see a way forward.

Chapter 23

INSIDE THE POST office, the women are waiting again. Now they are bringing in Tommy's dad's dog so Tommy can see him. Blythe doesn't know how this will help anything, but she is not a negotiator, so she assumes there is a purpose in it, a plan that will lead to them all being freed. She gets that he wants to see the dog. He obviously has some emotional attachment to it, which she understands more than anyone in the room. She would do just about anything to see Murphy one more time. She feels tears prick the corners of her eyes and blinks them back. She will not think of Murphy now.

Her eyes stray to the counter where Tommy is hovering, using his fingers to drum out a beat. He is keeping away from the windows but still monitors law enforcement's movements from afar, occasionally peering over the partition behind him to make sure no one is attempting to access the back. Tommy stops drumming, stares at the poster of the USPS logo for a moment. She watches him looking at the poster and wonders what he is thinking. Is he thinking that his wife knew more about that logo than anyone else in the room? Is he thinking that he hasn't given her enough credit? Is he thinking about how that eagle is looking forward, but because of what he has done today, he doesn't have much to look forward to? Is he even capable of such deep thoughts? Blythe doubts it.

When he looks away from the poster, his eyes flicker across her, but she pretends not to notice, looking down at the fabric of her jeans, focusing on how many different variations of blue are woven together. She pretends to be absorbed in her jeans when really what she wants is to get her phone back and see if Bryan has texted her again, even though she should not care. Bryan is not Aaron. Aaron is her fiancé. If she's thinking of anyone, it should be Aaron. She decides not to think about either of them until she gets out of here. She heard a long time ago never to make a big decision when you're hungry, angry, lonely, or tired. Right now she is all of the above.

She looks up to see that Tommy has gone back to rummaging through the mail, the things other people carried in here today, dropped off, and left behind without a moment's thought, never appreciating how close they came to being held captive. If Blythe had run her errands in a different order, if she'd left instead of waiting in line when it was taking too long, if she'd never let her mom plant this crazy idea in her head in the first place . . . She decides not to think of the what-ifs. It is what it is. She is here; she is trapped. She looks around at her fellow hostages. They all are.

All of a sudden Tommy lets out a whoop and stands up, holding the bottle of liquor aloft, his eyes dancing as he unscrews the cap with a flourish and tilts it to his lips. The four women watch him, their faces impassive. To react, they all seem to understand, would only be to fuel him further.

Not getting the attention he wants, Tommy makes a big smacking sound with his lips. "That hits the spot right there!" he says.

Still none of them respond. He takes another dramatic sip, and then, in what can only be a desperate attempt to get their attention, he slams the bottle down hard on the counter. Too hard. It is not the sound of the bottle making contact with the counter that makes them all look up, though. It is the sound of the bottle cracking, of the liquid spilling out onto the counter and running over onto the floor. They all watch, Tommy in horror and the four women with barely disguised glee, as amber rivulets stream out like tributaries. They sneak glances at one another, smirking as Tommy stalks around cursing a blue streak.

"You should probably get something to clean that up with," says Nadine. "There's paper towels underneath the counter." Her voice is as impassive as when she explained what the logo meant. "And you'd better be careful picking up that glass," she adds, pointing at the windows. "If you cut yourself, you'll have to get those EMTs out there to come in here and give you stitches." A full grin breaks out on her face, then they hear her snicker, and the sound makes them all snicker too. In seconds they are all chuckling, though they try to hide it.

This makes Tommy even angrier. He flails his arms in the air. "You'd better get over here and help me. Every last one of you'd better stop laughing and come clean this up."

Nadine crosses her arms and keeps her seat. "What are you gonna do about it if we don't, Tommy? Shoot us? I can just hear it now when the police question you. So why'd you do it, Tommy? Why'd you shoot those four innocent women in cold blood? And your answer will be—lemme make sure I get this straight: 'They wouldn't help me clean up a mess I made.'"

"Innocent women," scoffs Tommy. "I doubt that." He crouches back down and peers under the cabinet, looking for the paper towels. He pops back up and tears off far more paper towels than needed for the task, balling them up and swiping at the mess, taking his anger out on it, which only serves to send the rivulets wider. Somehow they all know not to laugh as the alcohol spreads.

He looks up when the room goes quiet, his gaze sweeping across all four faces, his own face like stone, his eyes gone flat in his head. No one speaks as Tommy cleans up his mess, picking up the broken pieces of glass. Then standing over the bin, he drops them one by one. *Plink, plink, plink.* It is the only sound in the room. When he is done with his task, he goes back to the counter and stares down at the spot where the bottle was.

He looks up and their eyes meet again. Blythe looks away as fast as she can, but it is too late—a connection has been made, like the worst bully in the schoolyard singling you out. She sees his eyes spark.

"Hey," he says to her. "Weren't you the one mailing something when I came back in here?"

Blythe's heart begins to gallop in her chest. *No,* she thinks. Involuntarily her head begins to shake in the same direction as her thoughts.

He smirks at her. "Sure you were. I remember." He swipes his finger back and forth in the air. "You looked upset about whatever it was." He smiles, happy because they're no longer laughing at him. Happy because he can turn the spotlight of shame on someone else.

He begins to paw through the cart that holds the collected mail. "It was a box wrapped in brown paper," he says, pretending to talk to himself but taunting her nonetheless. "I just need to look for the return address with your name on it, *Blythe.*" He has been paying attention.

Blythe doesn't like her name in Tommy's mouth. It makes her nervous and nauseous at the same time. Her hands go to the stool. She grips it at the edges, clings to it tightly, the rim of the steel digging into her fingers. The pain helps her not to think about the inevitability of what Tommy is doing. She looks toward the door, no longer barricaded but locked. She sees Nadine see her looking for an escape. Nadine presses her mouth into a thin straight line as she shakes her head, a reminder. There is nothing they can do. Yet.

From her seat Nadine considers extracting the keys from her pocket and rushing for the door. With his attention focused elsewhere, she might be able to get there and get the door open in time. But would they all get out before he fired that gun again? Would he fire at them? In her mind she hears the bullet hitting the exit sign, the broken fragments raining to the ground where she stood. He'd fired high. He'd missed. But would he miss again?

She never would've thought Tommy was capable of shooting anyone, especially not after he'd lost his father to a gunshot. But Tommy had changed after his father died. "He's not handling it well," she would tell friends and family by way of explanation. But that barely scraped the surface of what became of Tommy. The loss had decimated him. She thinks of the obituary for Thomas Sr. "*He is survived by his only son*," it said.

But it seemed to Nadine that Tommy had not survived his father's death. Some huge part of him had died too. For months she thought of ending the marriage, then felt guilty, then felt she had to leave, then wondered what kind of wife would leave someone in the throes of grief. The emotions swirled, a whirling dervish of feelings.

Tommy finds the package, because of course he would. It was only a matter of time. Nadine recalls the way Blythe had teared up as she handed her the package. Nadine had pretended not to notice, but she knows, as Tommy holds up the package, that whatever is in that box is important, and personal. Tommy has no right. But Tommy has no right to do anything he's done today.

Nadine remembers standing in front of the preacher, exchanging their vows nearly four years ago, remembers the promises they'd made to each other. For months she's carried around the guilt of not keeping those promises. But Tommy broke his promises too. He stopped being the man she'd made the promises to. Maybe, if they make it out of here, people will start to understand that she only did what she had to do. The truth, the whole truth, she thinks, can finally come out.

Tommy strides over to Blythe, waving the package around as he proclaims, "Lookee what I have here."

As she watches him, Nadine feels a revulsion unlike anything she's ever felt. In the past year she's disliked him. She's pitied him. She's loved him. She's wanted to slap him. But in this moment, as he dangles the package just out of Blythe's reach, delighting as she grabs for it and misses, she truly hates him. She rises from her seat, ready to intervene. Sylvie and Morrow stand as well.

Blythe gives up on her attempts to retrieve the box and instead attempts to rationalize with Tommy. "Please give me my package," she says, her voice breathy and shot through with desperation.

In response Tommy clutches the box close to his chest, cuddling it like a baby. "It's not your package anymore," he tells her. "You handed it off to the United States Postal Service." He points at the poster of the Sonic Eagle. "You gave it to the Sonic Eagle," he says and cackles.

Nadine can tell that the shots of liquor he managed before the bottle broke are hitting his bloodstream at full force now. This is the part she hated, the moments when his grief and the liquor merged, creating an entirely different Tommy, rendering him unrecognizable. "Please," she would beg, "please get help," sounding much like Blythe does right now. Based on experience, Nadine can tell her that she's not going to get anywhere. Later he will be sorry. But later the damage will already be done. But what kind of damage? And when is later?

"I think that with things being the way they are, I have the right to change my mind," Blythe says. "So just give it back, and I'll keep it." She holds out her hand. Nadine can see her hand is shaking. Whether the tremors are from anger or fear, Nadine can't tell. "I'll take it home with me when this is all over," she adds, and Nadine guesses this is her attempt at projecting a positive outcome.

Tommy must think so too. He smirks at her. "Aw," he says, a fake affectation in his voice. "I love that optimism." He clutches his hand to his heart as if touched but keeps a firm grasp on the box just the same.

Blythe, undeterred, tries reasoning again. "Tommy," she says, "you don't need that package. It doesn't concern you."

Something flickers across his face, and his eyes grow larger. He presses his lips together as he looks down at the box in his hand. He shifts it this way and that, flips it upside down and back over again, appearing to read the writing on the front. He raises his eyes to look at Blythe again. "Who's Bryan Welch?" he asks her.

Nadine's own heart rate hikes up as she watches Blythe, who appears to be weighing her words. When she doesn't respond, Tommy points at her left hand. "That your fiancé?"

Say yes, Nadine wills silently. *Even if it isn't, say yes.* If she says yes, Tommy might leave it alone out of respect for another man. A man who is getting married, a man who still has a shot at happiness, unlike Tommy, who has ruined his own.

But Blythe goes for honesty. Nadine's heart sinks as she watches Blythe shake her head no. "He's an old . . . friend. The package is something that was . . . once his." She waves her hand in the air.

"It's a long story," she says. "That doesn't involve you." Exasperation colors her face a deep red. "Now please just give it back."

And that's when it happens. Tommy gives a gleeful little laugh as he uses his index finger to begin to tear away the brown paper wrapped around the box. With his vision averted he doesn't see Blythe lower her head like a bull charging and launch herself in his direction, making contact with his midsection as they both tumble to the floor, rolling around as she grasps for the box and he succeeds in keeping it from her. From the edges Nadine, Sylvie, and Morrow call out, "Stop! Y'all stop it!"

Finally, Tommy scoots far enough away from Blythe that he's able to stand up, still with the box tightly gripped. "Crazy bitch," he says to Blythe. He wiggles the box in front of her but keeps it away from her reach as she, panting from exertion, gets to her hands and knees, then slowly rises to her feet. As they all watch, she turns to face him.

"Please give me my box back, Tommy," she says.

He presses it against his chest and gives her a coy look. "Tell you what," he says. "I can either open it up, or you can tell me what's in here."

Blythe puts her fist to her lips, closes her eyes, and swallows. Then she speaks. "And then you'll give it back?"

Tommy pretends to think it over, which makes Blythe want to plow into him again. But she keeps still. "Sure," he finally says. She holds out her hand, but he waggles the fingers of his free hand at her. "Not so fast. You've got to tell us first."

Blythe huffs in frustration as she looks from one woman to another. She never intended to tell anyone about this. Had she had more time to think about what her mother had proposed, she never would've gone along with it. She would've come to her senses. At least that's what she hopes she would've done. But that's not the way it's gone. And now here she is.

The phone rings, but Tommy ignores it. All eyes stay on Blythe, who takes a deep breath before she begins to speak.

"I came here to send part of my dog's ashes to my ex-boyfriend. We got the dog—Murphy was his name—together back in college. And when we broke up, I kept him with me because Bryan—that's my ex—went off to law school. So it just made more sense for me to be the one to keep him. And, well, Murphy was . . ." A tear slips down her cheek. "They say dogs are man's best friend. And he was. To me. I've been pretty devastated since he died." She swipes at the tears that have followed the first one. "This is hard for me to talk about," she says, so quietly they can barely hear her.

"Tommy," says Nadine, "you're an absolute ass for making her do this." Though they don't say so, Morrow and Sylvie agree. They would hate to be forced to tell the others what they brought in here to mail.

Tommy shrugs and makes a motion for Blythe to continue. Blythe swallows, acquiescing because to tell her story is to fix a mistake. Maybe it is fitting, she thinks, that she must confess before she gets her package back. Besides, she will probably never see these people again. So she goes for broke.

"When Murphy died, I posted about it on Instagram—a reel of pictures throughout his life and a quote about loving a dog. Just, you know, something I wanted to do as a tribute to him, to what a good dog he was. Then a few days after that, Bryan messaged me. Just to, you know, say he was sorry to hear about Murphy and that he often thought about him." She swallows. "And about me." She looks up, scans the faces in the circle. "It kind of, um, went from there."

Tommy cocks his head and crosses his arms. "So you were talking to your ex behind your fiancé's back?"

Blythe looks down, nods. "I know how it sounds. I didn't

mean for it to unfold the way it did. I just—well." She pauses, thinking about how to explain why she kept talking to Bryan when she loves Aaron. "Bryan was sort of 'the one who got away.' He's this successful attorney now. He's done well for himself, and my fiancé—" She stops talking as she sees Tommy's facial features start to contort. "My mom keeps saying I can do better," she says. She puts her hands over her face but keeps talking through her fingers.

"Look, I know how bad this sounds. I don't want to be the kind of person who does something like this. It's just that last night my mom was in town, and she wanted me to have wine with her. I'm not a big drinker, so the wine went straight to my head, and I ended up telling her that I'd been talking to Bryan." Blythe pictures her mother's face in the moonlight as they sat on her gran's porch, how she leaned forward, eager, as Blythe spoke.

"She came up with this plan for me to offer to send him some of Murphy's ashes since we got him together and he *has* seemed genuinely sad about Murphy dying. She thought I should play up our shared past and maybe that would, like, move things to another level. She just got so excited the more we talked. It was like she saw me differently and I— Well, she's always disappointed in me. What I do for a living, where I live, who I'm marrying. And I just—for once—wanted her to be proud of me, to be hopeful for me. So I went along with it. I reached out to Bryan last night and asked if he'd like me to send him the ashes." She shakes her head. "In the sober light of day, it sounds every bit as ridiculous as it is. But he said yes. He seemed really touched by it. And this morning when I woke up, I felt I had to go through with it. Because I said I would." She pauses. "And because my mom was counting on it."

She holds up her hands, forces herself to make eye contact

with Tommy. "So that's what's in the package. That's why I'm here."

She waits for Tommy to rail at her. She deserves it. Instead, he says, very quietly, "Do you love your fiancé?"

"Very much," Blythe says as she spins the engagement ring around on her finger. It is only a half carat, but it was all Aaron could afford. Still, she loves it, is proud of it. Or she was until her mother frowned at it.

"Then why would you do something like that to him?"

Blythe feels tears sting her eyes. She blinks them back as she answers. "Because I love my mom too. I feel caught between the two of them. I just wish she could see what I see in Aaron. For my mom, it's all about money and status. And . . . marrying Aaron means I'm not going to have either."

The phone rings again, but again no one moves to answer it. When it stops ringing, Tommy speaks. "So why marry him?"

Blythe's smile is reflexive. "Because he's kind and caring. Because he makes me laugh. Because we make each other happy, and when I'm around him, I feel better. About myself. About life. He's my person." She thinks about the dinner held in their honor the night before. "And he's got this big, noisy family—they bicker and laugh and tease one another and tell funny stories, and I love being around them. They don't have much either, but they . . . love each other. It's only ever been me and my mom. And my gran, but she died a year ago. What Aaron's family has is what I've always wanted. When I'm with them I feel like I'm part of something bigger."

Tommy looks to Nadine, who looks down. No one speaks until Tommy walks over to Blythe and hands her the package. "You're right," he says. "You need to take this back." He points at her. "Don't be stupid and ruin a good thing just to please your mom. Let her figure out what matters for herself. And if she doesn't, well, she'll be the one who's miserable. But at least you'll be happy. You'll have what you want." He tries to get Nadine to look at him, but she keeps her head down. He continues anyway. "Finding your person is a miracle. And miracles don't come along every day." The phone rings again, and his eyes stray in the direction of the ringing before settling back on Blythe. "Besides, it wasn't his damn dog anyway."

Chapter 24

Outside the post office Hope listens as the phone rings and rings but no one answers. She was hoping to get the suspect on the phone, but Hope, on high alert, no longer cares who answers as long as that person can tell her what's going on inside the post office. The lookouts are reporting that some sort of fight broke out, but based on what they can see, it is not the suspect who was the aggressor.

Perhaps the hostages are taking control. Perhaps, thanks to their actions instead of her own, the suspect will give up and they can all go home. There was a time when such a resolution would've ruffled her feathers. She would want the victory, the winning points on her side of the board. Now she doesn't care about the board.

Things are devolving, becoming more desperate the longer those five people are trapped inside that post office together. She needs more support. Especially with nightfall approaching, which always makes things seem worse. She looks at Bo, still beside her. He is well intentioned, but he isn't much help. She needs eyes on this situation in real time, an experienced SWAT team at the ready. Help is on the way, she has been reassured. It can't arrive soon enough.

She exhales as someone finally answers. But it is not Tommy.

"Is everyone okay?" Hope blurts, then thinks better of it. "Sorry," she says. "Who am I speaking with?"

"This is Sylvie. Yes, everyone is okay. We just had a, uh, misunderstanding."

"I'm hearing there was some sort of altercation in there?"

"Yes," says Sylvie. "But it's over now."

Hope doesn't like depending on the impressions of a hostage. "I'd like to speak with whoever was involved," she says.

"Okay," says Sylvie.

Beside her, Bo whispers, "Ask to speak with them all."

Hope looks at him, raises her eyebrows in question.

He nods. "Get a gauge on how everyone is doing."

In the background she hears Tommy ask for the phone. "Wait," Hope says. "Put him on first."

"I will," says Sylvie. "But tensions are pretty high. We're all a little weary and edgy, as you can imagine." Sylvie clears her throat before continuing. "I know I'm not the one who can make demands, but I think perhaps some food might be helpful. And water would be nice as well."

"Okay," says Hope. Not knowing the protocol for this in Sunset Beach—or if there even is a protocol—she has no idea how she will go about making that happen, but she will figure it out. "We'll get some sort of plan together." She pauses, then adds, "We'll make sure you all are taken care of." She hopes her promise brings some sort of comfort.

"One more thing," says Sylvie. "If you don't mind, I just wondered if perhaps someone could make contact with my husband. He's at home, and I know he never expected me to be gone this long, and he's . . . well, he might be . . . anxious. After all this time."

Hope makes her voice sound confident and reassuring. "I know the chief is at the station working on informing and updating the families. I can ask him if he's made contact with your husband when I talk to him again."

"Yes," says Sylvie. "That would be nice. I'll try to get Tommy to come to the phone now."

In the ensuing silence, Hope and Bo exchange glances, the seriousness of the situation reflected in both their countenances.

"That's tough," he says. "What she's going through."

Hope nods, feeling the pang of not being able to help that nice little old lady, of not being able to set her free right here, right now.

"But," Bo adds, interrupting her thoughts, "Tommy's getting tired. Making poor decisions. What just happened is proof of that."

Hope nods a second time.

"That's good," Bo says.

This wasn't what Hope expected him to say. "Good?" she asks. Hope fears Tommy's impulsive actions will lead nowhere good.

"In my experience, that's how surrenders happen. They get tired, bored, frustrated that nothing is coming of their standoff. *Then*"—Bo stresses the word—"they give up. It's less about the fine art of negotiation and more about good old human nature. People give up on things all the time."

Tommy's voice comes over the phone. "Yeah?" he asks, sullen.

"I don't really understand what went on in there, but Sylvie tells me things are fine now. Do you agree?" she asks him.

"Yeah. It's handled," Tommy says, not offering further explanation, and Hope doesn't press. She moves on to what Bo suggested. "I've spoken to Sylvie, but I'd like to speak to the other women in the room." She does not call them hostages. "Just to connect with each of them and make sure they're okay."

Tommy sighs. She thinks he's going to refuse, but then he says,

"Fine," and she can hear him handing the phone off to someone. A female voice says, "Hello."

"Who am I speaking with?" Hope asks.

"This is Blythe."

"Hi, Blythe. I'm Hope. I just wanted to check on you."

"This is about the fight, isn't it?" Blythe says. "I shouldn't have done that. He made me so mad, I just—"

Now Hope knows who the person involved was. She looks over at Bo, and he gives her a thumbs-up. "I wasn't asking about the fight," she says. "I know tensions are running high and things are bound to flare up. We're going to try to get some water and maybe some food in to you guys as soon as possible. We want to make you as comfortable as we can." She fears she sounds like a concierge instead of a negotiator.

"Well," says Blythe, "it's settled now. So that's good."

"That is good."

"And some water would be great," adds Blythe.

"I'll start working on it as soon as we hang up. But first I'd like to talk to—Morrow, is it?"

"Yes," says Blythe. "I'll get her."

There is a shuffle, and a new voice comes on the line. "Hello?" she says.

"Am I speaking with Morrow?" asks Hope.

"Yes, this is she," says Morrow.

"Hi, Morrow. This is Hope. I just wanted to speak with each of you, get a gauge on how you're feeling and any urgent needs you have."

"I urgently need to get out of here," quips Morrow.

Hope gives a little laugh. "I understand that completely. We are working behind the scenes here to make that happen. I appreciate you hanging in there."

"Has my—" Morrow stops.

"Has your what?" prompts Hope.

"It's silly. I doubt you'd know the answer. I just—I was wondering if perhaps my daughter has contacted you guys? If she knows about this?" Part of Morrow wants Hope to say yes, and part of her wants Hope to say no.

"I know the chief of police is liaising with family members, as well as with the media and other branches of law enforcement. So he would know better than I would if she's been made aware. I will say, based on the media turning up and members of the public coming by, there's a good bet that she does know." Hope does not say that this is the biggest thing to happen in Sunset Beach in quite a while, and it's likely the whole town knows by now.

"Okay," says Morrow.

"Would you like me to get a message to her if I can?"

"No, that's okay," says Morrow. "I'll . . . tell her myself soon enough."

"I like that positive attitude," says Hope. "Now, if you could just give the phone to Nadine, I will have spoken to everyone."

"Okay," Morrow agrees.

There is more shuffling until Nadine speaks, her voice wary as she asks, "Yes?"

"Nadine, is it?" Hope asks. This is, she knows, the woman at the center of the dispute, the unwitting catalyst. Hope thinks of the last negotiation. There'd been a woman at the center of that siege as well. But she'd never gotten to speak to her. The suspect never allowed it. In that regard, this is progress.

"Yes," says Nadine. She rushes to add, "I just want to say I'm sorry about all this. I should've torn up the papers when he asked and been done with it. Now I've gone and caused all this trouble."

"*You* didn't cause all this," says Hope. She wants to say more;

she wants to preach a sermon on whose fault this is. But she holds her tongue. "I don't want you to worry about that. Just try to relax while you wait on us to get you out."

"You never know what could happen," says Nadine. There is innuendo in her voice, but Hope isn't sure what she's getting at. She wonders if Nadine is up to something, and if so, do the others know? She feels a little zing of excitement travel through her. Perhaps the hostages are plotting something. If they are, Hope hopes it's a safe plan, preferably risk averse.

"Can you put Tommy back on now?"

"Yes," Nadine says. "And, Hope?"

"Yes?"

"Thank you."

"I haven't done anything yet," protests Hope.

"You will," says Nadine.

Before Hope can respond, Tommy's voice comes back on the phone.

"Okay, thank you for letting me speak to everyone. That was helpful," Hope says, pandering to him.

"Uh-huh," says Tommy.

Realizing that's all she's going to get from Tommy, Hope continues. "When I spoke to Sylvie, she had a good idea. She thought perhaps some food would be helpful. Maybe some beverages."

Tommy gives a little *heh, heh* sort of laugh and says, "I can think of a beverage I'd like."

Hope ignores him. She thinks of the last negotiation. They'd sent in pizzas. The suspect had agreed because his children were getting fussy, and probably because he was hungry too. It was to be his last meal as a free man. She thinks of the letter Alex told her about just a few hours ago, an honor bestowed when she has felt anything but honorable. She had done good that day, but it had all been forgotten the moment she returned her father's call.

She forces herself to focus on the here and now rather than the past.

"Why don't I have some pizza and bottled waters sent in?" she asks.

Tommy's voice perks up a little. "You can do that?"

"I'll have to go through some approvals, but I think we can make that happen. Why don't you ask the ladies what kind of pizza they like, and I'll call back in a few minutes?"

Tommy agrees, then hangs up without saying goodbye. *Some people*, thinks Hope, *have no manners.*

Chapter 25

INSIDE THE POST office, the women comfort Blythe while Tommy is focused on his conversation with Hope. They get her a paper towel to wipe her face, pat her shoulder, and murmur consolations to her. All the while, Blythe keeps a tight grip on the package she fought to get back.

When Tommy ends the call and turns around to speak to the women, everyone already knows what he's going to announce because Sylvie told them. "They're going to send pizzas in here," he says, acting like it was all his idea. "And waters."

Sylvie can't help but wish Blythe would've gotten in a good, hard kick to his gonads while she was rolling around on the floor with him.

"So what do you like on your pizza?" Tommy continues. "I'm supposed to find out and let the girl know."

The girl, Sylvie thinks, *has a name. Her name is Hope.* But she doesn't say that aloud. Instead, she says, "I really shouldn't have pizza. It gives me acid indigestion." She makes a show of looking at her watch. "Especially if I eat it this late in the day."

Tommy frowns at her. "That's easy for you to say. You already had something to eat." He points at the basket, still toppled on its side.

"No one stopped you from doing the same," Sylvie retorts.

Tommy waves his arm in the direction of the basket. "There's nothing in there I want to eat. Not when I can have pizza." He makes a dismissive motion in Sylvie's direction. "If you don't want it, you don't have to eat it."

Nadine speaks up. "Well, I'm not eating dairy." She crosses her arm over her stomach. "It hasn't been agreeing with me lately."

Tommy looks at her quizzically. "Since when?"

"Since none of your beeswax, Tommy Harrell."

"Well," says Blythe, hurrying to interrupt lest a marital spat get them all off track. Her stomach is already rumbling at the thought of pizza. She hasn't eaten since her trainwreck of an engagement dinner last night, where she only picked at her food. "I'm vegetarian," she tells them. "So I can only do veggie toppings. If there's, like, even the oil from a pepperoni on the pizza, it's a problem."

Morrow speaks up. "I have to agree with the others. I'm on a diet. And pizza is definitely not on it." They all nod in sympathy. They have all been on a diet at one point or another.

"Perhaps they could send something else?" Morrow asks. "Something everyone could enjoy? There's a good deli in Calabash." She gives a little laugh. "It's called Calabash Deli, actually. They have lots of salads and sandwiches and—oh!—they make the best soups." She places a finger on her temple. "I need to think about what today's soup special is." She looks at the other women, who all look riveted by the prospect of soup. "They change it every day," she explains to them.

Tommy, who has been shaking his head since they all began speaking, has had enough. "It doesn't matter what the soup special for today is! This isn't DoorDash! It's the Sunset Beach Police Department offering to send in some pizzas! Geez!" He runs both hands through his hair and closes his eyes.

As she watches him Sylvie thinks, *If we asked him nicely right now, I bet he'd let us go.* She opens her mouth to do so, but before she can get the words out, he opens his eyes. "I'm telling them cheese pizzas. No toppings." He looks at his wife. "You can pull the cheese off if you need to." There is a gentleness underneath his words, a softening of his face as he speaks to her. He says nothing, Sylvie notices, about anyone else's aversions. But then again, none of them are the wife he's desperate not to lose.

Chapter 26

Tommy answers eagerly when Hope calls back. The talk of pizza has made him hungry, which is good. She will not send the pizzas in right away, Hope decides; she will let the hunger grow. People will do almost anything if they get hungry enough. She recalls a Bible story from her Sunday school days, a stiff dress that itched and patent leather Mary Janes that pinched and the story of Esau selling his birthright for a bowl of stew. There are many kinds of hunger, Hope thinks, many kinds of birthrights for sale.

"I'll place this order and start making the arrangements to get the pizzas to you," she tells Tommy. "I'll also get some bottled waters. Anything else?" she asks, not expecting a response.

There is a long pause, and if she couldn't hear his breathing on the other end, she might've assumed he hung up. But then he speaks. "There is something."

"What?" she asks, doing her best to sound unfazed by this unexpected turn.

"Hang on," he says. She hears movement, footsteps. He must be moving away from the women, out of earshot. His voice goes low, so low she can barely hear him. "I need something stronger than bottled water," he says. "Maybe like a fifth of Jack Daniel's? I was thinking you could send it in here with the food."

"Tommy?" she asks. "I can barely hear you." This is not true. Even though he's talking softly, she can hear him just fine. "Can you speak up?"

"No," Tommy says, continuing to whisper. "I don't want them to hear."

"Why not?" She realizes she is lowering her voice to match his.

"Because they won't want me drinking," he says. "Especially my wife."

When she says the next words, she uses her full voice. "Why doesn't she like you drinking, Tommy?"

"Because I do stupid sh—" He amends his choice of language, and Hope wonders if this is just his southern upbringing (never curse around a lady) or a sign of respect for her.

"Sometimes I don't make good choices if I've been drinking," he says instead. Hope can't help but think this a direct quote from his wife.

"Are those choices why we're all here today?" she asks, thinking of birthrights and bowls of soup.

Tommy goes silent again. "Maybe," he says finally. Then, "Yeah."

"So you think drinking more in front of her might help that?"

"I don't know. I just need it to get through this." He huffs his exasperation into the phone. "You ask me what I want, and then when I tell you what I want, you argue with me about it."

An idea pops into her head. Maybe she could agree to this. Or at least pretend to agree with it to get him thinking about another option. "Okay," she tells Tommy. "I'll tell you what. You let one of the hostages go, and I'll get you that bottle." She sees that Bo, who had walked over to the post office to get eyes on the hostages again, is coming back toward the car. She watches as he looks over his shoulder, then keeps walking, his face etched in concern.

She continues with Tommy. "But you need to hang up now and decide which one you're going to let go. I'll wait for you to call me back once you've made a decision."

Across the room, as Tommy is speaking to Hope, Sylvie takes advantage of the opportunity to offer some words of encouragement to lift her fellow hostages' flagging spirits. Even as, privately, her own worries about Robert continue to bombard her, she pushes them aside as she surveys the other three women. Blythe looks like she is about to dissolve into tears at any moment. Morrow looks perpetually concerned. And Nadine just looks broken.

Sylvie feels like a coach in the locker room at halftime. "This will be over before we know it," she says. "He's getting tired, starting to wear out. Which is what we want. We want him to lose hope." She glances over at him to check that his back is still turned. "Because then he will give up," she says. "He will surrender." She smiles at them. "Or we will outsmart him, whichever comes first." Nadine pats her pocket, and they all trade quick, conspiratorial smiles.

Across the room, Tommy hangs up the phone and turns to study the women, considering who he should release. They are back to sitting on their stools, talking quietly among themselves. He knows the right one to release is the old lady, but he feels a fondness for her he doesn't feel for any of the others. She reminds him a little of his grandma, who would be—*will be*, he thinks with a pang—so disappointed in what he's doing here today. The next oldest woman is closer to his mother's age, with long dark hair and a serious expression on her face. He can take her or leave her.

Then his eyes land on the woman who fought with him over her package. *Yes*, he thinks, *her*. He will send her and her package packing. He smiles at his own joke. The smile stays on his face as he thinks about taking the first swig of liquor, how it will burn as it goes down, warming him from the inside. He needs the liquid courage, a reason to keep going, something to look forward to. If only he hadn't broken that bottle.

When he returns to where the women are, they go quiet. He scans the ring of them like a coyote checking out a pack of lambs, then claps his hands together. They flinch at the sound.

"So the food's on the way," he says. They all sit up straighter. "I've asked for one more thing when they bring it, though." He points at the windows where there is, conveniently, an ABC store right across the street. "I asked them to run over there and get me a fifth of Tennessee's finest." He smiles without showing any teeth. "Just to take the edge off."

Sylvie drops her head into her hands. She wonders just how experienced this Hope person is and what she could possibly be thinking in saying yes to this scheme. Then Tommy says something that makes it make sense. "So I told them that, in exchange for the booze, I'd let one of you go."

I get it, Sylvie thinks. One less hostage means one less liability. And in letting one go, he will potentially be able to see himself letting the rest go. It is a step toward resolution.

She thinks about asking to be the one let go. She is the oldest, after all; it would make the most sense. She envisions herself getting home in time to fix dinner. If that happens, she wonders if she will even tell Robert. Probably best not to upset or confuse him. No, she decides, if she's the one released, she will keep this whole thing from him, just like she's kept the reason she came here today to herself. Shc thinks about the envelope she never mailed and wonders what she will do with it now. It is still sitting, innocuously, under her stool. She can take it with her when she walks out of here and mail it another time, though likely she will go to the post office in Shallotte instead. She's not sure she will ever come back here again.

"Maybe I should let you guys decide who gets to walk out of here," Tommy says and smiles again, like this is funny, or fun. He is clearly enjoying the power as he points at each one of them. "Eeny, meeny, miny, moe," he says.

"Shut up, Tommy," says Nadine. There is fire in her eyes. She wanted to be the one to free them with the keys hidden in her pocket. She liked being the one who took charge, who got him to take down the barricade so they could walk out together. On their terms, not Tommy's. A look passes between the four of them. A look that says if one of us walks out of here and he gets more alcohol, then the rest of us could be in trouble. Nadine gives a little shake of her head, the movement almost imperceptible but the sentiment clear: *No. We don't go along with this.*

Sylvie sees the other three make a silent, but certain, agreement, knowing they expect her complicity. She has assumed she will be the one let go. But what if she isn't? What if he lets Blythe or Morrow go because they're the ones who've fought him and he wants to be rid of them? Her freedom is not guaranteed. She thinks again of the envelope under her chair, of what it contains and what it means. And she knows what she must do. Maybe she really is stronger than she thought she was.

With a single nod, she adds her assent, and then Nadine speaks up for everyone. "If we walk out—" She corrects herself, saying, "*When* we walk out of here, we walk out together. No one's leaving here alone."

Tommy's face gives away his surprise. He thought he was losing one of them but gaining a fifth of whiskey. He'd already made the trade in his mind. He shakes his head. "That's not the way it works," he says, a whiny tone creeping into his voice. "I promised to let one of you go. We agreed."

"But *we* didn't agree," Nadine says. "We didn't, and we don't." She looks at her fellow hostages, at Morrow and Blythe and Sylvie. "We're in this together. We're staying together. Right, ladies?" They nod in resolution, their decision certain. They are proud and afraid all at the same time.

Morrow knows they have done the right thing in sticking together. At least she hopes they have. She feels a surge of camaraderie, a bond forged akin to the kind that soldiers find in foxholes. She wants to hug each one of them, but she stays in her place. They all do, even as Tommy storms around cursing and muttering at their mutiny.

This event, Morrow thinks, *is something I will only ever have in common with the women in this room.* This matters, though in the moment she cannot gauge how much. Perhaps they will walk out of this—she has to believe they will walk out of this—and never see one another again. Still, as Tommy goes back to the phone to tell the negotiator they don't have a deal after all, Morrow hopes they will stay in one another's lives after today. She thinks of what she came here to mail and how satisfying it would be to have friends like these to talk to about it. She hasn't found friends in this town like she'd hoped, yet it was her dream to move here, to live by the sea.

Sometimes she thinks it was inevitable, being named for a woman who wrote a famous book about the ocean. She does not remember a time she was not drawn to it. Perhaps her mother planted the idea in her head when she was a baby, whispering to her about all the gifts the sea could give her. She likes to picture her mother holding her, the two of them looking out at the water together as the waves crash and the seagulls call to one another. She likes to think that happened often, but she never got the chance to ask her mother. By the time she was mature enough to think of such questions, her mother was gone. Whether it did or didn't happen, her love of the beach is something that has defined her for as long as she can remember. Throughout her life, she did anything she could to get back to it, living fifty-one weeks a year for one week every summer.

So after being a good sport through countless moves for Kevin's job, when he took a remote position and told her she could choose where they would live, the decision was a foregone conclusion. They moved to Sunset Beach the year Maya started high school. Other than Morrow, no one in her family was really thrilled with the decision.

While Kevin liked the proximity to golf and the water, he complained bitterly about the lack of direct flights every time he traveled, which was a lot. Their son was out of the house by then, so he didn't really have a stake in where his parents lived. But Maya, her baby, her only daughter, barely spoke to her during her entire ninth-grade year, giving her the silent treatment for moving her away from her friends and her school. The move had come at a cost—Morrow still has sticker shock—and yet she has what she's always wanted. Or what she always thought she wanted.

She feels that niggling sense that perhaps her life would be better if she hadn't decided to move them here. She wonders if she made a mistake choosing her wants over her family's. As a young mom she used to hear that you should take care of your own needs first, then the needs of your family, citing that airplane example about the oxygen. But that really only applies if the plane is crashing. In Morrow's experience it doesn't always work that way. The people you love can come to resent you for choosing yourself, silently judging you for prioritizing your wants over theirs.

But at the time, when presented with the option, Morrow couldn't help but think, *If not now, when?* She didn't want to wait for retirement to live in a place she loved, only getting the best part of her life at the end of her life. So when she had the chance, she took it. And now she is here, in the place she loves most of all, a place she longed to be, in a hostage situation. The irony is not lost on her.

Chapter 27

While they wait for the pizzas to arrive—it is taking a lot longer than Sylvie expected—Tommy has gone back to rifling through the mail, threatening again to open the envelopes and read what is inside. "It's illegal, Tommy," Nadine scolds him. "A federal offense."

Tommy points at the poster of the USPS logo. "Ohhh nooo. The Sonic Eagle is gonna get me!"

"Just leave it alone," Nadine says. "People sent those letters expecting them to get where they're going. You don't have the right to interfere with that."

At least a year ago—maybe longer, time runs together—Sylvie had watched an interview about a man who had picked up thousands of pieces of mail that had been strewn about on the side of the highway. The man had said that when he called the post office to report what he had found, they told him those letters had been deemed undeliverable. The man was upset and held up what looked to be a personal card, perhaps for a birthday or graduation or in sympathy, lamenting that whoever sent that card, and whoever it was intended for, would never know what happened to their attempt to communicate.

Since then, Sylvie had thought of that news report from time to time. She could still see that pink envelope in her mind, the man's sad face as he held it up for the camera. It had been tossed aside like trash. Yet someone somewhere had gone to a store, taken the time to select the card, written a message in it, found a stamp and addressed it, then sent it on its way. That person had trusted that it would reach its intended recipient, only to have it left on the side of the road. Even now they might be wondering whatever happened to it.

It was just another example of how humans try, and fail, to connect with one another. And yet we persist, reaching out in hopes of receiving love, acceptance, validation, forgiveness in return. She thinks of Tommy's efforts to reach Nadine, misguided as they are. She thinks of her own reasons for coming to the post office today, of how by pleasing one person she loves, she will be hurting another. She doesn't know how to prevent what feels inevitable.

She should've known her son was up to something when he asked her to go for a walk with him at the town park when he visited last weekend. A lovely piece of land that sits right on the Intracoastal Waterway, the park features swings that overlook the water, paths for walking, and picnic tables. Many times she and Robert have gone there to have a picnic. It is a peaceful spot, a place ideal for reading or reflecting or gathering.

The town market is held there every Thursday, which is where Sylvie gets her produce since she no longer gardens. And on Wednesday nights from Memorial Day to Labor Day, there is a free concert. They try to go at least a few times each summer, choosing the performers who sing the oldies. "Oldies for oldies," Robert says. Once they stumbled upon a wedding being held there, and once they saw a gaggle of girls taking their prom pictures down by the water, all willowy beauty and bright eyes.

She and her son had strolled along the sidewalks, enjoying the spring weather. She'd been happy, grateful for a little alone time with her only child, apart from his wife and daughters, who had gone to the beach. Lulled by his ruse, she'd been blindsided when their conversation turned. "Dad seemed out of it last night," her son had said, seven words that sank her. Sylvie willed herself not to stop in her tracks, to keep putting one foot in front of the other. She thought she'd covered for Robert, that Robert Junior and his family were none the wiser.

Robert Junior, who goes by Rob, continued. "He's called me before and been confused. One time when he spoke to the girls, he couldn't remember their names. They were pretty rattled by it." He glanced over at Sylvie, but she made no comment, so he kept talking. "I know you love living here, but I'm not sure the two of you should be so far from family," he'd said. "You're all on your own here."

Yes, Sylvie had thought. *And we like it that way, the two of us against the world. It was the way we started, the promise we made on our wedding day.* But she hadn't said it. She hadn't said anything, so Rob did. "You have to think about the what-ifs—"

"Put that stuff down and come sit." Nadine's voice pulls Sylvie out of her recollection. "The pizza should be here soon."

Tommy looks up. "I don't have anywhere to sit," he says, sullen.

Nadine gestures to a space near where they are sitting on the stools. "You can sit on the floor and lean against the cabinet."

Sylvie watches as he acquiesces to Nadine. Sometimes it seems that Tommy forgets that he's in charge, that he's the one with the gun. She gives Nadine a sly wink, a reminder of what she'd said in the bathroom. The stage is set. Seated, with a place to rest his head, he can eat the pizza, get full and sleepy, and nod off, and then they can flee. A surge of optimism courses through her. It is almost over. Where *is* that pizza?

"In my day," she says, just to fill the quiet and try to make the time go faster, "everyone wrote letters. There was no email. No cell phones. You called someone at their home or, if it was long distance, you wrote a letter. That's how you kept in touch."

Morrow chimes in. "I remember. We had pen pals. We wrote thank-you notes. We passed notes in school. I would meet kids at camp in the summer, and we'd exchange letters all year long until we went back to camp the next summer." She pauses. "I wonder where all those letters are now." She smiles. "They'd be fun to read."

"There was something satisfying about receiving a letter," Sylvie agrees. "The anticipation of wondering what was inside, what bit of news or unexpected declaration might be waiting."

Morrow, who guesses she's probably the only other person in the room to recall a time before email existed, nods.

"I was a schoolteacher before I retired," Sylvie continues. "Used to be letter writing was an actual unit that was taught as part of English, which is what I taught. The students had to learn how to write a formal letter, a friendly letter, a thank-you letter, and the different parts of each one. We were quite formal about it all."

Now we aren't formal enough, Sylvie thinks. *Everyone is so casual about everything. Too casual.* But she does not say this. Instead, she says, "I would have each student write a letter to the business of their choice and ask for something, something that had to do with that business." She gives a little laugh. "Oh, the things we got in return. It was such fun!"

Tommy looks particularly skeptical. "Like what?"

"Once I had a student write to an executive at Coca-Cola, and they sent us free cans of Coke for the whole class." She can't think of any other examples just then, but she knows there are many, as she taught school for many years. She wonders if they still cover letter writing in school now. She doubts it.

"Whoop-de-do," says Tommy. "Free cans of Coke."

Ignoring him, Sylvie asks Morrow, "Do you still remember the parts of a letter?"

Morrow makes a stricken face. "Oh goodness. Let me think. Um . . . there's the part where you write, like, where you are and . . . the date? Right?" She looks to Sylvie, who nods.

"That's the heading," Sylvie says. She makes a little motion for Morrow to continue.

"And then there's the part where you say 'Dear so-and-so.' And that's the . . . greeting!"

Sylvie claps her hands together and nods her affirmation, remembering her years in the classroom. She did love teaching, but she does not miss it as much as she misses that time in her life, the whole of it. The work and the family and the day-to-day routine she took for granted. Sometimes in her dreams she goes back to that time, to the house they raised their son in. She is never doing anything special in the dream, just going about her normal life. She is always sad when she wakes up. This would likely surprise her younger self if she knew that someday she'd literally dream about that harried, hurried time in her life.

Morrow continues, caught up in the challenge and glad for something to think about besides the situation. "And then there's the part where you just say what you have to say." Again, she looks to Sylvie. "But I don't remember what that's called."

"That's the body of the letter. It's actually in three parts: your introduction, your main points, and your summary. Or, as I used to tell my students: Tell them what you're going to tell them, tell them, then tell them what you told them."

Tommy pretends to snore, but they all ignore him.

"Ha. I've never heard that," says Morrow, who is thinking that if people communicated this succinctly now, maybe more would get accomplished. She wonders if, when people lost the art of letting writing, they lost some core part of culture. But she doesn't add her commentary; she just says, "I remember being tested on this."

"You got tested on letter writing?" Tommy interjects, and Sylvie turns to him, ignoring his comment and lobbing a question at him instead. She did this with the troublemakers in her classrooms too.

"Okay," she says. "So what do you think comes after the body?"

"The grave?" Tommy says, then laughs at his own joke as they all roll their eyes. Even still, Blythe feels a little shiver go down her back as he says it. No matter how much it was said in jest, it's never good for the man holding you captive with a gun to be making jokes about bodies and graves.

Sylvie ignores him again and continues with her impromptu lesson. "So we've got the heading, the greeting, the body. But there are five parts total. So"—she looks over at Morrow—"don't you answer this. Let's see if the young people can guess." Morrow smiles and nods.

"So you've said what you want to say. Now what's next?"

"You have to close it out?" asks Nadine.

Sylvie claps her hands together. "Yes! Exactly! The closing!"

"No fair," says Tommy. "She probably already knew that because she works here."

Nadine turns on Tommy. "I did not! I guessed it. I mean, if you've said all you have to say—if there's nothing left to be said—it's time to end it."

Nadine stops talking and chews on her lip as her words seem to reverberate through the room. For a moment no one says anything as Tommy and Nadine look at each other. For once Tommy doesn't look angry. He just looks sad.

Blythe speaks up before things can go in an altogether different direction. "So what's number five?" she asks. She doesn't care what the fifth part of a letter is. She just wants to move the conversation past this awkward moment.

Sylvie is no longer caught up in the lesson. Perhaps she should've kept her mouth shut and not started this. It seems there is nothing in this room that cannot turn on a dime. Her voice is quiet when she says, "The final part is the signature, and we know what that is."

For a time no one speaks. But then Tommy does. "What about the PS?" he asks.

All four heads turn to look at him; then, blinking, four sets of eyes return to Sylvie. One thing she always understood about teaching: It is a responsibility, one to be taken seriously. Where you lead, your students will follow. At the moment she feels this acutely.

"Yes," she says. "You're right. The PS can be part of a letter. It stands for postscript, and it's something that can be added on after the end, below the signature line." She treads carefully, weighing her words before she says them. "It can be something you forgot to say earlier that you'd like to add, or a reminder to the person you're sending it to. Something you don't want them to forget."

Tommy nods and looks down at the gun that rests in his lap. "I thought so," he says. "I thought there was still something left."

Chapter 28

Outside, hope and Bo wait for the pizzas to arrive. She has stretched the wait out long enough. Hope would like the pizza delivery to be wrapped up before the convoy from county arrives, which, according to an update from Hank, should be anytime now and, likely, the end of the road for her. She will no doubt be relieved of duty once the higher-ups get here. There is talk that the Feds are en route as well. They definitely won't need her then.

She wonders if Bo will head home too. He seems invested in seeing it through to the end, maybe because he is a retiree with nothing better to do—this will probably be the highlight of his year, or at least his month—or perhaps because he is genuinely concerned about the outcome. No matter how much she tells him to stay with her, he keeps wandering toward the post office, questioning the personnel closest to the building about what's going on inside. For now she has him corralled in Brower's car.

"You know it snowed here," Bo says. He is talking to her but watching the post office through the windshield. Hope has learned that he's not fond of prolonged silences and is prone to talking just to talk. But it helps pass the time. Suspects aren't the only ones who get bored and tired during a negotiation.

"Not this past January but the January before. Newspaper said it was a once-in-a-lifetime event. This area doesn't get much, or really any, snow. So you can imagine that it shut this whole place down. Everything closed. Our neighborhood amenities closed. No one dared go anywhere at all."

He clears his throat loudly, which Hope has also learned he has a habit of doing. "The thing is, that's the way it is in a town like this. They're not outfitted for snow—and why would they be? It's a lot of expensive equipment to have on hand for something that will likely never happen." He gestures at the scene in front of them: the ambulances, the fire trucks, the clusters of cops milling around waiting for something to happen. "Makes sense they wouldn't have everything they need for something like this either." He holds up his hands. "Why would they? This is a once-in-a-lifetime event too."

Hope can't help but chuckle. "I'm sure everyone in this parking lot hopes you're right."

He nods. "Pretty sure I am."

He pauses, but she knows he is still thinking. She can almost hear the old gears of his mind grinding away. She never knew her grandfather, but her mother used to talk about him, and from how she described him, Hope imagines he would've been like the man sitting beside her. It would've been nice, she decides, having a grandfather like Bo.

"You know," he adds, "the thing about that snow was that it was so unexpected. When they first started forecasting it, no one believed it would happen. Then when it did, it made everyone feel inspired. Like, if this can happen, then anything could happen. That snow gave us hope." He elbows her. "Get it? Hope?"

"Yes," she says. "I get it." She points at a car slowly approaching, the little sign strapped to the top indicating the pizza delivery. They can see the driver's head swiveling as he negotiates the phalanx of emergency responders. She picks up her phone and hits Redial, putting the phone on speaker for Bo. She watches the supervising officer greet the delivery person, taking the pizzas so they can bug the boxes before turning them over to Hope and Bo. Now they will at least have ears on the hostages. More progress.

Tommy answers quickly this time. "Your pizzas are here," she says. "So we need to go over how we are going to get them to you."

"Okay," says Tommy.

Hope looks to Bo, and he nods his assent to their plan. "We've got a retired officer out here who has volunteered to take the pizzas in himself. But he will be surrounded by other officers for his protection."

"Am I supposed to just—what?—walk out there and take them from him?"

"No," says Bo, speaking up. "Not you. We need to make contact with at least one hostage. We need to get eyes on someone who's been in that room, or we can't leave the food." He gives Hope a half smile at this fib. They could leave the pizzas by the door just like they're going to do with the water. But she sees what he's doing: making Tommy engage with both law enforcement and his hostages through this transaction, stretching his boundaries just a little further. *Smart,* Hope thinks.

Bo continues. "So you'll need to send out one of the hostages." He thinks about it for a moment. "Send the old lady out. She's the least likely to attempt anything sudden or risky."

Hope wrinkles her brow at this. The old lady? Why put undue stress on her when there are younger, more agile women in there? But Hope doesn't argue. It's not what she would've done, but it does make an odd sort of sense. Two old people exchanging pizzas seems harmless.

"The police will first leave the waters by the door," Bo continues, "and once they've done that, I will enter the vestibule, hand off the pizzas, and leave." He pauses. "I don't expect any funny business from you in the meantime. Even a hint of something going any differently than what we've discussed and this is over. No pizzas. No waters."

Then Tommy says something that surprises Hope. He says, "Yes, sir." They end the call, and then it's time for Operation Pizza Delivery.

Hope sees the signal from the supervising officer that the bugs have been attached to the undersides of the pizza savers in each box. If all goes well, pretty soon they will be hearing what's going on inside that post office in stereo. Before they climb out of the car, she looks at Bo one more time. "And you're sure about this?"

"Trust me," he says, patting her on the shoulder. "I'm the least threat to him, which means I'm the safest bet to go in." He points at the post office. "That kid in there isn't going to shoot an old man. I've been doing this a long time, and I know it. Now, let's go deliver some pizzas."

Inside the post office a little zing of anticipation ripples through the women as they watch the approach of a cadre of law enforcement officers from the front windows. At the center of the escort is an older gentleman with a determined expression carrying the three boxes of cheese pizza.

Tommy and the women move from the front windows to the side windows as the ensemble enters the building. Sylvie takes a step toward the door as she has been instructed to. She didn't understand why they chose her, but she wasn't going to argue about it. She was in favor of an excuse to escape the confines of the room they've been in for hours, even if for a moment. But now that she can see the old man who is walking the pizzas in, she understands fully.

She goes to take another step, but Tommy stops her. "Hold on," he says, his hand on her shoulder.

Together they watch as, on the other side of the glass, the officers enter the vestibule, guns drawn as they survey the area. They come to a stop in front of the post office and peer into the glass, their eyes locked on the hostages and their captor. One officer slides a case of water bottles across the floor like a hockey puck across the ice. It thunks against the post office door. The officer with the largest rifle nods over his shoulder. It is all very serious and very tense. *All this for some pizza and water*, Sylvie thinks.

Tommy's phone rings, and he answers. They have moved from the post office line to his personal line, and this is its own kind of progress.

"Tell them I just want the old dude in here," he says to Hope. "None of these guys with guns."

Sylvie thinks this is ironic considering he is holding a gun even as he says this. But the rules don't apply to Tommy today, just other people. She wonders if, when he thinks back on this day, he will remember it fondly, if this moment in time will be his apex. That would be quite the tragedy if so. He is, she decides, too young for this day to define him for the rest of his life.

Standing so close to him, she can clearly hear Hope speak. "They're just clearing the area, making sure it's safe to send in the civilian. They won't all stay in there, but I have to leave a few to guarantee his safety."

"Fine," says Tommy, knowing when he's bested. "Once most of them have left," Tommy says, "I'll pull the waters in and send the old lady out."

"My name is Sylvie," grumbles Sylvie. "Not the old lady." She has never been called old this much in her life, and she's getting sick of it. Until today she didn't really think of herself as old. Old*er*, maybe. But not old. Her neighbor across the street is approaching ninety. That, she thinks, qualifies as old. It is funny how the older you get, the more old age becomes a moving target.

Hope must give some sort of command from wherever she is because they watch as the man carrying the pizzas enters and all but two of the officers exit. Sylvie goes to take another step toward the door, but Tommy reaches out to halt her a second time. "You know what to do," he says.

She wants to tell him to shut up, but instead she just nods and listens as he gives her his instructions again: no sudden movements, no going anywhere near the main door, no opening the pizza boxes before she gets back in. She knows that telling them all what to do makes Tommy feel powerful, perpetuates the myth that he is in charge here. So she lets him say his piece even as her shoulder strains against his grip. When he lets go of her and unlocks the door, he pulls the waters in and she walks purposefully toward the vestibule, her eyes trained on the man standing there. She had not expected this. But she should've. These last few months, she has forgotten what he is capable of.

She comes to a stop in front of him. "You're Sylvie?" he asks her. She has no doubt he is wearing some sort of wire, or the pizza boxes are bugged, or both. Either way, she understands this is not a private conversation.

She nods. "You're Bo?"

He gives her a sheepish look. "Yes," he says. He has used his nickname from back in his early precinct days, back before he went to the FBI.

"Pizza delivery, at your service," he says, lifting the stack of pizza boxes and giving her a little smile. His hands are large enough to hold them all, his thumbs anchoring the top box and his pinkies the bottom one. The other fingers hold the center box in place. She cannot take her eyes off his hands, how strong they look, how capable they make her feel, even now, in spite of the protruding veins and age spots. They are still his hands.

His wedding ring glints in the harsh fluorescent lighting of the lobby they are standing in. She wants to toss the boxes to the side, take his hands in her own. They could make a run for it. She doubts that Tommy would pursue them, that he would shoot two old people as they flee.

But Sylvie stays put. She and the other women have promised to walk out together, and she will keep her end of that promise. The smell of the pizzas wafts up between them, filling the air and reminding her of the time they went to Italy.

They look at each other for a few silent seconds, saying with their eyes what they cannot with their mouths. If the pizza boxes are indeed bugged, then from now on the people outside will be able to hear everything that's going on inside the post office. More progress.

He looks past her, peering into the glass at Tommy, who stands watching them, the gun in his hand. "Everyone okay in there?" Robert asks.

She nods, because for a moment she cannot speak. It is the kindness in his voice, the voice she knows better than her own, that catches her up short, sparking tears. He has found a way both to be here and to let her know that he is here. She thinks of the envelope under her stool and questions anew what she came here to do today.

"We're okay," she says, her voice barely above a whisper because it's all she can manage. "Everyone okay out there?"

He looks at her, gives her a little smile. "County will be here soon, and I'm betting once they are they'll have this in hand pretty quick. Meanwhile, I'm trying to be of assistance. I came the minute I heard. I'm a former FBI agent," he says. "Retired now, but I was in law enforcement for forty years."

Sylvie smiles at him. He misses it, she knows, the work, the respect, the purpose it brought. "I'm sure they appreciate the help," she tells him.

"We're all just doing what we can. We're out there for you, working to get you free."

She nods and—a reflex—goes to reach for him, wanting his arms around her more than all the pizza in the world. When she does, he thinks quickly and pretends she has reached for the pizzas. He fills her arms with the warm boxes instead of himself.

Tommy uses the gun to rap on the window. Her time is up.

She sees Robert's eyes go glassy. "You be safe in there," he says, giving her a wink that is so fast it is barely perceptible as he turns to exit the building, to leave her behind. She does not watch him go, turning instead toward the door that will take her back into captivity, carrying sustenance that makes her, for the moment, a hero to the other women inside. She hears Tommy turning the key in the lock as the door closes behind her.

"Do you know him or something?" Tommy asks, following her. "You sure did talk to him a long time."

Sylvie busies herself with setting the boxes on the counter, one, two, three, an excuse to keep her back to them as she works to compose herself and come up with a good lie at the same time. She carefully takes the white plastic pizza savers out and places them to the side, scooting them just behind a large packing tape dispenser nearby. Robert hadn't designated her because she is old. He'd designated her because she would know what to do. She's been a cop's wife her entire adult life. She's learned a thing or two.

"He just asked about each one of us," she says. "He wanted to make sure everyone is okay, no medical needs or anything like that." She looks over her shoulder at the other women. "I told him we were fine, which sounds a little silly if you think about it."

She moves her hand in the air over the pizzas like a game show hostess showing a contestant what they won. "Now, let's eat while it's still hot!"

But then there is a noise at the windows, the sound like the bird that flew into Sylvie's front window just a few weeks ago. It is like that, but louder. Startled, everyone wheels around to see what happened, momentarily forgetting the pizzas, some of them wondering if it was a gunshot or the police trying to come through, some sort of surprise attempt when Tommy's guard is down. But at the window they don't see a bird or any officers or a bullet hole.

Instead, they see a girl, standing on the other side of the glass, banging her fists against it and yelling. Morrow blinks at the face as her mind registers that the girl is her daughter and what she is yelling is "Mom!"

Morrow rushes to the windows, but before she can reach her, Maya is dragged away, kicking and screaming, by several officers. She thinks about Maya as a toddler, how many times she had to drag her away from something she wanted, kicking and screaming much the same. But this time what she wanted was her. Morrow stands and watches Maya until the police take her out of sight. Behind her, she can hear Tommy opening the pizza boxes, unfazed by the disruption since it poses no threat to him.

Beside her, she feels a hand on her shoulder. "Your daughter?" Sylvie asks her.

Morrow's eyes are shining with tears as she turns to her and nods. "Their attention must've been diverted after the pizzas got delivered, so she saw her chance, I guess." She looks back to the windows, scanning for a glimpse of Maya somewhere out there. "I didn't even know she was here."

"I'm sure this is scary for her. You trapped in here like this. Her unable to get to you."

Morrow only nods, unable to speak, as she thinks of the morning, the regrets that have been taunting her all day. She'd thought she'd be the one to bridge the gap between them as soon as she could manage it. But Maya had found a way to her instead. She must've also wanted to make sure they didn't leave things the way they were.

"She's a brave girl," says Sylvie. Morrow nods again, smiling through her tears. "You must be very proud."

Morrow thinks about the moment she saw her daughter for the first time, when she held the tiny, swaddled bundle of her, how beautiful she was. Maya took her breath away. After struggling with secondary infertility, Morrow couldn't believe she finally had her long-awaited second child, and a little girl at that. She absolutely loved her son, but she'd become especially enamored with her daughter once she finally had her, filling her empty arms.

"I am," she says.

"Let's get something to eat," Sylvie says, gently tugging on Morrow's elbow. "She'll be okay until you get out of here."

Morrow allows herself to be led away from the windows and steered toward the pizza because there is nothing she can do now. And she is hungry. The scent of oregano and tomatoes and yeasty dough fills the enclosed space and makes her stomach growl. She thinks being held hostage is a good enough reason to abandon her diet, just this once. For now she knows Maya is safe, she is aware of what's happening, and she has shown up for her. For now that is enough.

Chapter 29

INSIDE THE POST office the hostages and their captor sit in a circle to eat their pizza and drink their waters. They make polite conversation between bites, unaware that outside the post office chaos reigns. Just as the police completed Operation Pizza Delivery, a family member of one of the hostages saw her chance and made a mad dash for the building. (Though what she thought she was going to do once she got there, Hope has no idea.) They intercepted the kid before anything could come of it, but no sooner did they handle that situation than the county team showed up.

Now, in the parking lot of the building next to the post office, the NOC is being set up, SWAT is mobilizing and scoping out the building for access points, and Hope is being asked a barrage of questions before she hands over the reins and leaves them to it.

It is for the best that a team that does this regularly is taking over. Hope stepped in when she was needed; she did what she could. And nothing awful happened on her watch. That, she tells herself, is a good day's work. And yet she has a nagging feeling that she is abandoning these people, leaving them in the hands of strangers.

Two team members take charge: Adam and Chris. Chris sees the concern on her face and tells her that he will take good care of the hostages, that he will work toward a peaceful surrender with no one harmed. Though they both know he can't promise that, she goes along with it because at least he has the intent. In the background the other team members are getting all the technology up and running with a no-nonsense efficiency.

When the hostages' voices, coming from inside the post office, fill the command center through the speaker box, Hope has to resist the urge to applaud. This is what they've needed the whole time. The ability to eavesdrop will bring intel, give them an advantage, and hopefully bring this day to an end soon.

Hope looks around for Bo, but he has slipped away. She wonders if he, too, feels that his work here is done. She's sure it's been exciting for him to come out of retirement for a few hours. In a way, she feels like she has done the same.

"Excuse me," she says to the members of the team. "I just need to go find my . . . partner. He might have more to add." They nod, turning back to the frenzy around them.

Hope steps out of the NOC, which is a huge semitruck with an RV-like setup inside. The quarters are tight in there and the interior dark in contrast to the sunshine she steps into. She shields her eyes as she scans the area but doesn't see Bo anywhere. She checks to make sure his car is still there, and it is. She didn't think he'd leave without saying goodbye. She walks across the parking lot to the place where the witnesses smoked cigarettes and told their story when she arrived hours ago. She stops there to scan the perimeter again but still doesn't see Bo.

She keeps walking and looking, walking and looking, until she finds him. When she finally spots him, he's hunkered down, his lanky body like a collapsed folding chair, as he speaks to the kid they'd dragged away from the post office. The girl is sitting on the curb out by a mailbox near the main road, put there for customers who just need to drop their mail and go. Hope draws closer yet stays back, not wanting to interrupt whatever he is saying to the girl. Hope watches as Bo comforts her, handing her a paper napkin to dry her tears. A man stands off to the side, also watching the two of them, his brows knit together and his mouth a grim line. He must be the girl's father, the husband of one of the hostages. *Morrow*, Hope thinks, recalling the brief report she read early on. *This is Morrow's family.*

Bo sees her, stands, and gives her a smile. He points to the girl on the curb. "This is Maya. Her mom is inside. She and I were just talking."

Hope steps toward the girl but doesn't sit on the curb beside her like Bo had. She needs to get back to the NOC and facilitate the transition. "Nice to meet you, Maya," she says.

Bo points to Hope. "This is . . ." He stands still for a moment, searching her face, his own blank. Then he says, "Faith. She's a negotiator. She's the one who's been talking with the man who's inside so he'll start to feel good about coming out."

Maya peers up at Hope, keeping her from processing what Bo just said. He had forgotten her name, then called her by a different one. "Are you going to get my mom out of there?" Hope hears the hope in her voice.

There is no sense explaining that a new team has come to relieve them and that she and Bo will soon be going home. The only thing, the right thing, is to tell this girl yes. Yes, for sure she is going to get her mom, and the other women, out of there safely. The sooner the better. Maya has nothing to worry about.

Maya seems placated with the platitudes, and Hope decides not to correct Bo about her name, chalking up his gaffe to the stress of the day. She is not the only one who needs a break. Hope and Bo excuse themselves, waving goodbye to Morrow's family, falling into step as they head back to the NOC.

"You will, you know," says Bo.

"I will what?"

"Get them out of there safely. You just need lady luck on your side."

"Lady luck?" she asks. She thinks of the old Frank Sinatra song. She and Alex used to go to an Italian restaurant in Philly where they played nothing but Sinatra. It was one of their favorites. Homesickness and longing swell inside of her, unbidden and, at the moment, inconvenient.

"Something to happen that will open him up even more," he says. "Something that connects you, something you can't plan or manipulate. It just happens. I've seen it many times." He gives her a wink. "You'll see."

But she won't see. Because she is going home. And so should he. "I came to find you because I thought you'd like to take part in the debrief before we turn things over to the experts," she says to him.

He gives her a look. "Turn things over?"

"Yes," she says. Doesn't he understand that the county is the relief team, that they're dismissed? "We can go," she explains.

He keeps shaking his head. "No, we can't. I mean, I could leave and no one would miss me. But I'm not going to." He shakes his finger at her like a schoolmarm. "And neither should you. You've built rapport with Tommy. And that's not nothing."

"Someone else can build rapport with him. And besides, I don't think they want us here. They want to handle it," she says. "It's their job." She feels a tremble in her throat and swallows against it. It's ridiculous to let emotions in over this. She's completed her assignment; now she gets to go home. Rufus will need to go outside. Rufus! As she thinks of her dog, she realizes she has forgotten to mention Tommy's request.

"I forgot to tell them about Covey!" she says. "They're going to need to know about that." She checks her watch. "Tommy's stepmom will be here anytime. We—I mean, they—will need to figure out how to go about letting Tommy see the dog. We—I mean, I—promised him that."

She quickens her pace. Hope hopes that agreeing to the dog was the right thing to do. She's counting on the dog to break something open in Tommy, to pave the way toward the resolution they all need. If she's right, she's a hero. If she's wrong, she's an idiot.

"You negotiated that," Bo says. "You need to be here when it happens."

She shakes her head, insistent. "They'll handle it."

She expects him to argue with her, but he says nothing, just keeps his head down as he trudges to the NOC, to the people inside it waiting to take over the negotiation.

Inside the post office the hostages use the boredom to their advantage, hoping and praying that Tommy will do as Nadine said and fall asleep. They talk in low tones about boring things on purpose. They do not make jokes so there are no loud outbursts of laughter. Sylvie asks Nadine a lot of questions about the post office rules and regulations just to increase their odds. When Nadine starts to tell a story about the time someone tried to mail live chickens, Sylvie shakes her head, a quick, subtle redirection. No funny stories.

The mood is deliberately quiet and subdued. So much so that they feel themselves getting sleepy. So surely Tommy must be as well. Tommy, sitting where Nadine told him to, has eaten a whole pizza by himself. Finished, he leans his head back, resting it against the cabinet. They take turns glancing at him. They notice his eyelids growing heavy. He has to work to keep them open.

They all think, *Any minute now.*

Sure enough, there finally comes a time when Tommy's eyes close and do not open again. Nadine silently pumps her fist in the air as they all exchange smiles, their heads swirling with the thought of the freedom that awaits. They find themselves leaning forward as they look to Nadine, expecting her to get up and run to the door like they'd talked about. But instead, they watch, their faces contorted with confusion, as she crawls toward Tommy. Blythe wants to cry out, "No! This isn't what we agreed on!" but she cannot say a word. She has to sit silently as Nadine reaches for the gun that rests in Tommy's lap.

She's going to get that gun and shoot him with it, thinks Blythe. She can't say that she would blame her. But Nadine is potentially risking their freedom for the sake of revenge. Blythe claps her hand over her own mouth to keep from calling out as she watches Nadine use her pincer fingers to slowly, gently slide the gun from his lap. The room holds its collective breath as she inches it across the fabric of his jeans.

Tommy's eyes fly open and his hand clamps down on Nadine's at the exact same moment. Then everyone is hollering—Tommy hollers at Nadine, Nadine hollers at Tommy, and Blythe, Morrow, and Sylvie just holler, whether in fear that Tommy will shoot them or in outrage that they are not free doesn't make a difference. They had a chance, and now that chance is blown.

Blythe wants to yell at Nadine too. She wants to scream out, "Why didn't you just unlock the door like we planned?" But to ask that in front of Tommy is to divulge that they had a plan, which would only anger him further. And it would reveal that Nadine has her own set of keys, which he still doesn't know. Maybe at some point she will get the chance to ask Nadine what she was thinking, but now is not the time.

She thinks of her own impulsivity in attacking Tommy when he had her package. That wasn't smart either, but she got her package back. She looks to it, as if to confirm that it is still there, tucked under her stool. She goes and picks it up, brushes her fingers across the seam, smoothing down the little tear that Tommy made. In the midst of the melee, she thinks about Murphy and how glad she is that she is keeping all of him all to herself.

Chapter 30

The hostages' yells erupt over the speaker as the incoming team scrambles to place their first call to the suspect even as the SWAT commander insists they can enter through the back and put an end to this with minimal risk. SWAT likes to end things with force, but negotiators like to end things with words. Sometimes it seems that the two sides are at odds, but they are all fighting the same battle. Usually they find a way to meet in the middle.

Pushed to the side, Hope and Bo watch them search for that middle, Hope silently fearing that any ground they've gained today is now lost. Until the screams erupted it had been silent. Whatever just happened inside the post office has shifted the environment from quiet sanity into mad uproar. If they'd had eyes and not just ears on the situation, they'd know what happened. Now that the county is here, they will likely be able to use drones or robots. Or maybe the dog could have a camera mounted on his collar? She will mention this to the team as soon as she can. But first they need to make contact. She watches as they make several failed attempts to contact Tommy. They try his cell phone and the post office landline to no avail.

The hope is not so much leaking out of the room as whooshing out of it like a tire blown. She could leave, but she needs to tell them about the dog first. She wants to explain to them what

Covey means to the suspect. She will refer to him as the suspect because, to them, he is still just that. But in the last few hours he's become Tommy to her. Tommy who asked for his dad, the one thing he knew he couldn't have. She understands this better than most people. She wants to make sure that Tommy gets to see the dog. As unconventional as it is, it makes sense to her. She just hopes she can communicate this in a way that will make sense to them.

Beside her, Bo shifts his weight from side to side. She can almost hear his old bones protesting as he does. He probably shouldn't be on his feet for too long. "You could go, you know," she whispers to Bo.

She watches his face harden as he shakes his head. A single muscle in his jaw flinches. "I'm staying put."

Hope doesn't argue further. She looks away, sees Adam from the county team looking at her with his finger crooked, beckoning her. "I'll be right back," she says to Bo.

Adam is all business. "It's kind of tight in here," he says. "I think we've got it under control if you'd like to take off."

"Oh, I know." Hope can take a hint. She would feel the same if she'd relieved someone but they kept standing around in the close quarters inside the NOC, which is growing warmer by the minute from all the body heat. "I just wanted to tell you before I go—I almost forgot about the dog."

"The dog?" asks Adam, narrowing his eyes. Hope sees him motion for his other team members. As they walk over, Bo does as well. She appreciates the gesture of solidarity.

With everyone looking at her, she finds herself fumbling with her words. "Tommy—the suspect," she corrects herself, "asked to see his father, which turned out was just a bluff. His father is deceased. But I didn't find that out until I tried to get in touch with him. I did speak with the stepmother, and when she found out what was happening, she offered to bring the father's dog here, in case that would help."

As she speaks she recalls the earnestness in the woman's voice. She'd wanted to do something, to help somehow, like so many people want to do in cases like this. In police work it is expected to see the worst of society. But Hope has also seen the best of it too. At times it is easy to forget one and dwell on the other.

"The suspect is apparently quite close to the dog. It seems that after his father died, he really wanted to have the dog come live with him. There was some sort of custody battle over the dog, for lack of a better term. And there was some bad blood between the stepmother and the suspect as a result. I think her offer to bring the dog is her way of trying to mend fences."

The group nods and Hope continues. "The trouble is the dog is all the way in New Bern, and she had to get ready, then drive more than two and a half hours." Hope shrugs. "At the time I honestly thought the situation would be resolved before she got here. But it seemed like she needed to make the effort as much as the suspect needed to hear that she was bringing the dog. So I went along with it."

Chris wrinkles his nose like he has caught a whiff of something foul. "I'm not sure I feel comfortable with him having access to the dog. Especially if there's bad blood between him and the stepmother. He could be setting up some sort of revenge ploy. And even if he isn't, it could provoke him further. The emotions this could trigger feel too loose."

The teammates exchange glances. "We run a tighter operation than that," Adam adds, siding with his teammate because of course he is.

"I get it," says Hope. "No pun intended, but I don't have a dog in this fight. Not anymore." In her peripheral vision she sees Bo frown as she adds, "But I truly didn't think it would go this far."

"And if it did, you knew you'd already be gone." Adam pretends to say this under his breath, but it is loud enough to be heard by everyone standing there.

Hope feels a flash of anger but wills herself not to show it. She knows it's the right thing to allow Tommy to see the dog—she feels it deep inside—but gut instincts are hard to explain. She must be willing to stand up to the scrutiny of her decision.

And then she can go home. Well, she corrects herself, not home.

More and more, she wants to go home-home, not just to Alex, but back to her team in Pennsylvania, who would have her back the same as this team has one another's. She can't blame them for their unity. She'd be the same with her team. *Except*, she thinks, *you left them behind.* She blamed the work for what happened and abandoned her job, which included the people she'd worked side by side with for years. Driven by grief and plagued by PTSD, she ran away, sought shelter here. *It was supposed to have been safe*, she thinks. *That was why I came.*

"She shouldn't leave," Bo speaks up, interrupting her thoughts and making her heart rate hitch at the same time.

Adam turns on Bo. "Remind me again what department you're with?" he asks, crossing his arms and squinting at him.

Nonplussed, Bo answers, "I'm retired FBI, here of my own volition, with the authorization of the Sunset Beach police chief." He gives Hope a sideways glance, then returns his gaze to Adam. "I came to act as a consultant since the situation here was sort of . . . unprecedented." He rocks back on his heels. "I've met the chief a few times, and when I heard about this, I gave him a call, offered my services. He was glad for the assistance, especially since your team had . . . delays." He reaches over and pats Hope's shoulder. "Turns out I wasn't really needed. This young lady had it all under control without me." Hope notices he's still not using her name and wonders if he still can't recall it.

Adam frowns. He opens his mouth, perhaps to argue some more, but he is silenced by the interruption of a ringing phone.

"I guess that's for you," says Bo, looking in the direction of the back of the truck where Adam and Chris are to sit for the negotiation, one to talk, one to coach. They nod and rotate on their heels at the same time, moving toward the ringing and into their positions. Hope reaches for Bo's sleeve and pulls him with her, getting out of their way so the team can work.

She moves until she can go no farther, resting her aching back against the walls of the semi. She watches the negotiation from a distance, feeling detached from what is happening. She should just leave already. In truth she is relieved to be relieved. Though nothing really bad has happened so far, she knows all too well that things can go sideways without warning. She would rather be back at 108, relaxing with Rufus, if it does. Caught between the team's desire for her to go and Bo's insistence that she stay, she stands immobile. *Just wait a bit longer*, she tells herself. *Appease Bo. And then you can go.*

Chapter 31

"WHO IS THIS?" Tommy shouts the question instead of a greeting into the phone. He is back to using the post office phone, his cell phone shoved into his back pocket and his gun tucked into his waistband. The women are grateful it is no longer in his hand. He'd been so angry over what Nadine did—the kind of angry that can make a person do reckless, regrettable things. They'd feared—real, certain fear, unlike anything they'd felt up to that point—that he would kill her.

Instead, he'd just paced and cussed, paced and cussed, ignoring the ringing phone, intermittently talking to himself. "They're back there trying to get in. I can hear them." He walked over to the counter, stepped behind it, and craned his neck to see into the back part of the building, looking backward and forward, from his hostages to the area where—he wasn't wrong—they could all hear people doing something to the building.

If they gained access and came in, the women wondered, would he shoot them? Himself? Was that the way this would end? The thought brought on more fear. Sylvie thought of Robert. Morrow thought of Maya. Blythe thought of Aaron. Nadine thought about her secret, of dying without ever telling it.

They were all lost in their private thoughts when Tommy moved to the phone, picking it up like it was what had wronged him as he waited for someone to answer. When he yelled, "Who is this?" they all jumped in unison and looked wide-eyed at one another before looking to Tommy. Now they watch him listen to whoever is speaking, each one still trembling and rattled. They don't want anything else to set him off.

"Where's the girl?" he asks, spittle hitting the receiver. He is holding the phone so tightly his knuckles are white. They cannot hear what is said in return. It was better when he was using his cell phone; they could at least sort of hear what the person on the other end was saying. "I'm talking about the girl I've been talking to all day," Tommy says. There is more silence as he listens again. "I ain't talking to you, dude. I want the one I've already been talking to. I need to speak to that girl."

He needs Hope, Sylvie thinks. *We all do.*

Outside, in the NOC, thanks to the technology available to the new team, everyone has listened to Tommy's ravings through the speaker, the escalating anger they tried and failed to talk him down from. Finally, Chris gives up further attempts at discussion and turns to scan the outer area, finding Hope on the back wall. With a frown on his face, he waves his arm to summon her.

She goes to take a step toward him, but Bo places his hand on her arm to halt her. "I told you," he says. "Rapport. It's not easy to establish, and it isn't something you can just hand off to someone else." He raises his eyebrows at her. "Now you just need lady luck on your side."

Hope hums the Sinatra song as she walks away from him and enters the back area to take Chris's seat. Across from her, Adam watches as she puts on the headset. She has done this many times before, in a different NOC, with a slightly different setup, with a different face across from her. And though she ran away from it, she can do it again.

"Hello, Tommy?" she asks. She is pleased there is no waver in her voice. There is, she realizes, no waver inside her at all. A resignation, a determination, has replaced all nervousness. She has been assigned a task, and the task is to see this thing through.

"What's the deal?" Tommy asks. "They said you're leaving?" Tommy doesn't have a waver in his voice either. But he does have anger with an undercurrent of desperation.

"There's another team here now," she explains. "From the county. They are more . . . set up to handle things than we are."

"Seemed to me we were doing just fine without the county," Tommy huffs.

"Well, if that were true," she says, "then your hostages would already be released."

There is a silence. Then, "And I'd be in jail for the rest of my life."

This she remembers how to deal with, her training ingrained in her no matter how long she has ignored it. Time to minimize. "You won't go to jail for the rest of your life. Not if I have any say about it." She pauses. "And I do. I will."

"If you don't mind me saying, you didn't have any say about whether you got to stay here and talk to me. So I'm not sure you've got much say in what they do to me after this."

"Actually, there's lots we can do. And the sooner we resolve this, the more bargaining power we have."

"Who's we?" Tommy asks.

She smiles, thinking of Bo, of his belief in the rapport between her and Tommy. "You and me," she says.

There is another spate of silence as he takes this in. She needs him to believe she is there for him, that she is on his side. She glances over at the team who wanted to be where she is right now. In some ways, she is on his side and not theirs. Needless to say, once this is over and Tommy is in custody, that can no longer be true. But Tommy doesn't need to know that. He won't know until it is too late.

"When's Covey going to be here?" Tommy changes the subject. "You promised."

"I did," she says. "And I always keep my promises. Do you remember the promise I asked you to make?"

"Yes," he grouses.

"Are you still going to keep that promise?" A silence follows, and she imagines that he is looking at the women, remembering his promise not to harm them.

"Tommy?" she prompts. "You can't expect me to keep my promise if you're not going to keep yours."

"Yeah," he says, his voice gruff. "I'm gonna keep it."

"Good," says Hope. "I'm glad to hear that."

On the screen in front of her a text box pops up. It is Adam asking, What did he promise?

She types her response, That he would not harm anyone. Across from her, Adam gives her a thumbs-up, looking relieved. But also surprised. *He thinks*, Hope suddenly understands, *that I'm a rookie, that I'm just winging this and I've never negotiated before. No wonder this team is so anxious to move me out of the way.*

"I don't have an exact ETA on Covey's arrival, but your stepmother said she was going to get here as fast as she could. She said she needed to get ready first, and then she had to make the trip here."

Tommy gives a dismissive little laugh. "That woman won't go anywhere without her face on."

"In my experience, that's true of a lot of women," Hope says. She thinks of her mom, who always fussed at her for not wearing lipstick. She hears her voice even now: "*You need color or you look sick.*" Even on her deathbed her mother had insisted Hope help her sit up and apply the bare minimum of makeup. "*Wouldn't want anyone to think I'm dying,*" she'd quipped. Sometimes Hope was able to laugh when she said this. Sometimes she had to excuse herself and cry. After her mother was gone, Hope stopped wearing makeup altogether. She stopped doing a lot of things. But she cannot think about that now.

"Tell me about Covey," she says, to keep Tommy talking.

"Not much to tell," he says. "He's a Boykin spaniel, a hunting dog. He was . . . with my dad when he died. They say that he came and sat right by my dad when he . . ." She hears the emotion pinch off his voice and gives him time to compose himself, listening to the pain that radiates through the air between them. A big part of negotiation, she knows, is just listening to someone whom no one has listened to in a long time.

"Back when I still lived at home," he resumes, "I helped train him. I went on his first hunts. So he was sorta my dog too. And after my dad was . . . gone, I wanted to bring him to live with us, but Jane—that's my stepmother—she said she couldn't part with him. Said he was her emotional support animal now." Hope can almost hear him rolling his eyes. "We went back and forth over it, but in the end there wasn't really anything I could do about it. So he lives with her, and my dad is gone, and I—" She can hear him swallow back the tears. "I'm here," he finishes.

"I'm sorry for your loss," she says to him for the second time, feeling as inane as the words sound.

"Why are you sorry? It's not your fault." She can hear him trying to make things lighter, to banish the heavy feelings welling up inside him, threatening to spill over. He doesn't want the women he's holding hostage to see anything but the bravado he's been relying on all day. But Hope sees the crack and decides to stick her finger in it.

With all the compassion and gentleness she can muster, she says, "It's not yours either."

His retort is quick. "You don't know that."

Hope looks at the screen in front of her, at the words Adam typed, taking in the shape of the word *promise*, the roundness of the *p*, the dot on the *i*.

"What don't I know?" she asks.

There is another long silence. For a moment she thinks that he will hang up on her, that she has pushed too far. But then he speaks.

"I wasn't there," he says. "The day of the accident. I could've been, but . . ." Hope realizes she's holding her breath, waiting on how he will finish the sentence. She exhales at the same moment he says, "It doesn't matter."

Behind her, from the outer area, she hears shuffling, breathing, little human noises that remind her they are all out there listening to this, each with opinions, she is sure, of what she should be doing or saying, each deciding what they would do if they were in her shoes. But they aren't in her shoes. She looks down at her feet, scrunches all ten of her toes as she does what comes next, what feels natural. "*Trust your instincts*," her mentor Rich used to say, "*your instincts and your training*."

"It does matter," she says. "I know that better than anyone." Tommy says nothing in response, so she continues talking. "I wasn't there when my mother died," she admits, telling Tommy and a roomful of eavesdroppers the thing she hasn't been able to say to anyone in eight months.

"I was at work even though I wasn't supposed to go in that day. She was dying, and I was supposed to be with her, to help my dad with her care. But there was a situation that developed, and I—I told myself I'd just go see what was happening and then I'd go be with her after. But once I got there, things . . ." She stops talking, thinks about her choice of words going forward. She will avoid the details of the hostage situation that day, another domestic, but this one involved a man, his estranged wife, and their two children.

She continues. "Once I got there, I found out they really needed me. And I couldn't leave. Or at least I felt like I couldn't leave." It was the children that made her stay. She had to do whatever she could to make sure those kids got out of there safely. And they did—after nine and a half hours of terror, threats, and fear, they did.

She thinks about that day. Talking to the man with the gun who was threatening the lives of his family even as her personal phone buzzed in her purse, torn between needing to be in two places at once. She hadn't answered the calls, reasoning that she'd check on her mother once the siege was over. She thought her dad just wanted her help. He was afraid of being left to care for her mother alone; he wanted Hope there all the time. She hadn't known—she couldn't have known, as Alex has pointed out to her again and again—her mother had taken a sudden and unexpected turn for the worse and he was calling to tell her to come if she wanted to say goodbye. Though she never *wanted* to say goodbye, she'd missed her chance to say it anyway.

"I broke a promise to her that day," she tells Tommy now.

"What was the promise?" Tommy asks, his voice breathy, his mouth closer to the phone than it was before. This is the connection Bo was talking about. When two total strangers find something in common, something that will bind them.

"I promised I'd be holding her hand when she went. When

she received her diagnosis—it was cancer—she made me promise that she wouldn't die alone."

"But you had to work." He rushes to her defense because in that moment she represents him too. They are united now, just two people who tried their best yet fell short anyway.

"You couldn't help it. I bet she understood that," he says. And now he is comforting her, or trying to.

Hope wants to smile and cry at the same time. She won't tell him that she could've helped it, that she could've let someone else step in. It is beside the point now. "Just the week before, my mom asked me to take a leave of absence. It was time I had coming to me. I kept telling myself I would. And at the same time I kept assuring myself we still had time."

"You didn't want to admit that you didn't," says Tommy.

"You're right," she says.

Another long silence elapses. Hope stares at the screen until she loses focus. When Tommy finally speaks, his voice is barely a whisper. "My dad asked me to go hunting with him that day."

Hope bites down on her lip, just enough to feel pain. "And you didn't go?"

"No," he says. She is getting used to the little defensive laugh he uses as an attempt to disengage. "I had to work. Sound familiar?" There is a pause, and then he adds, "But that wasn't even true. I just told him that because I didn't want to tell him the truth."

She takes his cue. "And what was the truth?" she asks.

"I couldn't go because I'd promised my wife I'd spend time with her."

In the background there is a noise that is a combination of exasperation and frustration. She hears a woman's voice that could only be Nadine's growing louder as, Hope imagines, she runs toward him. In the text box on her screen, Hope types, We need eyes on this situation ASAP.

"Tommy!" she hears Nadine say. "Don't you dare blame this on me! It's not my fault! I never asked that of you! I would never—" Hope hears a scuffle of some sort, then a loud clatter. And then the line goes dead.

Hope sits there stunned before rising and going into the front of the NOC with everyone else. Though the conversation with Tommy has ended, they can still hear the women and Tommy. (If Tommy was a savvier criminal, he'd have known to check the pizza boxes for bugs, but Hope is thankful it must've never crossed his mind.) She smiles as she hears the women's voices coming through loud and clear. It seems the hostages are ganging up on their captor, berating him for what he said about Nadine. There does not seem to be any danger to anyone, except perhaps to Tommy.

"Well," says Chris, "I didn't want to interrupt you since you had a good thing going there, but the dog is here." He claps his hands together. "So I guess we'd better make a plan for how we're going to let him see it."

Hope looks from the team to Bo, then back to the team. She thinks of what Bo said about lady luck, about the parallels between her experience and Tommy's and the strides she just made as they talked. If Nadine hadn't intervened, she was close enough that she might've talked him into surrendering right then and there. And an idea she'd had—and dismissed—reasserts itself more insistently this time. "I think I know what I want to do," she says.

Chapter 32

INSIDE THE POST office, it falls to Sylvie to try to restore order. She almost feels sorry for Tommy, who, in the crosshairs of Nadine's outrage, is backed up against a wall as Nadine unleashes months of her pent-up anger. Sylvie doesn't understand much of what Nadine is saying and doubts anyone else does either. The last thing she fully understood was "Is this why? Is this why?" But Nadine didn't wait for an answer from Tommy before she ranted some more.

Tommy winces about every fourth word but doesn't defend himself. He looks around for an escape route, but there is nowhere he can go to get away, as she will surely follow him around the room until she either wears herself out or runs out of words. Tommy is as trapped as they are.

Unless, thinks Sylvie, *I offer him an out.*

"You could let us go." She has to raise her voice to have any hope of him hearing her over Nadine. He doesn't respond, so she says it again, changing one word. "You should let us go."

"*I always start off by simply asking them to let the hostages go*," she remembers Robert saying. All those years that he was a cop, she was a teacher. He had the more exciting job, so his stories shared over the dinner table, riding in the car, or sitting on the beach just a few miles away from here were usually better than hers. She'd listened closely to all of his stories, many more than once. Though she never thought she'd have to, today she is putting some of what she'd gleaned to use.

Tommy's eyes meet her own, and for a moment, Sylvie sees him consider her suggestion. But then he shakes his head no. Still, there was a moment he wanted to let them go. That moment means something. He is getting closer to giving up. She needs to de-escalate the situation, restore calm, and give Tommy the chance to mull over her request a little more. Perhaps Tommy will, with a little more time, reach the right conclusion, do the right thing, and surrender.

She moves closer to Nadine, places her hand gently on her arm. The sensation startles her, and she whips her head around, wild-eyed, until she sees that it is just Sylvie. "Honey," Sylvie says to her. "I think that's enough for now." *Sometimes*, Sylvie thinks, *it pays to be the old lady.*

Nadine's face goes slack as she takes a step back from Tommy, who uses the moment to slide away from where she had him pinned. Nadine tenses, but Sylvie takes her hand and leads her away, back toward the stools. "Why don't we all just have a seat?" she says.

She poses it as a question, but it is really a command. Sylvie uses her teacher voice, calm but firm. In some ways, she used to tease Robert, their jobs weren't that far apart. Every day teaching middle schoolers was a protracted negotiation, the siege lasting the length of a school year. Robert liked to joke that he didn't know which of their jobs was more dangerous.

Sylvie is pleased that Blythe, Morrow, and even Nadine yield to her suggestion. Except for Tommy, everyone moves back toward the stools, the heightened energy in the room dissipating some with the change of location. Once they are perched on their stools again, Sylvie says, "Why don't we have a nice conversation. Maybe get to know one another a bit better?"

Blythe and Morrow nod agreeably, but Nadine looks unconvinced. She glances over her shoulder at Tommy, who has moved as far away from them as he can get without leaving the room. He has turned his back to them as well. *Good*, Sylvie thinks. *Give him time with his thoughts, time to hopefully form a plan to end this.*

Morrow fumbles around in her bag for a moment before extracting a small box from it. She holds it up. "I have these cards we could use," she says. "They're conversation cards." She pulls a face. "They were meant for my daughter. An attempt to get her to talk to me. She's a teenager, so . . ." Her voice trails off as she looks down at the box. "Anyway, she took one look at the box and said it was a lame idea." Morrow turns the box over and studies the back of it. She shrugs and looks up. "They've never even been opened."

"But she came here," Blythe says. "She came to the window." Blythe thinks of her mother, wondering if she stayed or left after Blythe never came back from the post office, if she even knows what's happening. She wishes her mother had come to the post office window and pounded on it, had called her name.

"That's true," says Morrow. "She did. It surprised me, her coming here." She looks toward the window. "I wonder if she's still out there or if they made her leave."

The other women shrug. No one in the room knows what is going on out there. As the day has dragged on, they've looked out the windows less and less. Seeing the free world is its own kind of torture. Blythe lets herself imagine walking out of here. She might just fall to her knees and kiss the parking lot asphalt when she does.

"She looks like you," Nadine speaks up. Her voice is ragged and hoarse from all her yelling.

"Oh," says Morrow, sitting up a little taller. "You think so?"

"Yeah, I mean, what I saw of her, she did."

Morrow gives them an odd smile. "Well, that's nice to hear, considering she's adopted."

"Oh, I had no idea," says Nadine. "I'm sorry."

"Don't be sorry," says Morrow. The odd smile on her face is replaced by a genuine one. "I like hearing it, actually. There've been so many times I've studied her face, trying to find something of me in there, even though I know it's genetically impossible." She pauses. "Genetics," she says, wistful. "That's actually the reason I came in here today."

"Genetics?" asks Blythe.

Morrow runs her hand halfway down her ponytail, then stops and rummages in her tote. She produces the package she's checked on numerous times since she entered the post office. "This," she says, as if that is an explanation. She chuckles at the blank stares looking back at her. "Sorry. I'm not making any sense." She gives the padded envelope a little shake. "It's a DNA test. My daughter's DNA test. She wants to find her biological mother. Or, as she says, her 'real' mom. Her real mom who will, no doubt, let her get a tattoo."

"A . . . tattoo?" asks Blythe.

Morrow makes a scoffing noise. "My husband and I made a rule a long time ago. We had a friend who got a tattoo as a teenager, and later in life she regretted it, thought it looked childish and unprofessional. We watched her go through a pretty long, pretty painful process to have it removed. It led us to make the rule that our kids weren't allowed to get a tattoo till they have graduated from college to, you know, have more time for their brains to develop."

Morrow thinks about this before she adds, "We made the stakes pretty high. If they get a tattoo before they graduate from college, we stop paying for college." She shrugs, then continues. "Our son never questioned it. Even now that he's an adult, he's said he's glad we made him really think about the permanence of the decision the way we did."

She shakes her head. "And then our daughter comes along, and getting a tattoo is the only thing she seems to want in life. She brings it up all the time, thinks we're so backward and uptight. All her friends are doing it, and why can't she? She doesn't get the part where we are just trying to think about her, for her own good."

She looks down at the envelope she is holding, squinting at the address printed on the front. "We've been fighting about it a lot lately. We fought about it last night. And later, when I went up to check on her before bed, I found her with the DNA test. She freaked out and chased me out of the room, and, well, we haven't really talked about it since. I tried to get her to talk to me this morning, but she just stormed out of the house and left for school."

"And you're sure she was taking the DNA test so she can find her biological mother?" Sylvie asks the question gently, her voice softer than usual.

Morrow purses her lips. "Maybe not her mom specifically. We have talked about it in the past, submitting her DNA to one of those genealogical sites. You know, just to see if she has any blood relatives out there. I understand the curiosity, the wanting to know where she came from. I never stood in the way of that. But I thought it was something we'd do together, that we'd talk about it before she did it, at least."

"I know where I came from," Blythe quips. "And that doesn't necessarily make things better." The others chuckle and nod their agreement.

Morrow looks down at her lap, rubs her palms along her thighs. "But this whole thing with her desperately wanting a tattoo and me holding out has driven us apart. We used to be so close. We joked that she was my broke best friend. But then we moved here and she just withdrew. I thought she'd come around eventually. But it's her senior year. In the fall she goes to college and . . ." She drops the envelope back inside the tote. "I fear I'm losing her. And then I saw her with that test last night, and it was like confirmation that she'd rather have any other mother than me."

Nadine speaks up with confusion in her voice. "But then you were going to mail the test?"

Morrow nods. "After she left for school this morning, I thought about it—about what I could do to make things right. So I went up to her room and found the test. She'd thrown it in the trash, but I was able to pull everything together and get it ready to send off. I sat around all morning debating about whether I could go through with it. I mean, this is a Pandora's box I can't close once it's opened. Who knows what will come from it? Maybe she will find her bio mom. Maybe she will love her more and I will lose her for real. But the more I thought about it, the more I knew that—it's kind of like the tattoo—denying her this only makes it more enticing. And so, before I could change my mind, I got dressed and came here." Morrow thinks about being pulled over on the way there, but she leaves that part out. Still, the word *invalid* hovers in her mind.

Sylvie's head is nodding in approval. "I think you're doing the right thing," she says. Blythe and Nadine make affirming noises. "I think it's a good way to tell her you're there for her, no matter what."

"I hope so," says Morrow.

"I mean, she came here. She's clearly worried about you. She snuck past the cops and took a big risk to try to get to you. I don't think that's someone you're in danger of losing," says Blythe.

"I think it's just a kid trying to find her own way," Nadine adds. She looks around the room before looking back at the other women. "It's hard enough to find your way as an adult."

They all nod in solidarity, then silence falls for a moment until Sylvie says, "I almost got a tattoo when I turned fifty. My husband called it my midlife almost crisis."

"He didn't want you to do it?"

Sylvie thinks about her answer before speaking. "He wouldn't have forbidden it if I'd pushed to do it, but no, he preferred I didn't." She pauses again, then adds, "I still kind of wish I had. 'Course I'm too old now."

"Aw, you're not too old," says Nadine.

Sylvie shakes her head but says nothing. Her skin is thinner now than it was then. She has age spots and bruises easily. She's not sure putting needles and dye in the mix would be the best thing at this point in her life. But if she could go back and do it over, she would.

"What were you going to get?" asks Blythe. "If you'd gotten one?"

Sylvie pauses, her eyes moving as she thinks about her answer before they widen with a look of surprise. She looks from woman to woman. "I can't remember!" They all crack up laughing, less because it's that funny and more because, for a moment, it is a relief just to laugh. But then the ringing phone cuts through the sound of their laughter.

Chapter 33

Outside in the NOC, Hope is standing her ground as the county team argues with her about her proposal to take the dog, Covey, inside the post office, to enter the fray, as it were. She struggles to make them understand her conviction that this is the only way to do this. To parade the dog in front of the windows and let Tommy merely see him isn't enough to make an impact. To try to coax Tommy to come outside and engage with the dog in person with armed men all around will be a hard sell. She feels it in her gut: To assume the risk on her part and go in with the dog will change everything.

"What if something bad happens?" says Adam.

"It won't," she says.

"But you can't guarantee that," he counters.

"You're right," she says. "I can't."

"You need a team around you," says Chris.

Hope thinks, but does not say, that she hasn't had a team around her in eight months. Instead, she says, "I'll be with those women in there. The ones who've attacked him and yelled at him and manipulated him, the ones I've spoken to personally and worked to free for hours." Hope stands a little taller, looks from Chris to Adam. "They'll be my team."

Chris and Adam exchange glances. Though they are uncertain,

Hope is not. She knows that taking Covey into the post office is the way to end this thing. She feels it in her core, in the same place where all the things that matter reside, the things that remain. This is the instinct her mentor spoke about often. But it is one thing to feel it inside; it is another to act on it. She used to have a quote by Joan Baez hanging on her locker door back at the station in Philly that said, "Action is the antidote to despair." This has been a day of despair. Action is required.

She looks to Bo, who gives her a nod. She can't tell whether he thinks this is a bad idea or a good one. He probably thinks this is too big a risk like everyone else does, but he is keeping his thoughts to himself. The others have said plenty about how crazy they think this is.

The SWAT commander speaks up. "I can't let you go in there on your own. My team will all go in the building with you. They can stay in the vestibule and monitor from out there since that room's so small, but one of my guys *will* go in with you. That's the only way we can let you assume this risk."

Hope thinks about it. It's not ideal. It's not what she envisioned. But she can tell that this is as far as she's going to get. She will have to acquiesce on this one point. She nods her assent.

"And he has to put his gun on the counter in plain sight the whole time. If he so much as flinches in its direction, we will all go in."

Hope knows Tommy will balk at this. But it's the only way he will get time with his beloved dog. She thinks she can sell him on it. "Okay," she says. "Let's do it." She goes to the phone before they can change their minds.

Tommy answers immediately, and with just one word, "Hello," she can hear it: The fight is almost out of him. He is weary, both physically and emotionally. The conversation about his father only wrung him out further. The intel says he's standing far away from the hostages now, keeping his distance with his back turned to them, which is a change. He wants out, but he doesn't know how to get out. That's what she's here for. It is what she intends to facilitate when she gets inside. This is what she and Bo had talked about earlier in the day, the point of surrender. You just have to wait for them to be ready to give up. *Everyone gets there eventually*, she thinks. *Even negotiators.*

"Hi, Tommy," Hope says. "Covey is here. Are you ready to see him?"

"Yes," he says. "But how?"

"Before I tell you, I want you to reassure me of something," she says.

He sighs. "What?"

"That you remember the promise you made to me."

He sighs again. "I do."

"Then remind me what it is," she says.

"No one will be harmed today," he says, then mumbles something she can't make out.

"What'd you say?" she asks.

"Nothing," he says.

"Tell me what you said, Tommy, or I don't tell you about Covey."

He laughs a little. "I said you should've made these women make the same promise. *They* keep attacking *me*."

Just let them go and that won't happen anymore, Hope thinks. But before she can say it, he speaks again. "What does the promise have to do with Covey?"

"Because I'm going to bring Covey in there. It's important you keep your promise and this goes smoothly, with no harm done to anyone—not me, not the hostages, and not you. Or the dog," she adds.

"I would never hurt Covey," he says.

"Well, then I need reassurance about hurting the humans."

He exhales into the phone, his breath hissing across the line. "I won't hurt any humans. And it's just you? Coming in here with Covey? I don't want no cops."

"I'm afraid it's not that simple. There have got to be some rules, or the people in charge will never allow this. You have to go by those rules, or this doesn't happen."

There is a pause before he says, resigned, "What are the rules?"

"First, before I can come in there, you need to put your gun down somewhere out of reach and visible through the glass. An armed SWAT officer will be coming in with me and will be watching everything that happens. If he sees you go anywhere near the gun, it's game over. I'll bring Covey in on a leash, and you will need to unlock the post office door to allow us to get in. Are you following all this?"

There is another pause. "How do I know that the SWAT dude isn't going to overpower me the minute he gets in here? That you're not setting me up and using Covey as bait?"

Hope hadn't considered using the dog as bait. It hadn't even crossed her mind. "Because I wouldn't do that to you," she says.

"Okay," he says.

"One last detail. The SWAT team will accompany me into the vestibule just like the officers did with the pizza delivery. One of them will come into the actual post office with me, but the rest will stay in the vestibule area the entire time I am in the post office. Just to reiterate: You are not to pick up or move toward your gun at any point."

She pauses but then continues, her words coming in a rush. "I'm taking a huge risk here, Tommy. It's not normal for a negotiator to enter a barricade situation. Most of my colleagues out here think I'm crazy." She softens her voice intentionally. "But I know that seeing Covey matters a lot to you. And I didn't think just seeing him through the window would be the same."

"It wouldn't," Tommy agrees.

"So promise me that you're going to fully cooperate with everything I've said."

"I already promised you," he says, the whiny tone creeping back into his voice.

"That was a different promise," she says.

"Fine," he says. "I promise."

"Where are you going to put your gun?" she asks.

"On the counter, I guess," he says.

"When SWAT gets in there, they're going to watch through the glass while you put the gun down and move away from it. They won't allow me and the dog to enter the building until you've done so. Okay?" she says.

"Yeah," he says, "I got it. But I'm going to put those women around me so no one can take a shot at me without going through them."

Hope decides not to fight him on this but sees the irony of using his captives for his own protection. "Okay," she says. "I'll see you in a minute."

After reviewing the plan one more time with the SWAT commander, she walks outside, where Covey is waiting with Tommy's stepmother, Jane. Overhead, the sun has dropped a little. With any luck the hostages will be free before it gets fully dark. The dog will be the change agent they've needed all day. Though she never considered using Covey as bait, she is definitely using him as an emotional manipulator.

"I could take him in," offers Jane, who grips Covey's leash with a worried expression.

Hope reaches out for the leash and squeezes Jane's shoulder.

"We can't let you do that," she says. "Please don't worry. Everything will be fine."

Jane hands over Covey's leash. "Take good care of him," Jane calls as they begin making their way toward the building. She doesn't know which "him" Jane means—Covey or Tommy. It doesn't matter. Hope intends to take care of them all.

Chapter 34

INSIDE THE POST office, Tommy hangs up and strides boldly to the windows for the first time in hours. When the four women get up and join him there, he looks over at them with exasperation. "What are y'all doing? Go sit back down. This doesn't involve you."

Sylvie crosses her arms and repeats a sentiment from hours ago. "We are trapped in this room with you and have been for hours. So, yes, it does involve us."

Beside her Nadine asks, "What's going on, Tommy?" Though they'd tried to eavesdrop on his conversation, it was hard to understand what was happening based just on Tommy's curt responses. But something, it is clear, is happening.

"She's bringing Covey in here," he says.

"She who?" says Nadine.

"That woman I've been talking to all day."

"But . . . why?" asks Sylvie. She thinks, but does not say aloud, that this is highly unusual. She can't believe it's being allowed. She can't believe Robert didn't say, "Over my dead body," and put a stop to it immediately.

"Because it's what I wanted," he says. "She asked what I wanted. I asked to see Covey, so she's making it happen."

"I just assumed they'd bring him up to the window, let you see him and let you know he's here on the premises. Maybe they'd tell you that you could pet him if you come out," Sylvie says. "That's what I would've done if I was in charge."

"Well, you're not in charge," Tommy retorts.

"That's true," Sylvie agrees. "I'm not." She says no more but hums a few bars of "Amazing Grace" as they observe what's occurring outside. She expects Tommy to tell her to hush, but he doesn't. He's too intent on what's about to happen to bother.

"I sang that in church when I was a kid. A solo," says Nadine. "It's one of my favorites."

Sylvie keeps her eyes on the window, spots Robert in the distance. "Mine too," she says.

Outside the post office, Hope's assigned SWAT officer introduces himself as Dale and again goes over the protocol. The two of them, plus Covey, who has curled up at Hope's feet, hang back as the rest of the SWAT team prepares to enter the post office. Hope doesn't think about what she is doing. She doesn't think about the risk or the threat. Instead, she allows herself to think about the last negotiation she did. How, nine and a half hours later, when it was finally over, she grabbed her phone and called her dad back.

"Hey, Dad," she said. "The situation is resolved. I'm sorry I couldn't answer earlier."

"Did everyone make it out?" her dad asked. There was something in his voice, a broken strain she'd never heard before.

"Yeah," she replied, wary. She'd left him alone with her mom too long, that was all, she reasoned. He was just exhausted. "The mom and two kids are safe. And the suspect was taken into custody without incident."

"Good," he said. "I'm proud of you." There was a pause, and in that pause was a hole Hope felt herself begin to fall into even before her father told her what she didn't want to hear. It was a big black hole that, in some ways, she is still falling through now, here, today.

"We lost her this afternoon," he said. "She went peacefully."

"But they said . . . ," she argued, as if the right words could change the outcome. "They said it could be days. They said we had time."

"I know," he said. "We didn't expect this. You couldn't have known. You had to work, darlin'. It's not your fault."

But there had been a moment, not when her dad called the first time, but when he called the second. It wasn't like him. She should've answered. She should've let one of her team members step in to talk to the suspect. It would've been just that easy to hand over the reins and go to her mother, to keep her promise to her mother instead of her commitment to her job.

In that singular moment she had a choice. And she'd chosen her job. She'd walked off after she'd hung up with her dad and never returned. She'd blamed the job, then run from it. But it is really herself she blames, and she can't seem to run from herself.

She holds up a finger. "I just need a second," she says, handing off the leash to Dale and running back over to Brower's car. She opens the door, reaches for her purse where she stowed it, and pulls out a piece of paper that's been folded and folded and folded again. She shoves it into her pocket, then races back over to Dale, reaches for Covey's leash, and loops it once around her fist.

Dale looks down at her. "You ready?" he asks her.

"Yes," she says.

Ahead of them, the group advances, guns raised, barking out commands as they reach the outer door and begin the process of entering the building. There are seven SWAT officers, plus Hope and the dog. The group inside the post office pivots to watch through the glass as an initial wave of three officers enters the vestibule. They come to stand in front of the glass, peering in.

Tommy indicates for the women to circle him, one in front, one behind, one to his right, and one to his left. "Come with me," he orders, and for once no one argues or has anything smart to say in response. It's hard to talk when your heart is in your throat. Tommy crosses the room, and with his hostages positioned around him as human shields, he goes over to the counter and lays down his gun, holds up his hands to show that he is no longer armed, and takes several steps away from the counter, the women moving in tandem. The officers outside scan the room before nodding that it's safe and giving a sign that the rest of the team can come in.

Together the five of them watch as Hope enters, gripping a leash that is connected to a medium-sized spaniel with curly brown fur. Blythe looks from the dog to Tommy, seeing him see the dog he asked for. She watches as his eyes fill with tears and feels unexpected tears prick at her own eyes. She cannot help but think of Murphy, his loss still fresh and sharp. She feels unexpected sympathy rise for Tommy, who lost his dad, which has to be worse than losing your dog.

Blythe wouldn't know. She never knew her dad. He abandoned her mother before Blythe was born. It is why, she thinks, her mother puts so much emphasis on being successful. She's never had anyone but herself. Blythe lets herself sit with this thought about what made her mom the way she is and what made Blythe the way she is. People are shaped by their circumstances, formed by what happens to them, for better or for worse, in lack and in plenty. She resents how her mom sees her. But she hasn't done such a great job at trying to see her mom.

She thinks back to last night on the porch, drinking wine with her mom, laughing and scheming and feeling a rare closeness to her. She never wanted that feeling to end. She would've done anything to hold on to it, including coming here and doing something she didn't want to do. Maybe there's still a way to have what they had last night, apart from departed dogs and old boyfriends. Blythe thinks about the song Sylvie just hummed. Maybe grace could still amaze her.

Chapter 35

HERE WE ALL *are now,* thinks Sylvie. *Here we all are, together. Still.*

Once Hope, her guard, and Covey are safely inside the room, the women climb back on their stools with a resignation that makes their shoulders droop. Hope drifts into the center of their little circle and stays there as she takes in her new surroundings. Then she goes to each woman, doing the physical version of what she'd done on the phone hours ago, making sure they are okay, that they have no urgent needs. When she gets to Sylvie, the older woman tells her, "My only urgent need is to get out of here by suppertime. I have a husband who will be waiting for me." Sylvie does not add that he is waiting just outside. She's betting Hope doesn't know that.

Hope gives her a thumbs-up sign. "I approve of this plan," she says and smiles. It might be unorthodox for a negotiator to go in with the hostages, Sylvie thinks, but having Hope with them makes things just a little bit better. Or maybe it's the dog in the room. Dogs make everything better.

Sylvie and Robert always had dogs. When one died, they observed a mourning period but inevitably went out and got a new dog. Through the years they had big dogs and little dogs, female dogs and male dogs, mixed breeds from the pound and purebreds they paid far too much money for. Dogs that were afraid of the rain, dogs that barked at anything that moved, dogs that chewed up furniture, dogs that slept with them, dogs that slept with their son. Each one still holds a place in her heart.

But when their last one died, they did the math. If a dog lives an average of thirteen years, they had reached the ages where the dog could outlive at least one of them. It was the most depressing calculation she'd ever done. So they did what they felt was the reasonable thing and remained dogless, yet another insult of old age.

Sylvie looks over at Tommy in the far corner of the room. He is on the floor beside the dog with his arms encircling him, his face buried in his fur. Seeing him curled around the dog the way he is makes Sylvie think of a Latin phrase: *incurvatus in se*, which means "curved inward on oneself." She cannot remember where she heard it. Just one of those tidbits she's filed away through the years. As she recalls, it basically means your only concern is yourself.

She thinks of another phrase, not Latin, but applicable: "He who lies down with dogs gets up with fleas." She bites back a smile and turns to Hope.

"How long are you going to leave him over there?" Sylvie points at Tommy.

Hope shrugs, then gestures at the officers outside. "I told them to give me some time. I'd like to convince him to surrender and walk out of here on his own, let it be his decision to let you guys go. But they're not going to wait forever."

Sylvie nods her approval as an understanding dawns on her. There is no way this ends without them being released, without Tommy surrendering. In that way, appeasing Tommy was also ending his siege.

"Gutsy move," Sylvie says. "Bringing the dog in here yourself."

Hope shrugs again. "Well, it came down to this being the best way to handle it. And since I've been the one talking to him all day, I was the most obvious choice. He at least sorta trusts me."

"I could only hear half of the conversation, but it seems like you really made a connection with him," Sylvie says.

Hope pauses before speaking, choosing her words. When she thought about coming in here, she thought about dealing with Tommy. She hadn't really given much thought to dealing with the hostages too. *Oh well*, she thinks, *I'm here now. The only way out is through.*

"We both lost a parent recently," Hope says.

Sylvie nods. "I thought that might be it. I heard his side and thought you must've been mirroring his feelings."

Mirroring, Hope thinks. *That's an odd choice of words, a negotiation term.* But she doesn't comment on that. "Well, it actually wasn't hard, or even intentional. We've gone through some things that are . . . eerily similar. Similar regrets, similar timing."

Sylvie keeps nodding along as her eyes stray from Hope and toward the windows that face the parking lot. A smile crosses her face. "Lady luck," Sylvie says.

"What'd you say?" Hope asks, her heart rate rising as, in her head, she hears Bo's voice saying the exact same thing.

"Nothing," says Sylvie, waving her hand. "Just something I heard once." But her cheeks are bright red.

"Where'd you hear it?" Hope asks. She notices the other three hostages lean forward on their stools.

"Oh, I don't know," Sylvie says. "Probably on some cop show or something. I watch a lot of *Law and Order*."

No, you don't, Hope thinks. But she doesn't say it. Instead, she says, "What did you mean by 'lady luck'?"

Sylvie holds her breath for a moment, then exhales it all out in a whoosh. "It just means that sometimes in life you find common ground in unexpected ways. There's some similarity that you hit upon with a total stranger that you couldn't possibly have orchestrated apart from—"

"Lady luck," Hope finishes. She gives Sylvie a one-sided grin, and Sylvie looks away. "You know, that's the second time today that I've heard that." She says this to Sylvie's profile. She waits a moment, but Sylvie doesn't respond. "I've never heard it before," she continues. "And now I've heard it twice in one day." There is a teasing quality to her voice as she adds, "Do you think that's also lady luck? A coincidence? Or is there someone out there we both know who has said it to both of us?" She waits again for Sylvie to respond. When she doesn't, Hope says, "Bo?"

At the sound of the name, Sylvie turns to face Hope, dispensing with further pretense. "Actually, it's Robert," she says. "Bo was an old nickname from when he was a rookie. He used it so he could be here today without you guys figuring out the connection."

Hope shakes her head as she recalls all the moments when, if she'd been paying closer attention, he gave clues. The concern in his voice whenever he spoke of the hostages, the way he reached out to the station and offered to come over, his constant walking over to see what was going on inside the post office, his volunteering to deliver the pizzas and even suggesting that "the old lady" be the one to receive them. He'd said it was because they would be seen as less of a threat, but it was just because he'd wanted to lay eyes on his wife. A senior citizen has fooled them all.

Good for him, Hope thinks. She gives Sylvie a reassuring smile. *Good for them.* He came as soon as he heard. He did what he could to look out for his wife. He couldn't bear to be separated from her, especially when she needed him.

She thinks of Alex, of how long they've been separated, a

choice she made apart from him. Steeped in grief and regret, she'd fled to Sunset Beach, but in doing so, she'd left her husband behind. Then when he offered to join her, she'd told him to stay behind. At some point he stopped asking why she doesn't want him there. He knows the answer will be the same one she always gives: "I don't know what I want."

An acute longing rushes through her as she misses her husband in a way she hasn't allowed herself to for months. She hasn't allowed herself much of anything since that day—not feelings, not comfort, not joy, not . . . hope. She looks over at Tommy, curled beside his beloved dog.

"What do you want?" she'd asked him when this all began.

What do you want? she asks herself now.

"Why didn't you tell us?" Blythe asks Sylvie, pulling Hope from her reverie. She looks back to the women.

Sylvie glances nervously in Tommy's direction and then back at the little ring of them. "I didn't want him to know," she says, lowering her voice. "I didn't want him to use it as some sort of leverage."

"When we were in the bathroom you could've told us," Blythe says. She sounds hurt, like she has been lied to.

Sylvie rushes to reassure her. "I didn't know when we were in the bathroom. I didn't know till he came in carrying the pizzas."

"That was him?" Nadine says with surprise in her voice. "He's way taller than you."

Sylvie smiles back and nods. "That he is. But we've made the height difference work out for almost . . ." Her voice gives out on her as she thinks of their approaching anniversary, of where things could be by then. "Almost fifty-five years," she manages to finish.

"Fifty-five years," says Nadine, incredulous. "Tommy and I didn't even make it three."

They hear the sound of the dog's collar jingle and all turn to look, expecting Tommy to be rushing over at the mention of his name, but he is still on the floor with his back to them. The dog's back and Tommy's back rise and fall in tandem. Sylvie wonders if Tommy has fallen asleep again. Now it doesn't matter. They will not need to attempt an escape with the negotiator and an officer in their midst.

So she asks Hope the question that's been on her mind all day. "Has Robert been . . . okay? Today?"

"Okay?" asks Hope. "What do you mean? Is he . . . ill?" She doesn't want Bo, er, Robert, to be ill.

"He's been having some problems with . . . forgetting things. It's reached a level of concern recently." She frowns. "I wrote it off as just aging at first, but . . . I can't anymore."

Hope's heart sinks. "You mean like dementia? Alzheimer's?"

Sylvie looks down at the envelope under her stool. "Something," she says. "We've not gone so far as to see a doctor about it. Though I know we should, it hasn't been going on that long and I've—" She raises her gaze back to eye level with Hope. "I've been pretending it isn't happening. Going to the doctor feels like admitting that it is, but then this weekend . . ."

She looks over to Morrow, to Blythe. "You two weren't the only ones here to mail something that you were uncertain about today." She slides off her stool, retrieves the envelope, then takes her seat again before holding it up for them to see.

"I'm supposed to be sending this to our son." She points to the address. "He's also Robert. Junior. It's papers to give him power of attorney over our affairs, to take the control away from his dad. He's insisting we sell our house here. He wants to move us to a memory care facility near where he lives in Virginia, which is where we're from." She stops, swallows.

"He and his family came to visit this past weekend for some

family time. Or I thought that's what they were coming for. But it was a ruse. He was really here to give me these papers to sign." She shakes her head. "He made me promise that I'd sign them and mail them back so he could"—she holds up her hands and makes air quotes—"get things moving."

Sylvie looks down and runs her hands along the envelope, and as she does, Hope sees a single tear hit the manila surface, then sink into the paper, leaving behind a dark circle. Soon more tears join it. No one says a word as Sylvie weeps silently. After a while she speaks, but she doesn't look up. "We waited our whole lives for this. To be here, in this place, full-time and not just for a vacation. To have time for just the two of us, without work or family or anything to get in our way. And now . . . our son wants to take it away. And maybe it's the right thing to do—I know it might be—but that doesn't mean it feels right. Or good."

"Why is he making you sell your house?" Morrow, who has been very quiet ever since she shared about her daughter, speaks up.

"He's afraid I can't handle Robert by myself. He says I need help, and I don't really have any here. No family, and the friends we've made are nice, but they're more like acquaintances." Sylvie presses her mouth in a thin line and lowers her eyebrows. "Keep in mind he's not volunteering to help. He's saying there will be people who can help at the place where he'd put us."

That's exactly what it feels like, Sylvie thinks. *Like he's shelving us, like a child who has outgrown his toys, so he puts them away.* But she does not say that to these women. What she's said just now is already more than she's said to anyone. Yet it feels natural to unburden herself, a relief of sorts. After all they've been through together, why not admit to why she was here in the first place?

"Anyway," she says, "I'm glad today is one of his good days."

Hope makes a face. "Other than one brief moment, I never

would have suspected there was any sort of problem. He's been a big help to me, actually."

"That's why he came here today," Sylvie says. "To be a help."

Hope shakes her head. "I thought that was why when he first showed up. But as I think back, I'm betting once he figured out you were here, he inserted himself any way he could."

Sylvie smiles at that. She wonders how exactly he'd put it together. He'd been watching—what else?—golf when she left the house. She'd only admitted to going to the grocery store. But maybe she'd thrown out that she needed to go by the post office as she walked out the door? She'd been flustered, her mind focused on her errand, on that infernal envelope. She can't recall just what she revealed.

She'd been more concerned about what she'd say to him after she returned than about what to say when she left. How would she tell him what she'd gone and done, and without asking him first? This isn't how their marriage was built. This isn't who they've been in all the years they've spent together. But things were changing, she'd told herself. She had to do what's best. And whether Robert agreed or not, their son was pretty convincing. So she hadn't consulted her best friend, her "life partner," as the young people say.

Then it came to her: the police scanner. He kept it running all the time. It sat on top of the TV cabinet turned to a volume so low she assumed he didn't really hear it. He just liked that it was on. She'd joked with him so many times that old habits die hard.

"So do old cops," he'd always joke back.

"What do you think you're going to hear on there?" she would tease. "Nothing ever happens here."

He'd shrug. "Keeps me company," he'd say. And she'd leave him to it.

But now it made sense. He heard the callout on the police

scanner. He searched her location on his phone or he recalled where she'd said she was going. She doesn't know exactly, but somehow he figured out his wife was in the post office they were talking about on the scanner. And he tried to come to her rescue. Just like he always had.

No matter what their son thinks, her husband is still there. He is still the man she married. After her conversation with the younger Robert, she'd almost lost sight of that. She'd focused on the present, discounting the history that preceded it. They are each other's own, and while their son came out of their union, he does not know their marriage the way he thinks he does. He does not know what they are capable of as long as they are together.

Sylvie realizes everyone is still looking at her and hurries to speak. "Thank you for saying that," she says. "I needed that reminder. Are you married?" Sylvie asks Hope, ready to shift the conversation away from her.

Hope looks down at her empty ring finger. She never wears jewelry to work. She is still standing in the middle of the circle, and with all eyes on her, she feels her face go hot, as if a spotlight has been trained directly on her. She'd thought only of the safety risk when she offered to come in here. Emotional risk never crossed her mind. She hadn't thought about what women do when they're with other women for any period of time. They tell their stories.

"I am, actually," she tells them. "He's back in Pennsylvania," she says, aiming to keep things succinct. She is not here to make new friends or bare her soul. "Where I'm from."

"Oh," says Sylvie. "So you don't live here?"

"I'm living here for a bit while I . . ." Hope does not know how to finish the sentence. While she does what? Sylvie was honest with her. She feels obliged to be honest too. She clears her throat, knowing that out in the command center, they're hearing her too. *Ah well*, she thinks, *I will probably never see any of these people again, not these women, not the officers outside looking in, not the team from county, not even Bo, who is really Robert.*

"I sort of ran away from . . . everything," she says. "I came here, to my family's place, to . . . figure some things out."

Sylvie gives her a conciliatory smile. "And how long ago was that?"

Hope's return smile is a concession of sorts. "Eight months ago."

"And your husband? He's okay with this?" Sylvie asks.

Hope shrugs. "He's just trying to be there for me, give me however much time I need. I went through a pretty hard time. I lost—" She feels the familiar knot that always fills her throat whenever she tries to talk about what happened. And here she is, talking about it for the second time today. She tries again, comes at it from a positive viewpoint. "I saved a woman and her children's lives," she says. "In a negotiation."

Sylvie's eyes grow wide, and she draws her hands together in a movement that is somewhere between a clap and a prayer. "Well, that's wonderful," she says.

Though no one in the room is aware of it, Hope feels Sylvie's validation hit her invisible shield and fall to the ground. She thinks about the award that Alex called about, the one they want to give her back home, recognition for what she did. But the people who selected her for the award don't know the whole truth about that day, how she succeeded at one thing but failed at another. Should she tell these strangers the whole truth? Hope opens her mouth to speak but closes it when a noise turns their attention to the corner of the room.

Closing

Chapter 36

Hope turns to see Tommy striding toward her, the dog right at his heels. He stops at the edge of their circle and the dog does too. "Are you going to tell them the rest?" he asks. "The things you told me? You can't leave out the rest, or it's not the truth."

"Oh, and you're the picture of virtue, Tommy," says Nadine. She points across the post office, at the small pile of discarded letters Tommy left on the floor. "He tore up people's mail. He even read some of it!" She looks at Hope. "That's a federal offense, isn't it?" She looks back at Tommy without waiting for Hope's reply. "You don't have any cause to tell anybody else about their business. You mind yours."

"Nadine, I swear—" Tommy starts, then stops. He gives her a hurt puppy look. "You didn't have to point out the mail stuff," he hisses at her.

"Oh, like they're not gonna find out after this is all over, Tommy. Like they're not gonna guess who did it." The dog gets up and goes to Nadine, jumping up to put his paws on her knees as she leans in for a nuzzle. "Hey, Covey," she says. She laughs a little as Covey licks her right across the cheek.

Tommy hangs his head. "Well, you didn't have to make it easy for them."

"It isn't like you've made it easy for any of us today," Nadine says. Covey returns to Tommy and flops down at his feet.

"And another thing," Nadine adds.

Oh no, thinks Sylvie. *It's never good when a woman adds "and another thing."*

"About that day with your daddy." Nadine looks from Tommy to Hope, making sure she's listening. "I just want her to know that it wasn't my fault that you weren't there. You made it out to her like I'm some shrew who forbid you to go hunting."

She stops. Her cheeks are red, but with embarrassment or anger, Sylvie can't tell.

Nadine narrows her eyes at Tommy, then looks back to Hope, continuing to plead her case. "He never even mentioned wanting to hunt that day. How could I have said no to something I didn't even know was happening? If it meant so much to him, then he should've said something." She points at herself. "I would've said, 'Sure, Tommy, have fun with your dad.'" She crosses her arms. "Unlike some people in this room, I can be a grown-up about things."

Tommy is silent and so is Hope. The only noise in the room is Covey scratching at his haunches and making his collar jingle. Tommy looks from Nadine to Hope, then back to Nadine, still managing to look wounded. *There was a time*, Nadine thinks as she holds his gaze, *that I would've fallen for that look. But not anymore.*

As if he has heard her thoughts, he looks away, turning to Hope again.

Sylvie holds her breath. *He's going to tell her to let us go*, she thinks. *At last.*

"I guess," says Tommy to Hope, "neither of us wants to tell the truth. Least not the whole of it."

Hope tries to swallow, but her mouth is dry. She wonders if any of those water bottles are left, but she doesn't look around for them. Instead, she focuses on Tommy, who needs to end this siege. Tommy, who is as tired of all this as his hostages are. She thinks of what Bo—Robert—said about surrender. "*You just have to wait until they are ready to give up.*" They are close, she thinks. This is the razor's edge of a negotiation. She has to convince him to let go rather than double down. She chooses her words carefully.

"I think sometimes people tell all the truth they can handle. It's not that they intend to lie. It's that to tell the whole truth—the real truth—is just too hard."

She reaches into her pocket, and when she does she sees Tommy's eyes stray to his gun and Dale bristle. "It's just this," she says, and waves the piece of paper in the air like a white flag of surrender. "It's funny, to share this in a post office," she says as she unfolds the paper, creased and softened with time and handling. "Because I wrote this letter, but then I didn't know where to send it."

She looks at the group. "It's to my mom," she explains. "I wrote it after she died. It's taken me a long time to come to terms with her death. In some ways, I'm still coming to terms with it. Even here, today, talking to you." She makes eye contact with Tommy, who nods.

"I won't read the whole thing," she continues, "because it's personal. But I will read this one part." Hope looks at the ink on the page, but the tears in her eyes blur the words. She blinks them away. She reads:

> I wasn't there for you, and I will never forgive myself for that. I broke my promise to be by your side, holding your hand, because I thought I had time when I didn't. I prioritized strangers instead of rushing to your side. I struggle with that decision every day, and I think I always will. I exiled myself here because of it.

> And the truth is, I don't know how to get back. The life I had before is gone. And I don't know how to build a new one. I don't want to build a new one without you.

Hope looks up at the group. "For a long time I told myself a version of the truth. A version that was close enough to live with. I told myself it was the job's fault. That if it hadn't been for the job, I'd have been there. I've lived with that version for a long time. But lately I feel it changing. And I think that's a good thing. I have to face the actual truth—look at all the facets of it—before I can move forward."

Tommy's face softens as he gives a single nod and reaches down to pat the dog's head. Covey licks Tommy's hand, bathing it with his long pink tongue. Tommy dries his hand on his jeans and looks at all of them, his eyes traveling past each woman before landing back on Hope. She bites the inside of her cheek to keep from speaking. *Let him work up to it*, she thinks. *One wrong word and he could be put off.*

"I guess I know the version you lived with," says Nadine, and Hope feels the energy in the room shift as her heart sinks. She knows that in any negotiation there is going to be ground lost and ground gained. But this feels like returning to ground zero. She wants to turn around and tell Nadine to just hush already. But she doesn't.

The other women all shift uncomfortably, like they'd also felt how close they were. But Nadine seems oblivious. She has a score to settle, and here before God and these witnesses, she's going to speak her mind.

"What do you mean by that, Nadine?" asks Tommy. His face, open moments ago, is now closed again.

Hope glances over at the window where SWAT is on the other side watching and waiting. She makes eye contact with Dale, who is standing just to their left and doing a pretty good job of being unobtrusive, considering he is decked out in tactical gear and holding a rifle. She's got almost no time left before SWAT does it their way, before they opt for force rather than words. With Tommy unarmed, she's surprised they've maintained restraint for this long.

"She said that people tell themselves whatever they need to in order to live with themselves—a version of the truth." Nadine looks to Hope. "Right?"

Hope nods.

"Well, today I learned that your version of the truth was that the reason you weren't with your daddy when he died was because of me. That I didn't *let* you go hunting." She hops down from her stool and jabs her finger in his direction. "You know good and well that isn't true." She turns and points at the ring of women around her. "You tell them that. You tell them it isn't true."

Tommy ducks his head, looking up at them from beneath his eyebrows. "You said you wanted to spend the day together," he mumbles.

Nadine huffs. "So?"

"So I wanted to make you happy," Tommy says.

"You could've told me we'd go out to dinner after you went hunting. That woulda made me just as happy."

Tommy thinks this over, shrugs. "We were both so busy with work and stuff that we never got much time together, so I figured it'd be better if I stayed with you."

Nadine crosses her arms and cocks her head at him. "You figured. But you didn't ask." There is a long pause as the two of them face each other, each searching for what to say next. Not surprisingly, it is Nadine who plunges ahead. "This was always your problem, Tommy. You never communicated with me. One simple conversation. That's all it would've taken. And none of this"—Nadine shakes her hands in the air, indicating where they are, who they're with—"woulda happened." She pauses, glancing over at the shreds of the envelope he tore up hours ago that still litter the floor. She adds, "None of it."

Hope clocks the moment Tommy's face goes soft again. She has to give it to Nadine; she got them back around. Nadine speaks again, her voice lower now. "After your daddy died, you were so angry at me. Suddenly everything I did was wrong. And you started drinking more and more, and that only made it worse. I told myself you were just grieving, to give it time. And I did. But then . . ." Her voice fades away. She swallows as a single tear trickles from the corner of her eye and glides down her face.

"But then, what?" Tommy asks, his voice ragged.

Nadine shakes her head. A few more tears follow the first one. She looks at the dog and blinks her way back to composure. She looks at Tommy again. "But then I just couldn't anymore," she says.

"It wasn't you I was mad at," Tommy says. "I was mad at me for not being there that day. I was mad at Jane for not letting me have Covey." He inhales, exhales, his nostrils flaring. "I was mad at my daddy for getting himself killed." Tommy looks up at the ceiling, squeezes his eyes shut. "I was mad at God for letting him die."

He looks back at Nadine. "I'm sorry I took it out on you. You didn't deserve that. Every day I'd tell myself to stop, but then something would set me off, and before I knew it I was blowing up at you, smashing the dishes, kicking the walls. I knew it scared you. So I kept trying to get the anger out, but it always came back again. It filled me up inside no matter what I did."

"Yeah, and look where it got you," says Nadine. "Where it got us both."

"I hope someday you can forgive me."

Nadine gives a bitter laugh. "Don't count on it," she says. Then a little smile crosses her lips.

And Tommy smiles too. It's the first time he's smiled, a real smile, not the sadistic one they've all seen earlier. He turns to Hope. "Can I still ask for something I want?" he asks her.

Yes, Hope thinks. *You can ask me to facilitate your surrender. We are here, finally.* "Sure," she says.

"I want my wife back," he says. With no warning he moves toward Nadine, taking her into his arms. For a millisecond her arms hitch slightly, as if she is going to hug him back. But then they go stiff and remain at her sides.

She looks up at him. "Tommy, what are you doing?" she asks, her face close to his. But instead of answering her, he leans down and kisses her.

Nadine immediately recoils at the kiss. She rears back, and her hand flies through the air, making contact with Tommy's cheek in a slap heard round the room.

Tommy, dazed, backs up as Nadine turns her head to look at Hope, her mouth an O of shock as they exchange wide-eyed expressions. In the moment that her gaze is averted, Tommy pulls her to him with one arm and pulls something from his pocket with the other, placing it at Nadine's throat. Hope sees that it is a box cutter. He must have found it at some point in the room and pocketed it. No wonder he didn't balk at surrendering his gun. He knew he still had a weapon if push came to shove.

Hope looks at Dale at the same moment he looks to her. She wants to ask Dale, "Didn't you pat him down? Wasn't that your job?" But then she thinks of how Tommy had surrendered his gun, then immediately gotten down on the floor to greet the dog when they walked in. Their collective attention had gone to the touching reunion without a thought of another potential weapon. But none of that matters now. Dale raises his gun and yells at Tommy to drop the box cutter. Blythe, Morrow, and Sylvie all come off their stools. Out in the vestibule Hope hears SWAT starting to make entry.

"Tommy, don't do this," Hope says. "You don't want to do this." She looks over her shoulder at Dale. "Give me one last try," she says to him. She turns and gestures for the SWAT leader outside not to enter, holding up one finger. Meaning what? One more minute? One more chance? But she can't have them storming in here. Not yet. Though they would no doubt take Tommy out, he could harm Nadine as well in the process. Hope won't let that be the ending they get, not if she has anything to say about it. She just has to keep believing in the power of words.

"Why not?" Tommy asks. "All I have on the other side of that glass is jail." He leers at Hope. "You can't give me what I want. No one can."

"But you promised," Hope says, hearing her own words as she says them, how childlike they are, how simple they sound. And yet she sees the flicker behind Tommy's eyes that shows he also remembers the promise. "You promised me that no one would be harmed today."

"So?" Tommy scoffs. In his arms Nadine squirms, but he only grips her tighter. At their feet Covey paces and whines.

"So this is your chance to not let your anger get the best of you. This is your chance to be the man you want to be, the man you just told Nadine you wish you'd been. You can still be that man," she says, hearing the pleading tone in her voice, the barely disguised desperation.

"It's too late," Tommy wails. In his arms, with the knife pressed to her throat, Nadine cries.

"It's not too late," says Hope. "There's still hope."

"No, there's not!" Tommy says and in one smooth motion

takes the box cutter away from Nadine's throat and presses it to his own as he releases Nadine.

"No!" The word is screamed above the sound of the outside officers ramming their way in. "You can't! You can't do this!" Hope sees that it is Nadine, who has not moved away from Tommy. She is standing with her fists clenched at her sides as tears stream down her face. "Please," she says, her voice softer this time.

"What do you care?" Tommy says, his voice rough. But his words are already a little softer than they were a moment ago, the box cutter a little lower. "You just want to be rid of me."

"I didn't know what else to do," she said. "And I had to do something. Because . . ." She stops and looks around, as if suddenly remembering she has an audience. Her eyes meet Hope's and Sylvie's and Blythe's and Morrow's. They have all told their secrets today. It is time to tell hers. She looks back to Tommy. "Because I'm pregnant."

The box cutter clatters to the floor. "What?"

"I wasn't going to tell you for . . . well, a long time. Not till I absolutely had to. I wanted for you to get yourself straightened out, and then I figured we could talk about it. I just . . . I didn't feel safe the way things were." She pauses, thinks about that day just a few months ago, recalling how it felt to be happy and scared and sad all at the same time. "When I found out I was pregnant, well . . . I had to get us out of there."

"Us . . . ," says Tommy.

Blythe studies Nadine's midsection. She doesn't look a bit pregnant to her. Maybe it's early days still. Or maybe she's one of those women who doesn't show till further along. Or maybe she's lying. If she is, it's an Oscar-worthy performance. But if it gets them out of here, then more power to her.

Nadine looks over her shoulder at Dale, who is still holding his gun on Tommy even though he has released her and dropped the box cutter. She turns back to Tommy. "What I'm trying to say is, you have to go out there"—she waves in the direction of the windows—"and deal with whatever comes next. And after that, well, you need to be here, to be this baby's father." Covey comes over and nudges her knee. She bends down and gives him a pat.

"Father," says Tommy. He breathes the word like a prayer.

"You had a good father," Nadine says, more to the dog than Tommy. "You can't see it now, but you'll be one too. I just know it."

When Tommy begins to cry, he is too wrapped up in the swirl of emotions he is feeling—loss, joy, sadness, and, yes, hope, even in the face of all that awaits him when he leaves this post office—to take notice of something that is happening in the room. If he looked around, he'd see that the women in the room are crying too.

Chapter 37

Hope stands in front of the hostages who, in a few minutes, won't be hostages anymore. She feels a ridiculous sadness at the thought of parting with them, chalking it up to this being the one—and it will be the only—time she's ever entered a barricade. Still, it has created some sort of bond. She likes these women and can't help but think that if they'd met under different circumstances, they would've all been friends. She certainly has shared more with them today than she has with anyone else. She feels a mixed sense of exposure and gratitude as she explains to these women how she's going to get them safely home.

"Tommy would like to walk out and surrender of his own free will," she says. She glances at Tommy, who is sitting on the floor having a few last moments with Covey as Dale hovers over him, watching his every move.

"So we are going to have each of you exit before he does that. You will walk out of here and go straight out the front door, where there will be a couple of squad cars waiting. Just walk out and get in whichever one is closest. There's a lot of press out there, and we don't want you getting bombarded. The officers will take you straight to the police station, where we will take your statements and get you home just as soon as we can. Your family members have been instructed to meet you at the station."

"So we'll just say goodbye to one another there, then?" asks

Morrow. She is, Hope thinks, feeling the same pang of parting. She's glad it's not just her. It's probably collective trauma bonding. But a bond is a bond. It's a place to start.

"Yes," says Hope, "you can say your goodbyes after you give your statements."

Blythe turns to them. "So let's none of us leave the station until we've all given our statements. Then we can, you know, like, exchange numbers. Or whatever." Sylvie, Morrow, and Nadine all agree.

Hope goes to the window to make sure the cars are indeed lined up and waiting for them. They are. She sees Robert, formerly known as Bo, standing by one of them. She gives him a little wave, but he doesn't see her. His eyes are trained on the door that his wife will walk out of soon.

Morrow thinks about Maya banging on the window and wonders where they took her afterward. She can hardly wait to hug her daughter. She thinks of Kevin, who will no doubt say, "What am I, chopped liver?" And smiles at the thought of her family waiting on the other side of this. Her imperfect, exasperating, loving family. She looks at Hope. "Can we do one quick thing before we leave?" she asks.

Hope raises her eyebrows. "If it's quick."

Morrow nods and reaches into her tote bag, pulling the small package from it. She holds it out to Nadine. "Would you be able to weigh this and put the right postage on it? So I can mail it later?"

Nadine takes the package from her hand and smiles. "I'd be honored." The women all move together over to the counter, back to where it all started. "I might be able to just run it through," Nadine offers. "I guess it would go out with tomorrow's mail if I did?"

"No, no," says Morrow. "I want to show it to my daughter

first. If we mail it—if that's still what she wants—I'd like us to do it together."

Nadine nods, then makes quick work of weighing and pricing the small box. That done, she starts to return it to Morrow but pulls it back as a grin crosses her face. She reaches under the counter and takes out a sticker that says, "Fragile: Handle with Care." She affixes it to the front of the package and hands it to Morrow with a wink.

"Perfect," says Morrow.

Beside her, Blythe pulls her own package close, grateful to have it back, ashamed of how close she came to mailing it off. Aaron will be waiting for her at the police station. She will tell him about the package, how sorry she is for what she almost did, and how glad she is that she didn't go through with it. If it wasn't for this situation, she wouldn't have gotten it back. She would've mailed off Murphy's ashes to someone who did not deserve them, who does not deserve her. She wonders if it would have changed everything. She's glad that now she will never know.

Sylvie goes over to the windows, looking out to see where Robert is. She feels a little rush of nervousness at the thought of seeing him, like a schoolgirl. He will want to know all about today. He will want to dissect it with her six ways to Sunday. And she will tell him all of it, as many times as he needs her to. Even if he forgets and she has to tell him all over again, she will. She will also confess what she came here to do today.

And then it dawns on her. He was out there with the others in the NOC, the bugged pizza boxes broadcasting every word she said about what was in her envelope. Maybe, she thinks, it is best that he knows the truth. Maybe, once she's finally by his side, they will just stand together and share the burden of an unknown future, just like she's wanted to do all along.

Nadine comes out from behind the counter, then stops long

enough to get one last look at the man she's been married to for three years, which is nothing compared to what Sylvie and her husband have had. Compared to them, three years is a drop in the bucket. But she and Tommy had a bucket. It was one she was sure they would fill together one drop at a time. She thought someday their bucket would be full to the brim. She'd counted on it. But then Tommy, in one of his fits of anger, kicked that bucket over, and all she could do was watch their little bit of water spill all over the floor.

"Before I go . . . can I say goodbye to him?" She hears a sharp intake of breath from either Morrow, Sylvie, or Blythe. She doesn't mind. She understands that they don't understand. They don't have to. The next time she sees her husband—and he is still her husband—will likely be when he is in jail. It will be different then, she knows. She wants one last moment before everything changes. Again.

Hope's eyebrows shoot toward her hairline as she considers whether to allow this. "You've got two minutes," she decides. She taps her watch, then shoos Nadine in Tommy's direction.

The three hostages shake their heads in unison as they watch Nadine stoop down in front of Tommy on the floor. Beside them Dale is on high alert, shooting questioning glances at Hope, who ignores him. Covey rises in greeting, but Tommy keeps his head down, focusing on the dog instead of Nadine, who begins speaking in low tones the others cannot hear.

"Why's she talking to him now?" Blythe asks no one in particular. "After all he's done to her?"

Sylvie watches Nadine and Tommy for a moment, then looks back at Blythe. "Remember what I told you earlier about surrender? About how eventually a person just gets tired of the waiting and they give up?" She takes a deep breath. "They give up because they just want the hard part to be over." She hitches a thumb in the direction of Nadine. "That's all she did. She got tired of being miserable, so she gave up." She raises one eyebrow. "That doesn't mean she stopped loving him."

"But she slapped him," counters Blythe.

Sylvie shrugs. "He kind of deserved it."

"He held a gun to her head," Blythe persists. "And a box cutter to her throat."

"And yet she may find it in herself to forgive him," says Sylvie. "I hope she does."

"You hope she forgives him?" Blythe is incredulous.

"Absolutely," Sylvie says. "He's the father of her child. And as we learned today, he's been through a lot himself."

"Still," says Blythe, "it's dysfunctional."

Sylvie laughs at that. "Oh, honey, we're all dysfunctional. That's what makes life interesting." Sylvie turns her head to look over at Nadine and Tommy, who are still locked in their own private conversation. She looks back at Blythe and Hope and Morrow, and points in the direction of the couple. "That's their marriage. Theirs alone. There's no call for us to judge from the outside looking in, because we don't know. We can't. Every marriage is a country unto itself. And there are only two people there who speak the language."

"Time's up," Hope calls to Nadine, who rises and walks back to the group without protest. For a moment no one speaks or moves, their eyes scanning the place that has been their prison for hours. Hope asks, "Everyone remember what I told you to do?"

They nod. Hope almost repeats the warning about how important it is that they do exactly as they were told, but she knows she doesn't need to. They will. They've been a good bunch of hostages. Exemplary. They could teach courses on how to be a hostage. She steps out of their way and, with a flourish, indicates that they are free to walk out. One by one they take their turn at stepping into the vestibule area, each taking deep breaths of the air as if it is an ocean breeze and not the exact same recycled air they've been breathing all day.

When it is time for Sylvie to go, she finds that she cannot without doing one more thing. Tommy is still sitting with the dog. Without asking Hope's permission, she rushes over to him and squats down, much the same as Nadine had done. At the doorway she hears Hope calling her name worriedly but ignores her as she leans forward and says, "I want you to have a PS."

He looks up, and her tired eyes meet his sad ones. "Remember, the letter doesn't end just because you sign your name." She raises her eyebrows, willing her student to recall the lesson. "If you have something to add, you can always write a PS." She reaches down and squeezes his hand. "And you have something to add," she says. "Don't forget that." Then she gets up and heads toward the door, toward her husband who is waiting for her, toward freedom.

Signature

Chapter 38

Once the cars carrying the hostages have disappeared out of sight, Hope turns to Tommy. "You ready?" she asks him.

Tommy nods, stands, and walks over to Hope, transferring Covey's leash back into her hand. "What now?" he asks her.

"Well, I will walk you out to the officers who are waiting out there, and they will place you under arrest and—"

"No," he says. "That part's pretty clear. I meant you. What now for you?"

"Oh, me?" Hope is surprised to be asked. "I guess I'll wrap up at the station, go home, take a shower, and crash."

Tommy shakes his head.

"What?" she asks.

"Never mind," he says.

"No," Hope presses. "What did you mean?"

"I meant, what's next? After all this. For you."

"I don't really know yet," she says.

They take a few steps before Tommy stoops down in front of the rack of tourism pamphlets, still in disarray. He looks up at her. "Mind if I finish this? I started fixing it earlier, but I . . . got waylaid. Won't take me but a minute."

"Sure," she says.

He makes quick work of arranging the remaining pamphlets

into neat little stacks, then pushes them back into their designated slots. "All the things we never did," he says, more to the pamphlets than to her.

He rises again holding one of the pamphlets and holds it out to her. "There," he says.

She looks down at what he's given her. It is a pamphlet about the Kindred Spirit Mailbox on Bird Island, a place she's heard about for years but never gone. People say it's special, mystical.

"You said you didn't have a place to mail that letter to your mom. You could put it here," Tommy tells her.

She looks up at Tommy. "Thank you."

"Maybe then you'll feel like it's time to go home," he says. "Like you did what you came here to do."

Hope thinks of the flowers she left behind, of the birthday she refused to celebrate, of the honor she was ready to refuse. She sees herself putting the letter she's carried for months into a lone mailbox on a stretch of undeveloped coastline, then turning and leaving it behind. "You might be right," she says.

"Stranger things have happened," he says as they exit the building.

Outside, Hope and Dale stand on the sidewalk and watch as the officers handcuff Tommy, put him into the police vehicle without incident, then drive away. Across the parking lot, the NOC is being packed up. Everyone is going home. It's over.

"Sorry about that oversight," says Dale. "I feel like an idiot for not patting him down."

Hope offers him some reassurance. "Well, it was an . . . odd situation. Protocol sort of went out the window when a negotiator walked in with a dog."

He chuckles at that. "Definitely a first time for everything. Still," he says, "everyone got out safe with no use of force. That's gotta feel like a win."

"Yeah." Hope smiles. "It does."

"Would you, um, feel like going somewhere to celebrate after we wrap things up at the station?" he asks. Hope watches two spots of color appear on his cheeks.

"Actually, I've got a very important phone call I need to make," she says. "To my husband."

He holds up his hands. "Can't blame a guy for trying."

"Thank you, though," she says, "for going in there with me."

She waves goodbye and walks away from the post office, toward Brower, who, relieved of her traffic duty, has returned to her car and is waiting to drive Hope back to the station. But first Hope finds the call from earlier, as she walked to work, and hits Redial. Alex answers on the first ring.

"I was thinking," Hope says, "that perhaps you could hand-deliver that piece of mail that came for me."

She hears him exhale his relief into the phone. "I thought you'd never ask."

Chapter 39

It is late by the time they all come together again. Hope had told them they could give their statements "real quick," but that was only wishful thinking. The only thing slower than a police station is a hospital or the DMV.

The women reconvene outside, clustering on the sidewalk that leads to the dark parking lot. The press, the county personnel, and any lookie-loos are long gone. Some of their families are there to take them home, but they hang back out of respect, giving the five of them a few minutes to say their goodbyes. The families know they will have all the time in the world to hear the story of this day.

The women exchange contact numbers, make promises to see one another soon, and exchange hugs all around. All five women—Nadine, Morrow, Blythe, Sylvie, and Hope—shed a few tears. They aren't guaranteed to see one another ever again, but as they part ways, each of them wants to. They have experienced something very few people have. They share something with one another that they will never share with anyone else. Lasting relationships have begun on less.

Nadine gets into her car and rolls down the windows. She can't get enough of the fresh air, gulping it as she drives home alone.

Her coworkers, Stacy and Martha, had sent word that she was welcome to come stay with either one of them, and Sylvie and Robert offered as well. But she wants time to herself. She's had enough togetherness for one day. Plus, she is tired and wants to sleep in her own bed. Her boss said she could have the day off tomorrow. She might just sleep all day.

Driving the short distance to her little apartment, she tries not to think about what's happening to Tommy at that very moment, tries not to think about what is to come. She was alone when this day started, and she is alone as it ends. But Tommy being incarcerated feels like a bigger alone, a more permanent one. Then she remembers, with a jolt, that she isn't alone.

She places her left hand on her stomach and drives with her right hand on the steering wheel as she speaks to whoever is there. "I think your daddy might be gone a long time," she says. "I don't know for how long, but you should know he'd be here if he could. He loves you. He even loves me too, hard as that is to believe. He just made—well, he didn't think, and now he's going to have to answer for that. I guess it sounds funny for me to say this, but deep down, he's a good man. A good man who did some dumb things, for sure. Things that will affect you. And I'm sorry for that."

Nadine feels the sharp sting of tears pricking her eyes at the thought of all that today has wrought. There are things she would maybe do differently if she could, but she can't. And that's the way it is. She takes a deep breath, filling her lungs with the night air that blows through her open windows. She thinks about that air oxygenating her blood, traveling to her baby and helping him or her grow.

"But I'll be here," she says aloud. "I won't be a perfect mama, but I'll do my best every single day. I'll make you that promise right here and now." *People*, Nadine thinks, *don't like to break a promise.*

Morrow decides to ride home with Kevin and Maya and collect her car tomorrow. She tells Kevin they need to make a stop on their way home, directing him to turn the opposite way they would usually go. Both Kevin and Maya give her quizzical looks in response.

"Mom," says Maya. "Everything is closed." It is true. They roll up the sidewalks in Sunset Beach as soon as it gets dark.

Morrow fishes around in her tote bag and produces the package. She hands it over the seat to Maya, who is sitting behind her. Maya reaches to take it at the same time she registers what her mother has handed her. She takes in the logo on the front, then looks at her mother.

"We can put this in the mailbox outside," Morrow tells her. "It's been weighed and has the correct postage on it, so it's all ready to go."

Maya stares down at the package. "This is why you were there?" she asks without looking up. "You were going to send this?"

From his seat, Kevin cranes his head to see what she's referring to, his eyes darting from the road to the back seat and back again. "What is it?" he asks.

"It's"—Maya looks up at her mother, gives her a smile—"a long story," she says.

Kevin slows down as they near the post office. "So am I turning in or not?"

"Shall we?" Morrow asks her daughter and points to the package.

"Eh," says Maya. "I'm pretty tired. Aren't you tired, Mom?"

Since they've arrived at the post office, Kevin turns in anyway, the headlights of their car illuminating the building. Morrow's stomach clenches in response to the sight. "I am pretty tired," she admits.

"Yeah," says Maya. "Let's just wait. We've got plenty of time."

"You're right," says Morrow. Her stomach relaxes and a smile fills her face. "We do." They circle past the post office and pull out onto the street that will take them home. Morrow watches as the post office fades in the side mirror, until it disappears entirely.

After she's said goodbye to the other women, Blythe finally has the chance to talk not only to Aaron but to her mother as well. It is a moment she's been waiting for ever since she got a glimpse of them together when she arrived at the station, just before she was hustled behind closed doors for her interview. The phrase "You could've knocked me over with a feather" came to mind.

She had expected Aaron to be there waiting for her but not her mom. And she definitely didn't expect for Aaron to have his arm wrapped around her mom, which is still the case when she joins them on the sidewalk. Aaron lets go of her mom so that she can be the first to embrace Blythe. "I called you once I heard, but you didn't answer," her mother says. "I was so worried."

Blythe, shocked, manages to say, "He took our phones pretty early on."

Her mom steps back to get a look at her. "My baby," she says. "You're okay?"

Blythe, her mind reeling, doesn't realize it's a question until Aaron answers for her. "Probably a little shaken up. But she's okay. Right, Blythe?"

"Huh?" She can't take in what's happening. "Oh, yeah. I'm okay. Or I will be."

Aaron takes her in his arms. He kisses the top of her head. "We're all going to be okay."

"I don't know what I would've done without Aaron today," her mom says. "He was my rock. He literally held me up at times. I've been a mess. A wreck. To think of that monster holding you hostage like that. He's just a horrible, horrible person. I hope they throw the book at him."

Blythe can't know for sure, but she has a feeling that one of the ways Aaron supported her mom today was by giving her wine. She steps back and gives him a look. "Did you take her to Grapevine?"

He shoots a grin at her. "Maybe," he says, then shrugs. "We had to wait somewhere. I thought it'd be good for her to see where you work. And meet everybody."

Blythe tries to picture her mom there, in her place of employment, in the midst of the people who work there, who have come to feel like family. She likes thinking about the people she loves surrounding her mother, loving her too. Even when she doesn't deserve it. Especially when she doesn't deserve it.

"Just so you know," her mother says, "I told Aaron about why you were at the post office."

Blythe's eyes go wide. "What did you . . . tell him?"

"Well, I told him the truth. That I sent you off on a ridiculous errand and that the whole thing was my idea. That I'd been tunnel-visioned about the absolute wrong person, when Aaron is so clearly the right one. Oh, wait!" Her mother gets a panicked look on her face. "You didn't mail that package, did you? Please tell me it all happened before you could!"

Blythe thinks about her brawl with Tommy, the intensity with which she fought to get Murphy's ashes back. "I didn't mail it," she says.

"I'm so relieved," her mother says, wrapping her into another hug. "You really are a lucky girl. This man will always be there for you. I can tell. He's a good one."

"Yes," Blythe agrees. "He is." Aaron and Blythe smile at each other over her mother's shoulder. She thinks about today, about Tommy and Nadine, and Sylvie and Robert, and Morrow and her daughter, and Hope and her mom, about love and all the ways it can go wrong. But sometimes it does go right.

Robert and Sylvie are the last ones to leave. They sit in their car in silence, thinking of, and discarding, words to say to each other. Sylvie holds the envelope in her hands, sees Robert look down at it and away a few times. Finally, she says, "I take it you heard me explain about this," she says. She lifts the envelope slightly. "When you were in the NOC."

He nods but says nothing.

"I'm sorry you had to find out that way. It wasn't what I intended."

"Nothing about this day has been what any of us intended."

"Ain't that the truth," she agrees. They sit in silence for a moment longer before Sylvie taps the tearstained envelope. "So, about this."

"Yes?" Robert's voice goes up with the question. He will not, she understands, ask her not to mail it, not if it's what she thinks is best. Not if it's what she wants. *What do you want?* she thinks, recalling the question being posed to Tommy. It's good to know what you want. But sometimes it's just as good to know what you don't want. Sylvie doesn't want to give up the home they love in the place they love. *Not yet. Not yet.*

"I'm not going to mail it," she tells her husband. "In fact—"

She smiles as she pinches the envelope and makes the tiniest tear, watching delight, and relief, cross Robert's face. She tears the two halves of the envelope into more halves, and then into more halves again until, finally, she stops and stares at the mess she has made. It looks like confetti scattered across her lap.

Sylvie recalls the question Nadine asked Blythe before she mailed her package all those hours ago. It is a question she's heard every time she's been in the post office, the question postal workers ask every customer who mails a package, repeated over and over, day after day. "Does the parcel contain anything liquid, fragile, perishable, or potentially hazardous?"

She gathers the pieces of the envelope and cups them in her hands as she thinks about the answer she will give the next time she's asked that question: *Don't we all, honey*, she will say. *Don't we all.*

Author's Note

While this story is set in a real place, it is a work of fiction. Constructing a story in which five people were confined in a small room for almost all of it was not an easy task, and at certain points I did have to take some liberties just to make it all work. Most notably, there is not a bathroom in the vestibule of the Sunset Beach post office, nor is there only one set of doors in the back of the building, according to what I've been told. (I was actually not allowed in the back of the building because of post office rules and regulations. I've only seen the part of the post office that everyone else sees, so I worked from there.) All this to say: In choosing whether to serve the story or stick to reality, I chose the story.

I also want to acknowledge the law enforcement and emergency personnel presence in this story. While it is true that the Sunset Beach police department is not set up to respond immediately to a hostage situation like the one depicted here—they would have to call in the county—I want to be sure to acknowledge the heart and devotion that these public servants show daily in keeping the town of Sunset Beach and its citizens safe. The delays, the errors, and the inexperience that happen in this story are also very much made up, all so that Hope can persist in her role and find her way back to hope. This is, after all, a story about hope.

Acknowledgments

I always aim to keep these short and sweet, yet they rarely are. But here goes . . .

This story would not exist if I hadn't been graciously permitted by Rich (who is named in this story) and his team to attend the Midwest Crisis Negotiators Conference, not just once but twice. I not only learned about the terminology, psychology, and procedures involved in a hostage crisis but also heard the real stories of heroes and gleaned from the forthright, detailed sessions I sat through. Specific thanks go to Adam and Chris (who are also named in this story) for taking me under their wing, answering my many questions, and just being good conference buddies. This book is dedicated to Ingrid Herriott, who was the first person I met at the conference and who lent parts of her own personal story to this story, plus spent hours on the phone with me answering what I'm sure were dumb questions.

Laura Wheeler and Julie Breihan, you two took my mess of a manuscript and made it make sense, which was no small feat, and for that I am so, so grateful. Amanda Bostic, without you neither this book nor the one before it would exist. Thank you for making that happen. And a big thanks to the production and publicity team at Thomas Nelson for all the ways you have shown up for me and other authors.

Thank you to my local friends who listened to me kvetch

about how hard this book was on many a night out: George and Lynn, Joe and Tina, Arlene and Fran, Kelman and Kim, Jeff and Dana, Deb and Jeff, Holly and Charlie. (An extra thank-you to Charlie for sharing his post office stories.)

A huge thanks to the Mabes family, especially George Mabes, for letting me "borrow" 108. Hope very much appreciated her stay.

To Jenna and Mac and the crew at Grapevine: It was you guys I was thinking of as Blythe reflected on what your restaurant means—not just to me but to so many. Thank you for taking us in when we washed ashore back in 2020. It'll always be white soda for me.

Dawn Miller, Candace Blackwell, and the staff of my local indie bookseller, Pelican Books: Thank you for including me in the bookish events you put on in our community and for always carrying my books. An additional thank-you to John and Tracy Hobgood for selling book after book year after year at Sunset Beach Trading Company. (Here's one set in Sunset!) And to all booksellers out there who are recommending and hand-selling books. I know I am not alone in my gratitude for your service.

To my friends who have been there for me throughout my writing adventures: Rachel Olsen, John and Jennifer Tuckwiller, Lisa Shea, Laurel Sauls, the SBGG (Kelly Clemmons, Pam Johnson, and Kelly Andrews), and the Birthday Girls (Karen Baker, April Adams, and Kimberly Young). Thanks for your grace those many, many times I couldn't get together because I was working. But hey! I'm done! (At least for now . . .)

To Lisa Patton, Patti Callahan Henry, Erika Montgomery, Joy Callaway, Kim Wright, Traci Keel, and T. I. Lowe: Not only have you been there for me throughout my writing adventures, but you also sympathize with them, which is grace upon grace.

Not many can say they have a significant Ariel in their lives. Even fewer people can say they have *two* significant Ariels in their lives. I count myself among those few. Sure, it confuses my husband regularly ("Wait a minute, which Ariel are we talking about?"), but he figures it out sooner or later. Ariel Lawhon, I don't think it's a stretch to say I never would've written my first novel without your encouragement. I'm grateful that we are still in each other's lives all these years later, still spurring each other on, or at the very least, listening to each other gripe. And Ariele Fredman, I am just so grateful you're my agent. Having you in my corner makes all the difference.

To my mom, Sandy Brown, who faithfully listened week after week as I updated her on how hard the work had been. That never changed, and neither did your unwavering belief in me. Thank you for encouraging me and praying for me throughout the writing of this book.

Thank you to Jack, Ashleigh, Matthew, Rebekah, Bradley, Annaliese, and now Cameron: You guys have shaped me, strengthened me, stretched me, surprised me, and softened me. I could not have written about these characters, or about hope, if not for you all.

To Curt, husband of more than three decades and best friend: Thank you for the date nights and beach walks, the tough talks and the encouraging ones. Thank you for reminding me that I've said all the things before and gotten through it before. And I will, again, with you. Ours is a story of hope.

And to you, dear reader, thank you for reading this book. I found this quote from Adam Haslett while I was writing *Handle with Care* that embodies what I tried to do through this story: "For years I've been writing about characters seeking to overcome isolation and connect emotionally with other people." For me, that is what the reading experience is all about—overcoming isolation and connecting emotionally. It is my sincere hope that I've done that here, not only for the characters, but for you as well.

And finally, to the Creator who imbues us all with creativity: Thank you for my portion. I need words, and you never fail to supply them. "But this I call to mind, and therefore I have *hope*: The steadfast love of the Lord never ceases; his mercies never come to an end; they are new every morning; great is your faithfulness" (Lamentations 3:21–23).

Discussion Questions

1. Hope plays a dual role as both a character and a symbol. How does her personal journey mirror the broader theme of hope in the story?
2. Tommy is portrayed as both an antagonist and a deeply flawed, grieving individual. How does the author balance his role as a threat with his humanity? Do you think the story succeeds in making him a sympathetic character, or does his behavior overshadow his motivations?
3. The hostages—Morrow, Blythe, Sylvie, and Nadine—come from very different walks of life. How do their individual backstories and struggles influence their interactions during the crisis? What does their bonding say about shared adversity?
4. Sylvie wrestles with aging, caregiving, and the fear of becoming obsolete. How does her perspective on life's "closing chapters" resonate with the novel's themes of legacy and meaning?
5. Each character carries a hidden burden, whether in an envelope, a memory, or an unspoken truth. How do these secrets drive the story forward, and what do you think the novel is saying about the power—and danger—of what we choose to hide?

6. Much of the novel unfolds in the ordinary setting of a post office. How does the contrast between the everyday environment and the extraordinary hostage situation heighten tension and meaning?
7. The author frames the novel through the metaphor of a letter, breaking the story into sections like "heading" and "closing." In what ways does this structure mirror the characters' experiences or the themes of communication, confession, and closure?
8. So much of the story hinges on timing—who ends up in the post office, who leaves just before the crisis, who decides to stay. How do you interpret the role of coincidence or fate in shaping the characters' lives?
9. The hostage crisis forces strangers to rely on one another. Do you think the novel suggests that true community is forged through hardship, or does it highlight the fragility of human connections in moments of fear?
10. The novel balances suspense with deeper questions of forgiveness, resilience, and community. What do you think *Handle with Care* ultimately suggests about the possibility of healing after trauma?

About the Author

Kristee Mays Photography

MARYBETH MAYHEW WHALEN is the author of *Every Moment Since* and nine previous novels. Marybeth received a BA degree in English with a concentration in Writing and Editing from NC State University a long time ago and has been writing ever since. Marybeth and her husband, Curt, are the parents of six kids, who are now all in various stages of adulting. A native of Charlotte, North Carolina, Marybeth now calls Sunset Beach, North Carolina, home.

Visit her online at www.marybethwhalen.com
Instagram: @marybethwhalen
Facebook: @marybethwhalen

For more from Marybeth Mayhew Whalen

"*Every Moment Since* is everything you want in a novel—a gripping story, nostalgia for lost childhood, exorbitant love, a deep sense of place, and page-turning tension."

—PATTI CALLAHAN HENRY,
New York Times bestselling author
of *The Secret Book of Flora Lea*

AVAILABLE IN PRINT, E-BOOK, AND DOWNLOADABLE AUDIO